Voice
ACROSS TIME

Voice
ACROSS TIME

a novel

LINDA TODD BUSH

Covenant Communications, Inc.

Cover images: *Dry Stone Wall and Mountain Farm* © 2011 FotoVoyager, Courtsey of iStockphotography.com; *Summer Portrait* © 2011 Piskunov, Courtsey of iStockphotography.com.

Cover design copyright © 2011 by Covenant Communications, Inc.

Published by Covenant Communications, Inc.
American Fork, Utah

Printed in the United States of America
First Printing: June 2011

17 16 15 14 13 12 11   10 9 8 7 6 5 4 3 2 1

ISBN-13: 978-1-59811-963-3

To Ron,
for his unfailing love and support

Acknowledgments

Thanks first and foremost to my family—my husband, Ron; our children, Ronda, Allison, Rebecca, Jillene, and Jennifer; and my grandchildren for their helpful suggestions, encouragement when I have struggled, and never-ending love and support. Without their confidence in me, this book would never have been finished. Thanks to my brother, Calvin, for sharing his expert knowledge about horses. And thanks to the many good friends who read, reread, and again reread the manuscript and gave me good recommendations.

Special thanks to John and Margaret Webster, who have become my good friends. They live near the small village in England where my Todd ancestors lived and were a good source of English history and customs.

Many thanks also to the wonderful staff at Covenant Communications for giving me the opportunity to publish this book. I am especially thankful to my editor, Samantha Van Walraven, for all her encouragement, help, and support in preparing my manuscript for publication. She has been wonderful!

And, finally, I give thanks for my pioneer ancestors who accepted the truth and light of the gospel and made great sacrifices in leaving their countries and families to finally settle in the beautiful Salt Lake Valley. Many of the pioneer experiences related in this book are their stories.

Prologue

May 1870

Wiping the perspiration from his forehead onto his shirtsleeve, Tom Fisher reached into the wagon to lift out the last trunk. He hoisted it to his shoulder and, balancing it with his hands, started back toward the new house, a feeling of thankfulness filling his heart. Two years ago Brigham Young asked him to move to St. George, Utah, to help with the building of the temple. Tom and his wife, Dorothy, had accepted the challenge without hesitation. Granted, Tom was no longer the young man he had been when working on the Nauvoo Temple, but he knew that if the Lord wanted him, he would be equal to the task. Besides, for him there was no finer joy to be found than in working on a house of the Lord.

The two years had not been easy. In the spring, rains and snow runoff from the nearby mountains brought the threat of flooding, and the roads and fields turned into a sea of red mud. The summer months in the southern Utah desert were hot and dry, the red dust blowing and shifting in the fiery winds and the sun overhead constantly blazing heat from the deep blue sky. Crops were hard to grow, and water was scarce. The Fisher family had lived in a sod house during those years, with Tom working on the new home when he had time. Dorothy was a meticulous housekeeper, and he knew the constantly sifting dirt from the sod roof and the bugs and snakes that found their way into their home had been a trial to her, although she seldom complained.

As he walked, he shifted the weight of the trunk and surveyed the new home in front of him with satisfaction, noticing the bright red of the clay bricks against the white gingerbread trim. Inside, he could hear the clatter of pottery and Dorothy softly singing as she placed her dishes in the new cupboards. Tom smiled to himself.

Entering the house, he walked upstairs to the large storage room. As he bent over to place the trunk on the floor, it slipped from his grasp and fell, the lid flying open and the contents spilling out around him. Giving a sigh of exasperation, he knelt down and began placing the items back in the trunk. The last thing he picked up was a wooden box. A flood of memories washed over him as he held it in his hands, and moisture stung his eyes. His finger gently traced the engraved leaves and hearts on the sides of the box, and he remembered the loving care he had taken when carving the images more than twenty-five years ago. He folded the box in his arms, drawing it close to his heart. "Catherine," he whispered as silent tears ran down his face.

Chapter 1

Present Day

"No, Scott," Abigail Peters said firmly, her green eyes flashing. "We've been over this before. I'm leaving in the morning, and that's final. This is just something I have to do."

Scott Shafer ran his hands through his hair and took a deep breath, trying to calm himself before replying. "Now, Abby, be reasonable. If you wait a few weeks longer, your mother will be able to go with you, and you'll finish the job faster."

Abby glanced over at Scott, noticing once again his blond good looks. Six months ago they had met at a dinner party her parents had given. He was a rising young attorney in her father's law firm, and after being introduced to her, he'd made a point of staying by her side throughout the evening. The next day he'd called and asked for a date, and since then, they had been together constantly. She admired his quick wit and confident, take-charge attitude, but tonight she wished he would listen to her instead of telling her what she should do.

A month ago her mother had received a telephone call from a Dr. Blake Matthews in St. George, Utah, informing her that Abby's grandmother Brown had suffered a fatal heart attack. After the funeral, Abby had wandered through the old home, remembering the summer vacations and holidays spent there with her grandparents. Her grandfather had died when she was in her early teens, and after his death, she and her grandmother had grown very close. Abby had planned on visiting her this past winter but postponed the trip because of looming contract deadlines with her busy real estate business. She had also been caught up in her romance with Scott and hated to be away from him. Now the feelings of guilt and loss were overwhelming. By the time they returned home from the funeral, her parents had decided to sell the old home, and Abby had volunteered to return to St. George to get the house ready to be placed on the market. She and Scott had argued for the last month over her decision to go. Tonight he had taken Abby to dinner at their favorite restaurant, and they had avoided the subject of her morning departure. On the drive back to Abby's condominium, however, Scott had once again tried to convince her to stay until her mother could go with her.

"I'm not going to change my mind, Scott, and this is a closed subject." Abby looked over at Scott again, disappointment showing on her face. "I just wish you understood how much this means to me. My grandmother was such a special person in my life, and I need to do this for *me*. There are so many wonderful memories I have of her that I can't believe she's gone. Besides, you know Mom will come as soon as she can, but I don't want to wait for her. I need time there by myself to find some peace with Grandmother's death."

Scott was silent as he pulled up in front of Abby's condo and turned off the motor. "Can I come in for a few minutes?" he asked, resignation flattening his voice.

She shook her head. "I don't think so, Scott. It's getting late, and I have last-minute packing to do." She leaned over and laid her hand on his, her voice softening, "You know I'll miss you and will be home as soon as I can." She gave a small laugh. "Besides, I can't be away from work forever. I have to be back for the Boulder Towers' closing, and that's scheduled next month. Hopefully, I'll be through in St. George by then."

He looked at her and nodded, sudden tenderness showing in his face. Unbuckling his seatbelt, he turned to face her and put his arm around her. "Just a minute, Abby. This isn't the way I planned to do this, but I guess it will have to do." With his other hand, he reached into his pocket and took out a small jewelry box and handed it to her. "I planned on being overly romantic when I asked you to marry me, but maybe the important thing is the way we both feel about each other. You know I'm in love with you, and if you're determined to go,

I want things settled between us. I'll feel better about your being away if you're wearing my ring."

Abby took the box, holding it carefully in her hand. Uncertainty washed over her. *Am I ready to make this commitment?* She raised her eyes and looked across at Scott. *I feel like I love him, but Grandmother's death is all I can think about right now.* Holding her breath, she opened the box. Inside was a ring with a large diamond surrounded by small emeralds. She smiled at him through eyes misting with tears. "Hey, it's nothing to cry about," Scott said. "I just hope you like it. Once I saw it, I knew it was the ring for you because the emeralds reminded me of your green eyes."

"Oh, Scott, it's such a beautiful ring. But please try to understand. Right now the timing is wrong for me." She glanced at the ring one more time and then carefully closed the box and handed it back to him. "My heart is so full of loss right now that I want to wait before making this type of commitment."

He looked at her incredulously, frustration again apparent in his voice. "What are you saying, Abby? That you don't want to marry me, that you're unsure of your feelings? We've talked about marriage before, and I just want to formalize our feelings for each other." He stared down at the ring box then shook his head. "No, Abby, I want you to keep it."

Abby sighed deeply, laying her head on his shoulder. "But, Scott, when we've discussed marriage, it has always been in the future, with the understanding that we need to give our relationship a little more time. You know how much I care for you; my feelings on that have not changed. So, please, keep this beautiful ring for me while I'm gone. I have too many other emotions to cope with right now. When I get back, I'll have closed one chapter in my life and will be more ready to talk about our future."

Scott put his hand beneath her chin and tipped her head back. He looked into her eyes for a moment, searching for an answer, then reluctantly took the box and placed it back in his pocket. "I know I've rushed things a little tonight . . . I'll keep the ring for now," he replied, his voice echoing the disappointment he was feeling. "Do I at least get to kiss you good-bye?"

"Of course you do," she whispered. "Oh, Scott, I really am going to miss you, and I'll call often." She turned on the seat and put her arms around him, bringing her face close to his.

"I'm glad you'll miss me while you're gone." He sighed then drew her close with his other arm. "Okay, Abby, I'll try to be understanding, but don't leave me alone too long." As he kissed her, he drew her even closer, not wanting to let her go. Finally, she drew back with a soft laugh. "I need to go in, Scott." She leaned toward him once again, giving him a quick kiss, then let herself out of the car and ran up the stairs to her condo. After opening the door, she turned and gave a final wave before going inside. Entering her bedroom, she glanced at the open suitcases on the bed then picked up the phone on the nightstand and dialed a number. The ringtone sounded just once before she heard her mother's voice respond, "Hello?"

"Mom, it's me. I know it's late, so I hope I didn't wake you."

On the other end of the line, Mary Peters smiled. Abby was always in such a hurry. "That's okay, dear, I haven't gone to bed yet; I've been waiting for your call. Are you ready to go in the morning?"

"I think so. I've just got a few things left to pack before I go to bed. I need to be on the road early. Mom, tomorrow morning would you mind calling Grandmother's neighbor, Mrs. Givens, and letting her know that I'll be there sometime in the evening? She wanted us to let her know when we were coming, and I've been so busy today that I forgot."

"I'll be happy to do that for you. Now, how was your evening with Scott?"

Abby took a deep breath before replying. "Full of surprises. We went to dinner, and it was really nice. But on the way home, he started his usual argument about me going, and that's not all. When we arrived back here, he asked me to marry him and had even bought a beautiful engagement ring to give me. I didn't know he was planning to do that."

Mary chuckled. "But, honey, you shouldn't have been completely surprised. You've mentioned several times that the two of you have talked about getting married at some point. In fact, he showed the ring to your father today at the office and said he was going to propose tonight. We both like Scott very much. So is it official then, and are we planning a wedding?"

Abby laughed too. "I guess you're right, but I was surprised. When we've talked about marriage, I haven't anticipated that it could be this soon. I feel I love him and just know that I care for him more than any man I've ever dated. But, Mom, don't start sending out invitations yet. I told him I had too much on my mind right now and wanted to wait until I returned home to talk about it. He wasn't very happy with my answer."

"He'll be all right, dear. Really, I'm glad you're not going to rush into anything right now. I'm sorry your going has caused problems with Scott, but your father and I appreciate your willingness to get Mother's home on the market. And, Abby, I promise I'll come to St. George as quickly as I can."

After agreeing to call when she arrived, Abby hung up the phone. Being an only child, she was very close to her parents and knew she would miss them. As she passed the dresser, her eyes fell on a picture of her and her grandmother, taken when she was ten years old. Picking up the picture, she sat down on the side of the bed, recalling the summer vacations spent with her grandparents in southern Utah. Those summers spent in the desert town of St. George were always hot but fun and had created lasting memories for her.

With her mind full of those memories, Abby stood up and set the picture back on the dresser. She added a couple more shirts to the full suitcases before she closed them and placed them on the floor. After setting her alarm for six o'clock, she changed into pajamas and climbed into bed. She tossed restlessly for several hours before falling into a troubled sleep.

* * *

Early the next morning, Abby packed the last of her things in her small overnight case then placed the suitcases in the car, along with a bag of groceries. The sky was dark and overcast with thick black clouds, and there was a smell of coming snow in the air. Closing the trunk, she glanced nervously at the sky, hoping the storm would hold off until she was through the high Rocky Mountains. She started the car, and as the engine quickly sprang to life, she gave a sigh of appreciation for her new deep-blue BMW. She had bought the car as a reward for closing a big real-estate sale a month earlier.

The drive to St. George was long and tiring. When Abby turned on her blinker to finally exit the freeway, she flexed her tired shoulders against the back of the driver's seat, grateful she was nearing the end of her journey. As she drove, she noticed that the clear evening sky had been slowly changing from the brilliant pink and coral of the setting sun to deep violet blues, the shadows becoming dark as the sun sank in final glory behind the western horizon. Taking a deep breath, she drank in the beauty of the desert sunset. What a difference from the cold, overcast world she had left that morning.

Abby turned her car into the driveway of her grandmother's home and shut off the motor. The moonlight of the early evening cast a soft glow of light over the old home. Tom Fisher, her fourth great-grandfather, had built the house, and it was a typical clay, adobe-brick, two-story pioneer home with a wraparound front porch and white gingerbread trim. The home had been added to and remodeled over the years by the generations who followed. Taking the old-fashioned key from her handbag, Abby stepped onto the porch, unlocked the front door, and walked into the small entry room, turning on the entry and hallway lights as well as the outside porch light. The old pioneer home filled Abby with nostalgia. She walked down the hallway that cut the lower level of the house in half. The downstairs of the home consisted of the hall running to the back of the house, with the front parlor, or living room, and dining rooms to the right of the hall. The large kitchen and her grandparents' spacious bedroom opened through doors to the left.

Tears filled Abby's eyes as she entered her grandmother's bedroom and turned on the light. "Oh, Grandmother, I miss you so much and wish you were here," she said with a sob in her voice as she whispered the words into the quiet room. She glanced at the open book on the bedside table and her grandmother's things still lying on the old-fashioned dresser as if the dear woman would be returning any minute. With a last look around, Abby turned off the light, backed out of the room, and closed the door. *I can't face all this tonight*, she thought. She peeked into the bathroom that had been added onto the back of the home and then retraced her steps to the entry hall and up the staircase that led to the second floor. She turned on the lights in the small bedroom where she had always stayed when visiting her grandparents, checked the bathroom, and then continued down the hall. She walked briefly into her grandfather's study. He had been gone for many years, but Abby noticed that no real changes had been made. She pictured him sitting at his desk but eagerly rising with a smile of welcome when she entered the room. Stale and musty smells greeted her as she peeked into the storage room at the end of the upstairs hall. It was a large room filled with old furniture, boxes, trunks, and other relics from pioneer days onward, and during her summer visits Abby had loved playing in this room. After draping her childish frame with dresses and hats from bygone eras, she would gaze at herself in the tall mirror standing in the middle of the room with smiles of delight on her face. She closed the door on the memories and started back down the stairs.

Abby loved the charm of the old home, with its echo of memories from the generations of her ancestors who had lived in it through the years. She loved visualizing the young women of the past in their long dresses, making their grand entrance down the old staircase to the young men waiting at the bottom for them. Often, she found herself listening for the sound of long-ago children's laughter as they ran through the house.

Tonight, though, the silent home felt very unwelcoming. With longing, she remembered the feel of her grandmother's welcoming arms and the music of their laughter as they talked of all the fun things they would do while Abby was there. Brushing a stray tear from her cheek, she returned to the car and picked up the bag of groceries she had brought with her then headed straight for the kitchen. She loved this room best of all. One of her grandmother's favorite expressions was that a kitchen was the heart of the home, and Abby felt it to be so in this house. As she glanced around, she noticed her grandmother's apron hanging—as it always had—on the pantry door. She remembered the times they had baked together and how her grandmother would find an apron for her as well, tying it around her small body several times so it would fit. A small stool stood just inside the pantry, and Abby thought of how many times she had dragged it to where her grandmother was working so she could stand on it and help.

Still holding back tears, Abby placed the bag on the countertop and then returned to the car for her other belongings. As she closed the car door, a porch light came on at the house next door, and at the same time, the front door opened and a figure stepped onto the porch.

"Is that you, Abby?"

Abby placed the suitcases on the ground and walked toward the neighbor. "Yes, it's me. I'm finally here, Mrs. Givens, but I didn't mean to disturb you."

Agnes Givens, her white hair shining in the porch light, was a small energetic woman in her early eighties. Her figure was still trim and straight, and her birdlike eyes were quick to notice what was going on around her. She had been one of Abby's grandmother's closest friends, and Abby had seen her many times when she was visiting. Mrs. Givens was a widow with three married daughters. Her keen blue eyes looked Abby over carefully before reaching out to gather her into a quick hug.

"I'm so glad you're finally here, dear," she said, releasing Abby. "Your mother called this morning to say you were on your way, and I've been watching for you for the last hour and trying not to worry."

Abby smiled at the older woman. "It's been a long day," she admitted, noticing that Mrs. Givens never seemed to change. She was still full of energy and health, despite her advancing years.

"I'm just glad you're safely here. I know you must be tired and hungry, dear, after your long drive, so I made a little casserole for your dinner tonight. I'm sure you're much too tired to think about preparing a meal." Giving Abby's five-foot-seven-inch form another look, Mrs. Givens shook her head. "All you young women today seem so thin to me, as if you never take time to eat."

Abby smiled at that but decided not to comment further on it. "It's been a long drive, and you're right, I'm tired and hungry." Abby rubbed her eyes as though trying to wipe the weariness away before continuing. "I just didn't think about how hard this would be, arriving and finding the house dark and empty. Usually Grandmother is waiting at the door for me. Believe me, a warm meal will help lift my spirits."

Mrs. Givens went to collect the casserole from her kitchen and followed Abby back to the house, carefully carrying the dish. Abby picked up the suitcases sitting by the car and carried them inside, dropping them in the entry hall and following Mrs. Givens into the kitchen. The delicious aroma of chicken and herbs rose in the steam of the casserole. Mrs. Givens set the casserole in the oven. "I'll just turn the oven on low, dear, and it will stay warm until you want to eat." She bustled around the kitchen, gathering utensils and laying a place setting for Abby at the table. Abby smiled, glad to have someone with her for the moment.

"I'll take my suitcases up to the bedroom and be right down," she told Mrs. Givens. She returned to the entry, grabbed her stuff, and went up the stairs to her bedroom. Abby placed the suitcases on the bed and looked around. She noticed that someone—probably Mrs. Givens, as she was the only one who had a key to the house—had cleaned the room and made the bed with fresh linen. A vase of lilacs and daffodils was sitting on the ancient dresser, and the heady scent of the lilacs filled the small room with the early smells of spring. New tears stung her eyes as she turned and started back down the stairs. She gave herself a mental shake and whispered to herself, "Come on, Abby, buck up. Don't be such a baby. You're twenty-six years old—old enough to handle what's ahead of you."

Entering the kitchen again, she put her arms around Mrs. Givens. "Thanks so much for everything, for dinner and for getting my room ready. It was hard to enter this empty home, but just your being here has made it so much easier."

Mrs. Givens hugged her back. "Oh, my dear, I'm so glad it helps. I loved your grandmother very much, and you're part of her. However, I know you're tired tonight, so I won't stay but will say good-night now and talk to you tomorrow. And, please, don't hesitate to call me if there is anything more you need."

At the door, Mrs. Givens gave Abby another quick squeeze before leaving. Abby watched until Mrs. Givens had entered her own home then returned to the car to bring in the last of the things she had brought with her. Feeling the emptiness in her stomach, she decided to eat before unpacking.

After dinner, she rinsed her few dishes and placed them in the dishwasher before turning off the kitchen light and heading upstairs to her bedroom. The quiet of the old house settled around her, and she gave a deep yawn. She was just too tired to unpack tonight. She would call her parents and Scott to let them know she had arrived safely, take a quick bath, and go to bed. Tomorrow would be soon enough to start going through the house.

Later, lying in bed in the dark, she tried to think of a plan for what she should do first, but the quiet around her and the weariness of her body caught up with her, and she fell into a deep sleep.

***

25 December 1844

My name is Catherine Anne Moore, and I was born to Benjamin Collins Moore and MaryAnne Carlisle on the fifteenth day of March in the year 1826, and I am now seventeen years of age. I am an only child, my parents being somewhat older in years when they married. I suppose that I should also describe what I look like. I am tall and slender, like my father, but my hair is black and curly like Mother's, and my eyes are green like hers as well. Mother says I have a somewhat stubborn nature when I feel I am right.

Today is Christmas Day, and Father has given me this journal as a gift. I love the idea of writing my secret thoughts and feelings in this small book. I should also mention that my father is the vicar of our parish and is much loved in our little village.

I live in the village of Fornham St. Mary, in the shire of Norfolk, England, and I love the gentle hills and fields of green surrounding my village. In the spring, the fields around our home burst with the color of wildflowers: daffodils, Queen Anne's lace, buttercups, daisies, and moss roses. On hot summer afternoons, I love to take a book and sit by the River Tas to read. The air is heavy with the rich smells of the earth and the lazy humming of bees as they fly from flower to flower. I love the song of the birds in the early morning when the world is slowly awakening and the day is new and fresh and I feel the wonderment of the creation. I love the old vicarage where I live, with its ancient flint walls covered with green ivy, and the gentle shabby rooms inside that ramble together.

Today being Christmas, the house is filled with the scent of pine boughs. The Christmas goose is slowly roasting, and the spicy smells of the

Christmas cookies that Mother and I baked yesterday linger in the air. Mother has made me a new dress for Christmas, and I wore it to church services this morning. The dress is of green wool with the collars and cuffs trimmed in white lace, and Father says the green matches my eyes.

Our old church looked beautiful this morning, with boughs of green pine twined around the bench railings, their pungent smell filling the room. I never tire of hearing the story of the baby born in the stable with only the stars from the heavens lighting the room and the animals the only witnesses to the birth. I love singing the Christmas carols, our old church filling with the music of worship, sounding as the heavens must have when the angels sang.

Tom Fisher was there with his family, and he stopped to talk to me after the service. Tom is two years older than I am, and he asked Father if he could walk me home. Tom's family lives on one of the farms in the village, and we have been friends all our lives. He is a tall man with blond hair and blue eyes. He has a somewhat serious nature, and I hoped he would notice my new dress. Tom's parents are kind people, and he has three sisters and two brothers.

As we walked home through the cold winter air, my heart was full of the joy of Christmas. It has been such a beautiful day—the ground covered with the new snow that fell through the night and the world around us turned into a sparkling fairy land by the light. Tom did notice my new dress and said he will look forward to seeing me at the party Elizabeth's family will be hosting next week to celebrate the New Year. Life is so good, and I am truly blessed.

Chapter 2

Abby awoke early the next morning to sunlight flooding through her windows. After the rush of the last few weeks in Denver, arranging her clients and job for an extended leave, the quiet of the morning seemed a gift from heaven. She lay in bed listening to the cheerful singing of the birds in the tree outside her open window before finally tossing the covers aside. She sat for a few seconds longer on the side of the bed and thought of the job ahead of her. Abby was grateful for the brightness of the morning, for it alleviated some of the sorrow she felt at the idea of packing up her grandmother's home. And so many memories. With a sigh, Abby stood up, stretched her arms, and walked into the bathroom.

After showering, she quickly blow-dried her short chestnut-brown hair then pulled on jeans and a yellow pullover sweater and went downstairs to the kitchen. As she poured herself a glass of orange juice and put a slice of bread in the toaster, the empty silence of the home surrounded her and she once again missed her grandmother's presence. The best cure, she told herself, was to keep busy and focus on what needed to be done. She retrieved a yellow writing pad and a pencil from her briefcase and sat down at the kitchen table to begin one of her famous "to do" lists. She couldn't count the number of times her grandmother had teased her about her need to make lists—lists of steps to complete a project, items to buy, or just reminders of things she did not want to forget. She pushed the thought aside. It had served her well so far, and now it would help her accomplish her current task. She knew she needed to buy groceries sometime during the day, but looking around the kitchen, she decided the first order of business would be to dust and vacuum thoroughly. She appreciated the start Mrs. Givens had made, but since the house had been empty for more than a month, it needed a complete cleaning. At home, her mother had a weekly scheduled housekeeper for cleaning, and she was sure she could find someone here as well. But today this would be a good outlet for the emotional sadness she felt. Abby ate her breakfast quickly then gathered cleaning supplies and started with the kitchen. She took a quick break at noon to eat an apple and went back to work. By late afternoon, the kitchen, dining room, and living room smelled fresh and clean, and she decided to leave her grandmother's bedroom for another day. She dreaded the thought of working in that room as she remembered her grandmother's personal belongings still scattered around the room.

As Abby was putting away the cleaning supplies, her cell phone rang. It was Scott, just giving her a quick call before he left his office. At the sound of his voice, she realized she already missed him, and she had only been away from him for a day.

"I'm so glad you called. I'm feeling pretty lonely right now."

"I hit a slight break at work and just wanted to hear your voice." He gave a soft chuckle. "Here I am, surrounded by all sorts of people and problems, and I'm feeling lonely too. So what's going on there?"

They talked for a few minutes before reluctantly saying good-bye. She was definitely homesick, and the job ahead of her seemed long and cheerless.

Putting her phone in her pocket, she ran upstairs to grab a sweater and her purse. She located her shopping list in the kitchen, locked the house, and started off to find a grocery store.

St. George had really grown since the last time she had come. Supermarkets, shopping centers, and big-box stores had opened and filled the city with new shopping opportunities. New housing developments had spread onto the bluffs and farmlands around the city. The traffic was also much busier than she remembered it being. True, it was early March, and many of the retirees or snowbirds, as they were called, who wintered in St. George were still here. After driving around for a bit, she found a supermarket she wanted to try.

Abby fished through her purse until she found her list and was just starting to fill her cart when she heard someone call her name. As she looked around, she saw a young pregnant woman with bright red hair and freckles pushing her cart toward her.

"Is that really you, Abby Peters? You remember me, don't you?" the woman asked.

"Of course, I remember you, Megan." Abby laughed, reaching out to clasp the outstretched hands. "How could I ever forget you, even though it seems forever since we were together? Didn't we have fun when I was staying at Grandmother's for the summer?" She sighed. "Those were really good days." Pausing a second to push her cart out of the middle of the aisle, she went on. "When I came the last time, I called your parents, and they said you were staying at college during the summer months. Then Grandmother wrote me that you were getting married. And now it looks like there is going to be an addition to your family," she continued, smiling at Megan, whose tummy bulged beneath her jacket.

Megan laughed, patting her rounded stomach. "You noticed, huh? This baby isn't too far away. Do you remember the huge crush I had on Ryan Fellows in high school? Well, he finally proposed, and I married him two years ago. I love married life!" She paused then reached out to take Abby's hands again, her eyes full of sympathy. "Seriously, Abby, I'm so sorry about your grandmother. Ryan and I were away when she died, and I felt bad I wasn't here to attend her funeral. I always loved being around her." She paused then continued, "I heard you were coming back to stay for a while, and I was going to come by tomorrow to see you. I bet it's lonely and difficult for you with her being gone."

"It is lonely, and I really do miss Grandmother. The house seems so empty without her, and I see her everywhere I look. My parents are thinking of selling the old home, so I'll be here until I have it ready to be placed on the market."

Megan nodded her head in agreement. "I'm sure it has to be hard for you. Just remember that I'm here if you need me. Now, what about you? Anyone serious in your life? I don't see a ring on your finger."

Abby laughed. "If you mean 'am I involved with someone,' then yes, there is a man I'm dating seriously, and we're talking marriage but have no definite plans as yet. Megan, it's so good to see you. Let's get together for lunch one day this week and catch up on what's been happening with each other. Could you get away sometime?" Abby asked.

Megan again nodded her head. "I'll make time because we definitely need to get together and have a good chat. I'm working as an accountant with Jones and Jones here in town, but I can get away for a long lunch this Tuesday if that will work for you."

"Tuesday would be fine. You know the town, so why don't you decide on a time and place and let me know," Abby said, handing Megan a card with her cell phone number on it.

"That sounds great," Megan replied, tucking the card into her pocket. "I'll give you a call." Glancing at her watch, she gasped. "I didn't realize it was so late. Ryan and I are celebrating our two-year anniversary tonight, and I'm cooking a romantic dinner for him, so I have to dash. But, Abby, it's so good to see you again, and I can't wait until we can really talk. See you Tuesday."

Megan waved good-bye as she wheeled her cart down the aisle, narrowly missing an elderly man who moved quickly to the side as she pushed past him. Abby smiled as she placed some pork chops in her cart and started for the checkout line. It was good to see Megan again. They had become close friends when she came to stay with her grandparents. They were the same age and attended the same ward, and though they saw each other only during the summer and occasionally at holidays, they were always able to pick up right where they had left off from the previous visit. Even though Abby came from a very affluent family and Megan from a farm family where money was always tight, they were kindred spirits. She and Megan had loved many of the same things: Barbies, reading, playing duets on Abby's grandmother's piano. They also both loved hot fudge sundaes and popcorn. Abby's favorite comfort food was still popcorn. The last few summers Abby had spent with her grandmother as a teenager, the girls had had increasingly differing goals, but it had never diminished their enjoyment of the time they spent together. Temple marriage and church had become less important goals for Abby as she and her parents had drifted into inactivity, but they had become more important for Megan. Abby also wanted to live her life in a big city with all the excitement that it would offer, whereas Megan loved the small town scene. Remembering Megan's crush on Ryan Fellows, she was glad they had married.

After dinner, Abby carried the clean casserole dish, along with a small basket of fruit she had purchased that afternoon, to the house next door. Ringing the doorbell, she looked around at the neat flowerbeds. *Mrs. Givens must still love to garden*, she thought.

"Come in, Abby," Mrs. Givens said with a happy smile on her face. She opened the door wider, gesturing for Abby to come in.

Abby stepped inside and handed Mrs. Givens the basket of fruit.

"Oh, Abby, how nice of you. I've been hoping all day you would stop by. Please sit down and tell me what you've been doing."

Abby followed her into the living room. Little had changed since the last time she had been in the home with her grandmother. The room was full of stuffed sofas and chairs. Curios and pictures of her daughters, sons-in-law, and grandchildren filled every available space on the tables and cabinets. The room was spotless, and she could only imagine the amount of time it must take to dust all the ornaments and bric-a-brac. Abby sat down on an overstuffed chair that faced the older woman. "It was a busy morning, but I had a nice surprise this afternoon. I met an old friend of mine, Megan Morris, in the supermarket. It was great to see her again. I guess, though, it should be Megan Fellows, since she's married now and is expecting her first baby."

Mrs. Givens smiled, nodding her head. "I remember Megan very well. She has such lovely red hair. Of course, all the children in that family were carrottops like their father."

"Yes, it's easy to see where her red hair came from," Abby responded thoughtfully. "I often wonder which ancestor gave me my green eyes. Mom and Dad's eyes are both blue, and my grandparents were combinations of brown and blue."

"Your green eyes are an unusual color, dear, that's for sure. But they do make a beautiful combination with your hair. Sometimes it's hard to know just where those genes come from," Mrs. Givens said, shaking her head. "I remember when Megan and her family were in our ward years ago, before the ward was divided. They were such a nice family. In fact, I went with your grandmother to Megan's wedding. That Ryan Fellows is a nice boy." She paused a moment to reflect then continued, "Yes, that was his name, and it was a lovely wedding, all done in shades of blue."

Mrs. Givens enjoyed telling Abby about Megan's wedding in even greater detail. Finally, when she paused for breath, Abby smiled and stood up.

"I guess I'd better get back since I still have a few more things I need to do tonight." Giving Mrs. Givens a hug, she continued, "Thanks again for the casserole; it was delicious. Also, thanks for making my room so nice for me. I especially loved the fresh flowers. Please let me know if there is anything I can do for you while I'm here."

"Well, actually there is," Mrs. Givens answered with a twinkle in her eye. "My car was taken to the shop yesterday and won't be ready until Monday. Would you mind picking me up for church tomorrow morning? It starts at nine, and I know you will want to go. Mary—your mother—still has many friends in town who will be glad to see you."

Abby groaned inwardly. It had been a long time since she had been to a Church meeting, and she had definitely not planned on going to church tomorrow. She wanted to start going through her grandmother's things and maybe work in the yard. *Oh well*, she thought, *I'll still have time after church. As kind as she has been to me, I need to do this for her.*

"Of course," Abby responded with a smile. "I'll be glad to take you. What time do you want me to pick you up?"

"Eight-forty-five should be fine, dear, and I'm so glad you can go with me. I'll see you in the morning." Mrs. Givens closed the door as Abby walked home. *Gosh, I hope this doesn't happen every Sunday*, she reflected.

It was such a beautiful evening that she couldn't bring herself to stay inside but walked straight through the house to sit on the patio in the backyard. She had only been outside for a few minutes that morning to shake some rugs, so she really hadn't taken time to see what outdoor work needed to be done. A block fence enclosed the backyard, giving it privacy from the neighboring houses. Abby could see that several changes had been made since her last visit five years ago. A rock waterfall had been added in one corner, and the patio had been extended with a covered lattice frame to give additional shade. She had always loved her grandmother's flower gardens and had spent many hours during summer vacations helping her grandparents with the weeding.

She walked around the yard, making a mental note to find someone to help with the heavier yard work. Her grandmother had not had time to prepare the flowerbeds for the upcoming season, and they were full of weeds. The roses also needed to be trimmed and cleaned. Abby wandered back to the patio and sat down on a chair, enjoying the last of the day's warmth, her mind remembering past summer evenings she had sat there with her grandparents. As the evening shadows lengthened across the lawn, she shivered, drawing her mind back to reality and the fact that with the sun going down, the air was turning cool. Giving a last look around, she stood up and went back inside the house.

Abby wandered in and out of the downstairs rooms, unable to concentrate on anything, which was unusual for her. She realized she was still lonely and missed Scott. He seemed to bring excitement with him wherever he went. She was proud of the fact that both business associates and personal friends liked him. At parties, he was usually the center of a large group, his quick wit and humor making him popular with both men and women. She was pleased with the meticulous care he took with his grooming and lean form. He was also very ambitious and aggressive with his law practice and had definite career and financial goals. Abby knew that when they married she would be assured of a financially secure future, although she loved her career and planned on working for many years.

When her grandmother died, Abby had asked Scott what church he belonged to, and he had replied that he didn't really have one, that he didn't know if he believed in organized religion. He had been baptized in a church when he was a baby and believed in a God but felt that if he lived a good and honest life that was all that was required of him. She had been troubled by his answer. Even though she didn't attend her church often, she believed religion was important, especially when they had children. It was one issue they would just have to work out together.

As she entered the living room, she noticed the old Steinway piano along the wall and walked over to it. She had taken piano lessons from the time she was six years old until she had entered college. As a teenager she had wanted to quit, but her mother had insisted she keep going. Abby had argued with her mother that her life was too busy with friends and school but finally gave up and kept at her lessons. Looking at the old piano, Abby was glad that her mother had encouraged her to continue; playing the piano was something she loved to do. She pulled the bench out, sat down, and opened the cover. She let her fingers run idly over the keys, noticing that the piano needed tuning. Then she started playing "Moonlight Sonata," her grandfather's favorite piece. As she played, she remembered that as a child she had sat on this bench with her grandfather, and he had taught her to play "Chop Sticks." He'd had a twinkle in his eye as he helped her find the right keys. That had been the beginning of her desire to learn how to play. She loved this old piano and was glad her mother was giving it to her.

Finally, she closed the cover with a sigh and went upstairs to her room. She was tired and would need to be up early the next morning for church. Stretching out on the bed, she punched in her parents' phone number on her cell phone. The phone rang several times before she heard her mother's voice.

After filling her mother in on all the day's news, she remarked on how lonely the house seemed without her grandmother.

"Every once in a while, I will enter a room and think I will see her there, and then I realize once again she is gone, and I miss her all the more. Mom, I wish so much I'd come last winter when I'd planned, and I worry that she didn't know how much I loved her, how important she was in my life." Abby paused. "I guess it also tells me that I need to let the people around me know how much I care, that opportunities to share love with others can end." With a catch in her voice, she said, "I guess I'd better go to bed. Mrs. Givens asked me to take her to church tomorrow, and I didn't know how to refuse.

I'd planned on using the day to start going through Grandmother's room, but I guess it will keep."

"I'm glad you're going, Abby," Mary answered. "Since Mother's death, I've been remembering how much the Church meant to my parents. I know our passive attitude toward the gospel was a silent heartache to my mother. I've been thinking about the joyful reunion that has taken place now that she's once again with your grandfather." Mary paused as if considering her words and then continued. "You know, Abby, when we have to face the loss of a loved one or go through a challenging trial, we seem more ready to recognize the need for spiritual help in our own lives. I'm sorry now for some of the choices your father and I made that took us, as a family, away from Church activity. Maybe it's time for all of us to make some changes, to rethink our priorities."

After ending the call, Abby was glad she had called home. Her mother's words of comfort and encouragement had helped ease some of the loneliness and grief she was feeling.

Placing the cell phone on the nightstand, she lay in bed and listened to the old home settle itself for the night as she mentally went over her day.

***

1 January 1845

New Year's Day, a day for new beginnings. Father has always said this is the day we need to look back at what we have accomplished during the year and make new goals and changes for improvement in our lives during the new year. Last night Mother, Father, and I went to a party at Elizabeth Brown's home. Elizabeth is my best friend, and she, under the supervision of her mother, had been planning this party for weeks. I wore my new green dress and brushed my hair until it shone and then pinned it up. Elizabeth and her family live in a very large home in the village. Her father is the squire, and the manor house is far grander than our home. I have shared lessons with Elizabeth in her home for years, and it has been a joy to me to read and study about the places in the world. Mother says I am also a dreamer, but I love to imagine myself traveling one day to faraway places. Elizabeth's mother is known in our village as a woman who speaks her mind regardless of whom she hurts, but I know she truly loves her family and is a kind woman at heart. Elizabeth has some of her mother's fiery temperament but is a good and loyal friend. She has been as close as a sister to me, and I love her dearly. She likes Tom's friend David, and we share secrets with each other.

This afternoon I helped Elizabeth decorate the drawing room for the party. We made fresh bouquets of pine and holly and placed them on the large table in the dining room, and it looked so festive with the dark green leaves and red berries of the holly branches lying on the snowy white cloth. Elizabeth and her mother had planned a fine dinner for us, and we ate dainty veal and ham pies, roast beef and Yorkshire pudding, roasted potatoes, parsnips and carrots in a cream sauce, and blackcap pudding and trifle for dessert. Elizabeth's father greeted guests as they arrived. He is a small, soft-spoken man who loves the country life and especially his fine stable of horses. During the fall and spring, the manor house is filled with visitors invited for the hunt activities.

At dinner, David mentioned that as he passed the village green that morning, two men were preaching about a new religion founded in America. They called themselves missionaries for The Church of Jesus Christ of Latter-day Saints and said the heavens have been opened and a new prophet has been ordained of the Lord to lead this new church. They further stated that new revelations had also been received that were important to all people on earth. The idea of new revelations sounded strange to each of us, and I cannot understand how anyone in our village will listen to them.

As Tom walked me home, he took my hand and nestled it in his large one. I felt so secure and special. He has asked Father's permission to court me, and I know in my heart that I care for him so much. My new goals for the coming year include ones that will help me to develop my character and skills to be a good wife.

Chapter 3

Sunday morning Abby woke early and hurried out of bed and into the shower. She was glad now that she had packed her green skirt and matching jacket. Giving her hair a final brush, she glanced at her reflection in the mirror. The deep green of the jacket brought out the green in her eyes and the deep red tones in her brown hair. She thought of the Sundays she had attended church with her grandparents, and on this bright beautiful day, she felt the peace of the Sabbath. As Abby was preparing to leave, a sudden memory surfaced, and she remembered that her grandmother always took her scriptures with her to Church meetings, so she hurried to the study to look for them. Her grandparents had given her a set when she turned eight and was baptized, but even if she had been home, she wouldn't have been sure where they were located. Looking quickly over the bookshelves in the study, she did not see her grandmother's scriptures. Going downstairs, she entered her grandmother's bedroom, and a feeling of deep loss filled her heart. She squared her shoulders and blinked back the tears threatening to flood her eyes as she continued searching the room. Finally, she located her grandmother's set of scriptures in the nightstand by the bed. Grabbing her purse and carrying the scriptures, she locked the front door and walked next door. Mrs. Givens was waiting for her, and together they walked back to Abby's car.

The drive to the chapel was a short one. Abby remembered that when she was young they had walked to church many times. She helped Mrs. Givens from the car, and together they entered the building. After being greeted at the door, Abby followed the older woman up the aisle to a bench near the front of the chapel. *Oh great,* she thought, *we're practically sitting on the front row!*

"This is where I always sit, dear," whispered Mrs. Givens in Abby's ear. "I like to be near the front so I can see the faces of the speakers. Besides," she added, pointing to the small hearing aid in her ear, "my hearing is not as good as it used to be."

Abby nodded her head in acknowledgment then sat back and listened to the organ prelude music. Just over a month ago, she had sat in this chapel with her parents for her grandmother's funeral. The pulpit and stand had been surrounded by fresh flower arrangements, the air full of their intoxicating and sweet fragrances and the atmosphere reverent and hushed. A lump came to her throat, and she quickly swallowed. Mrs. Givens, as if aware of Abby's pain, reached over and touched her hand. This small gesture comforted Abby, and she gently squeezed Mrs. Givens's hand. As the meeting started, she found she enjoyed singing the hymns, and she caught herself listening carefully to the speakers. After the closing prayer, Mrs. Givens guided her to the Relief Society room, where the Gospel Doctrine Sunday School class would be taught. On the way to class, many people stopped to introduce themselves to Abby, expressing how much they had loved her grandmother and were glad she was there. There were also several older members who remembered her mother and asked about her.

When they were seated in the Relief Society room, Abby was surprised to see that Blake Matthews was the instructor for the class. She remembered seeing him at church when she was here visiting her grandparents during the summer. When she was a teenager, she had developed a small crush on him, mostly because Megan had a huge crush on Ryan Fellows and Blake was his best friend. She had met him again at the funeral for her grandmother but recalled she did not have much time to talk with him because of the many people waiting to greet her. The one thing she had noticed as he had talked with her at the viewing, however, was the intensity of his blue eyes and the feeling that he understood her grief. She had thought him a quiet guy, but now, seeing him teach the class, Abby realized he was full of confidence and love for his subject. He was tall, well over six feet, with brown wavy hair, a square firm jawline, and those deep blue eyes. She acknowledged that he had become a very attractive man and wondered briefly why he was still single, since he must be about thirty years old. He was dressed in the usual dark suit and white shirt "church attire." She smiled as she noticed the leather cowboy boots on his feet. As if he were aware of her scrutiny, he turned his head, met her gaze, and smiled. Abby blushed and looked down quickly, surprised at her reaction. *Really?* she asked herself. *You haven't done that since you were a teenager.*

He was teaching a lesson from the Book of Mormon. As Abby opened her scriptures and thumbed through the pages to find the chapter they were studying, she saw how her grandmother must have loved her scriptures and read them often. Favorite and significant verses had been underlined, and notes and additional sources had been added in her grandmother's fine writing. Abby felt that lump in her throat rise again as she looked at the writing, remembering all the notes and letters she had received from her grandmother over the years. As she studied the written notations, she was impressed with the amount of understanding her grandmother had for the scriptures.

After class, as Blake left the room for priesthood meeting, he stopped to shake Abby's hand and welcome her to the class.

"It's good to see you again, Abby. I've been meaning to stop by and see if there's anything that I can do to help. Your grandmother was more than just my patient—she was my friend as well. After my father died, she made a point to stop and visit with my mother often, and after my mother died, your grandmother frequently took pity on me and had me over for dinner." He smiled down at Abby. "I've heard your parents are going to sell the house, so I know you'll need help getting that big yard in shape. Please let me help with that, as well as anything that needs an extra set of hands. I was going to come by this week and offer, so give me a call when you're ready for my assistance."

Abby took his card with his address and phone number and put it in her purse. "Thanks. I haven't had time to really make a list of what needs to be done outside, but I'm sure there'll be times I'll be glad for an extra set of hands." Smiling up at him, she added, "I really enjoyed the class today. It's been quite awhile since I attended church, but I'm glad I came today. You're a good instructor."

Blake grinned. "Thanks, I'm glad you came today as well, and just let me know, then, when you need my help. I'll be expecting that call." He gave her another quick smile then hurried off to his next class.

Abby also enjoyed Relief Society. The class consisted of a range of women of various ages, and she was surprised at how comfortable she felt there. She had never attended a Relief Society meeting before and always supposed it was an organization for older women. When she had come for her last few visits, she had arrived on Friday night and left early Sunday morning so she could be back to school on Monday. This schedule made it impossible for her to attend church with her grandmother. The instructor for the class was a young woman near her age, and she too gave a well-prepared lesson that invited active participation from the ladies attending the class.

After class, the Relief Society president, Sister Richardson, made it a point to stop and introduce herself to Abby. "I'm so glad you came today and hope you'll come often while you're here. It will be a little like having your grandmother back with us."

"Thank you, Sister Richardson," Abby responded, reaching out to shake the offered hand. "I enjoyed the lesson today. And thanks again for the luncheon the Relief Society prepared for us after my grandmother's funeral. It meant a lot to my family."

"You're welcome, Sister Peters. We were glad to be of help, and we appreciated the lovely thank you card your mother sent us after the funeral. Your grandmother was always one of the first to offer her services in our ward; whatever we needed, she was prepared to give." Shaking her head sadly, she added, "We all miss her very much."

Looking around, Abby realized Mrs. Givens was waiting patiently for her at the door, and with a quick smile added, "I'll try and come back before I go home, and thank you again." She shook Sister Richardson's hand one more time and hurried toward the door.

Abby pulled into Mrs. Givens's driveway and helped her from the car and into her house. After turning down an offer to stay for Sunday dinner, she got back in the car and pulled into her own driveway. The first thing she did after she entered the old home was open the windows in the downstairs rooms. That morning's promise of a beautiful day manifested itself in the light, pleasant breeze that lazily carried the scent of spring flowers through the air. The middle of March in Dixie, as St. George was commonly known, was one of the best seasons of the year. Lawns were starting to wear their vivid green coats, and the trees were a mass of color, from the pink and white blossoms on flowering trees to the bright spring green of new leaves opening their buds. Daffodils and tulips bloomed in a multitude of brilliant hues, and hyacinths raised their fragrant heads to the sky, their rich perfume filling the air. Breathing deeply of the scented fresh air as it drifted into the house, Abby felt her spirits lift even higher. She also opened the window in her bedroom and then quickly changed her clothes, pulling on casual cotton pants and a tailored shirt. Instead of returning the scriptures to her grandmother's bedside table, she put them on the nightstand in her own room. She had felt a comfort and peace today as she read with the class and decided to leave the scriptures close by.

Entering the kitchen, she felt this would be a good day to eat lunch on the patio. Taking bread from the pantry and deli meat and cheese from the refrigerator, she made herself a sandwich and grabbed an apple on the way out to the patio. As she ate her sandwich, she looked around the yard, mentally adding to her list additional projects that would bring order back to the flowerbeds. It also looked as though several of the trees needed to be pruned, along with the rose bushes. A couple of old shrubs were overgrown and needed to be removed. Abby was glad Blake had offered to help. If he could even give her a few names of someone to do the actual work, that would be a tremendous relief.

As she was finishing her lunch, her cell phone rang. She carried her plate into the kitchen and grabbed her phone.

"Abby, it's Scott," said the deep masculine voice. "I've been trying to reach you since nine this morning. Where have you been? I thought you were working at home today."

Holding the phone to her ear, Abby retraced her steps to the patio. "I'm sorry. I wasn't here," she answered. "Mrs. Givens, who lives next door, asked me to take her to church this morning, and I couldn't refuse. Actually, I quite enjoyed going. Scott, it's such a heavenly day. I just finished eating my lunch on the patio. Can you imagine it? And it's seventy degrees outside! I'm looking at an overgrown yard, but flowers are blooming, and birds are singing."

"Well, I'm glad you're enjoying your day," Scott grumbled. "It's thirty-five degrees in Denver and snowing lightly, and I'm still at the office working." She heard him give a deep sigh. "I'm sorry, Abby, I'm just tired. Your father and I have been working practically around the clock on this case. So I hope you've had enough time to analyze the situation there and give me a date for when you're coming back."

"But Scott—" she interrupted, her voice suddenly heated.

Scott quickly interjected, "Okay, okay, I'm sorry. It's just that it already seems like forever since you were here, and I'm ready to start thinking about our own future together. Let's change the subject, shall we?" She heard him take a deep breath before continuing. "Abby, you remember me talking about George Ross? He's an important client for the firm, and he's hosting a formal dinner party toward the middle of next month at his home. It's mandatory for me to attend, and I want you to go with me. Any chance you can at least come home for that if you're not through there?"

Calming herself, Abby plunged in. "Scott, I really hope I'll be through here by then, but I'm just not sure if it's possible. Remember, though, that I have to come back for the Towers' closing sometime next month, so I'll try to arrange it for the same time, if possible. Either way, I promise I'll be there. And I'll plan on staying in Denver for a few days before coming back here so we can have time together. Please, Scott, just be patient with me. I've only been here two days and haven't had time to do more than make a start. This really is important to me." In a softer tone, she added, "And I miss you too and wish you were here with me."

They talked a little longer about what Abby hoped to accomplish then signed off. Abby walked back in the house and put the cell phone on the counter. "So much for a quiet Sunday," she said to herself. "I'd better go through the house and make a schedule of what needs to be done in each room. That way I can get an early start in the morning."

She had just picked up her notepad and pen when her phone rang again. This time it was Megan.

"Abby, I hoped you would answer. I didn't know if you were going to church today but thought you would probably be home by now if you did. So, are you getting along all right, being there by yourself?"

Abby sat down again at the table. "Megan, I'm so glad you called. It's very different to be here without Grandmother, and, yes, I did go to church. Mrs. Givens asked me to take her this morning, and it felt good to be there. I just haven't gone to church much the past few years, and I think the times I was here and went with my grandparents were the best." Pausing for a minute, she asked, "Are we still getting together this Tuesday?"

"That's one of the reasons I called," Megan answered. "I thought we could meet at The Old Cottage restaurant for lunch. They have a really nice luncheon menu, so how about meeting me there at one-thirty? That way we can avoid the height of the lunch crowd. I have the afternoon off, so we can have a nice long lunch and catch up on all the news."

"That works great for me; I'll see you there on Tuesday. Thanks for calling, Megan. I'm glad you're still living here." Abby placed the phone in her pocket and picked up her notebook and pen. *Better start with the living room*, she thought.

At the end of three hours, she had made a detailed list of jobs. She knew, however, that she would spend the most time going through her grandmother's keepsakes and papers. Her mother had asked her to sort through her grandfather's personal papers as well to determine which should be kept; anything questionable was to be put in a separate box, and her father would look through them later. As she had gone through each room and made her list, Abby was once again filled with the emotion of loss for what had been and could now never be again. She pondered how strange it was that possessions and material goods last longer on this earth than people do, yet people spend a lifetime collecting and buying only to leave everything when they die.

Dusty and tired, she went upstairs for a quick shower. It was getting dark, and she remembered that when her parents were active in the Church they had taught her that the Sabbath was a day for rest, a day of putting aside the normal activities of the work week. Suddenly she thought of the Primary song she had learned years ago that taught how Saturday was the day to prepare for Sunday and found herself humming the tune. Yes, she had done enough for one day, more than what she should have done. She would make herself a big bowl of her favorite comfort food, popcorn with butter, and find a book to read.

***

On Monday morning, Abby started in the living room, sorting into boxes the pictures and knickknacks her grandmother had been so fond of. Abby found her own name on some of the things her grandmother had particularly wanted her to have. There were the Hummel boy and girl figurines she had always loved, along with several framed family pictures, and these she placed in a separate box. She stopped only long enough to grab a quick sandwich for lunch then went back to work. By late afternoon, she had finished the living room and decided to reward herself with a bubble bath before preparing her dinner.

After a relaxing soak in the tub, she felt refreshed and hungry. She was on her way downstairs when her cell phone rang. She quickly ran back upstairs to her room and grabbed the phone off the table by the bed. She was breathless when she answered.

"Abby, are you all right? You sound as if you've been running," her mother inquired.

Sitting down on the edge of the bed, Abby drew another quick breath. "I feel like I have been running all day, but I was halfway down the stairs when the phone rang and I had to run back upstairs to get it. Mom, I'm so glad you called. I've been sorting and packing the things in the living room all day, and it has made me think so much of Grandmother and Grandfather Brown. And when I was cleaning out Grandmother's curio cabinet, I was surprised to find the little lopsided ceramic flower vase I made for her in a summer art class. I think I was about nine years old. I can't believe she kept it all these years. It looked pretty sad to me!"

Mary laughed, "Yes, I remember that vase and how proud of it you were. Mother always treasured anything that someone gave her. I'm sure that this has been the first of several emotional days you will have as you go through things, so be patient with yourself."

"I'll try and remember that; so how are you and Dad getting along without me?"

"We're doing fine," Mary returned. "Missing you but glad you're there and willing to help. I really called to ask how you enjoyed going to church yesterday."

Propping herself farther on the bed, Abby smiled. "You know, I really enjoyed it more than I thought I would. Mrs. Givens is such a sweet woman, and she took good care of me. I met several people who asked about you. When I first entered the chapel, it reminded me so much of Grandmother's funeral that I had to fight back a few tears, and then I found myself enjoying the talks and lessons. It was also good to mingle with people again. I was surprised to see that Dr. Matthews, Grandmother's doctor, was the instructor for the Gospel Doctrine class, but he's a good teacher. He also offered to help with the outside work, so that's a relief to know there's someone I can call for help. How about you, Mom, what did you do yesterday?"

There was a quiet pause for a few seconds, then Mary said quietly, "I'm glad you have an offer of help, Abby. As far as yesterday, actually, I also went to church." She continued hesitantly. "Mother's death has made me recognize I need to make some changes for good in my own life. Your father was busy working at the office. The Chapman case will be going to trial next week, and he and Scott are busy tying up loose ends, so I went by myself. I'll admit that I felt alone when I entered the doors of the building." She paused before going on, and Abby could hear the sadness in her mother's voice. "You know how few times we have gone to this ward, and I wasn't sure if I would remember anyone's name. But once I was inside, I felt really welcome." She chuckled before continuing. "I wondered if Bishop Anderson would faint from shock at seeing me there, but he made a point of shaking my hand and telling me he was glad I had come. You remember our home teacher, Brother Wright? Well, he invited me to sit with him and his wife, Margaret. I'm sure he was surprised to see me there as well since we haven't given him any encouragement over the last few years. It's just too bad I waited until Mother's death before deciding that my spiritual life needed to be fixed. But it's like I told you Saturday night, Abby, the death of a loved one can help bring the spiritual focus back into our lives, to remind us of what's really important."

Changing the subject, they talked a few more minutes about what needed to be done in the house before saying their good-byes. As Abby started back downstairs she thought, *Grandmother would be proud of us both for going to church yesterday.*

***

20 January 1845

This morning I encountered the Mormons. They are called this because of a book they claim their prophet translated, the Book of Mormon. I was crossing the green on my way home, and they were preaching to a small group of people. They are men just past their youth, and their American accents sounded strange to my ears. I stopped to listen for a few minutes, curious as to what they might say. They were telling the small group of listeners about a supposed vision their Prophet Joseph Smith had received when inquiring of the Lord through prayer concerning which church he should join. They claim that God the Father and His Son Jesus Christ appeared to this young man and told him he would be the means of bringing back Christ's church here on the earth. I watched as they talked, and their humble faces and words impressed me in spite of my feeling they were wrong in their beliefs. I found myself wishing I had been able to hear more of what they were saying. They finished by inviting anyone interested to attend a meeting Friday night at Mr. Payne's home.

I told Father about seeing the missionaries and their meeting on Friday. He too has seen them in our village but has not stopped to listen.

It has started to snow again, and Mother and I are going to deliver soup and bread to several families in the village. I am glad I will see Tom tomorrow. We are going sledding with Elizabeth and David.

Chapter 4

Abby arose early the next morning and immediately felt the stiffness in her muscles as she placed her feet on the floor. She pulled on exercise pants and a sweatshirt then laced up her running shoes. Even though she had spent long hours cleaning and sorting, Abby could tell that her body needed some exercise. After a quick brush of her teeth and hair, she grabbed a light jacket and headed outside.

The sun was just rising, and as it cast its golden rays against the bluffs, they flamed into red and orange fire then gradually turned a deep blue as the sun began its upward journey. Taking a deep breath of the clean, fresh air, Abby did a few stretches then started out with a slow run along the quiet neighborhood streets. *How peaceful it is here*, she thought. *At home when I run, I dodge noise and traffic until I enter the park.* After a few minutes, she began running at the easy pace she enjoyed and gave herself up to the beauty of the morning. She slowed her pace as she neared the St. George Temple. The pristine white of the building sparkled in the morning light, and the grounds surrounding it were manicured, a beautiful display of color and order.

She had loved hearing the stories her grandmother told her of how her fourth great-grandfather and grandmother Fisher had been sent by Brigham Young to help settle this area and build the temple. She remembered her grandmother also telling her stories of Tom Fisher's work on the Nauvoo temple and then their journey west with the first group of pioneers to the Salt Lake Valley. When they were called to help with the St. George Temple, Tom and Dorothy, along with their family, had made their home in southern Utah. As

Abby's steps slowed to circle the temple, she marveled at the sacrifices the early pioneers made in both time and materials so this beautiful building could be built. That was a miracle in and of itself. She also recalled her grandmother telling her that Tom had told his children and grandchildren that when he worked on the temple, he felt as if his hands were divinely guided with extra skill and sureness as he cut and shaped the wood for the inside of the temple. To him, the work had truly been a labor of love, a chance to be a part of something that would last forever and be blessed from on high. As he had told his posterity, "Within its walls the sacred sealing of families, both living and dead, would be accomplished, their forever links to last though eternity."

Abby felt a deep sense of gratitude surface for the legacy of honor and courage that was hers. Promising herself that she would come back soon and go through the visitor's center, she turned her steps homeward.

By the time she arrived back at the house, she was tired but relaxed. Entering the kitchen, she fixed herself a bowl of cereal and sliced a few strawberries on top. Then she carried her breakfast to the table by the bay window. As she ate, she looked around the kitchen, noticing how the sunlight flooded the room and touched the rich sheen in the cabinets. The kitchen was a mixture of the old and the new. Her grandparents had modernized it several years ago, just before her grandfather died. The kitchen was painted a soft golden yellow, and the old linoleum floor had been removed to reveal the original oak plank flooring that Tom Fisher had lovingly laid by hand throughout the rooms of the home. It had taken a lot of work to clean and restore the old floor, but the results had definitely been worth it. The countertops were granite, and a modern range, double ovens, dishwasher, and honey maple cabinets had replaced the old stove and painted cupboards. The pine table and chairs where Abby was sitting were the ones Tom Fisher had made. He had been a craftsman, and the old home bore the evidence of his love of working with wood, from the beauty of the spindles in the railing of the staircase to the sideboard and the china cabinet in the dining room. "It is going to be so hard to sell this old home," she told herself wistfully. "It has a warmth and charm all its own, and besides, it's been in our family for such a long time."

After rinsing her bowl and putting it in the dishwasher, Abby walked outside to the garage. It was too beautiful a morning to work inside. Rummaging through the garage, she found her grandmother's bucket of garden tools and pulled on gloves before she set out for the backyard and her grandmother's flower beds. Reminding herself that she only had a few hours before meeting Megan for lunch, she sighed with pleasure as she knelt and started her weeding.

As she worked, she felt the warm sun on her back and experienced a feeling of peace as she pulled weeds, enjoying the feel and smell of the damp soil. As she dug and tugged at a particularly stubborn dandelion, she found herself thinking of Scott. Somehow she couldn't picture him kneeling on a damp lawn and pulling weeds. On a beautiful day like this, if he were free, he would be on a golf course. She wondered if, when they bought a home, he would want one where they could garden or a condo without any outside responsibilities. She tugged harder on the dandelion, and as it lifted away, she fell backwards. As she placed the weed in the bucket, she glanced at her watch and noticed that more than two hours had passed. Hurriedly, she put away the gardening tools then dashed into the house to get ready for her luncheon date. She showered and dressed quickly, thankful her short hair was easy to style with just a quick blow-dry. Grabbing her purse and car keys, she locked the house and headed out.

Fifteen minutes later, she entered the restaurant to see Megan waving to her from a table by the window.

"I can't wait to sit down," Abby exclaimed as she lowered herself into a seat opposite Megan. "I've been running on high all morning, and this is just what I need. I hope you were serious when you said you had the afternoon off!"

"I'm yours for the next few hours," Megan responded with a huge grin as she pushed her shoulder-length hair back from her face and leaned across the table to reach for Abby's hands. "It's so good to see you again, Abby. I've really been looking forward to this lunch date."

They both ordered the grilled chicken salad and then sat back to wait for their food. Abby, looking over at Megan, thought how little her friend had changed since the last time they had been together. Her hair was still the bright red of her teenage years, and her face was dusted lightly with freckles across the bridge of her nose and cheeks. The sky-blue shirt she wore brought out the blue in her eyes. The only difference she could see was Megan's rounded stomach due to her pregnancy.

Megan had been studying Abby as well. "You know, Abby, you haven't changed, except to become more gorgeous than ever." She laughed. "I used to be so envious of your clear, unfreckled skin. Do you remember all the concoctions we used to make trying to get rid of my freckles?" Wrinkling her nose, she added with a laugh, "Some of them really smelled awful, but as you can see, none of them worked. But it's okay now; Ryan calls them 'love spots.'"

The waiter placed their salads in front of them, and they gave themselves up to the enjoyment of eating and making small talk about the memories they had shared in the past.

Finally, Megan pushed her plate away from her. "Okay, I can't eat another bite; now I want to catch up on what's been happening with you since the last time we were together. What did you settle on for a profession? Did you become an attorney like your dad? Also, what about this big romance in your life? Is it really serious? If so, I want to hear all the details, so don't leave anything out!"

Abby pushed her plate back as well and leaned her elbows on the table. "One question at a time, Megan," she replied lightheartedly. "No, I didn't become an attorney like Dad. I graduated in Business Management and moved back to Denver after college. I decided to go into real estate and work for a large firm in the city, and I absolutely love it. There's something so exciting about working with people, and every new venture offers a different challenge. As for my serious romance, Scott is an attorney, and we've talked about getting married, but I'm waiting until I get home before committing myself." She paused for a few seconds, remembering their last night together, then went on. "Both our parents belong to the same country club and are good friends, so they are excited about our relationship as well. He's a very attractive man with a great sense of humor. He is also very ambitious and wants to make his first million by the time he's thirty-five, and if the long hours he works are any indication, I bet he'll do it. I think you would approve of him, Megan."

She looked over at Megan and said, "Now tell me about you. I know you are working as an accountant here in St. George, but what is your life like?" Looking at Megan's expanded stomach, she grinned and continued, "Has it been difficult to prepare for the new addition coming in your family?"

Megan flashed a radiant smile and folded her hands in front of her. "My life is so good, Abby, and the best thing in it is Ryan. Do you remember the huge crush I had on him during high school? Well, after he got home from his mission, we started dating again, and it didn't take long before we both knew we could not imagine life without the other. He's the best thing that has ever happened in my life. Ryan has one more year to go before he gets his master's degree in marketing. He's also working with his father; you remember his father was a building contractor?" Megan shrugged her shoulders and sighed happily. "And yes," patting her stomach fondly, "this baby is due about three months from now, and we are both so excited. I can't wait to be a stay-at-home mom."

Abby leaned back in her chair and crossed her legs. "I remember we were both going to marry wealthy men and travel the world. I'm still working toward that end, but I'm glad you're so happy. I love my career and can't imagine my life without it. Marriage and children will just have to work around my schedule. Lucky for me, Scott feels the same way and keeps encouraging me to push myself in my work. When we marry, we plan on waiting a few years before starting a family."

Megan looked over at her friend thoughtfully. "Well, I'm just glad that you're going to be here for a few weeks. I'm having a small dinner party this Friday night and would love for you to come. It will give you a chance to see Ryan again and for us to spend more time together. And besides, you'll need a break by then."

"I'd love to come," Abby replied enthusiastically. "Can I bring anything? What time should I be there?"

Megan beamed at her. "Around seven would be fine. As far as what you can bring, how about dessert? Just remember, I still consider chocolate to be an important part of any meal!"

Abby uncrossed her long legs and stood up, reaching toward Megan, who stood as well, and gave her a hug. "I'll be there at seven and will bring something totally fattening and decadent for dessert." She looked at her watch with surprise. "Gosh, the time has gone by so fast. Guess I'd better be going. I still have some errands to run before I go home. I'm so glad you're here. I need a friend in town right now."

They parted outside the restaurant, and Abby walked back toward her car thoughtfully. It had been a good lunch, and she was glad to be able to renew her friendship with Megan. *I'll have to think of something extra special to take Friday night*, she thought.

***

1 February 1845

It is evening, and I am full of conflicting emotions. Today Mother and I gave an afternoon tea at the vicarage. Mother always worries when Elizabeth's mother comes for tea because of the shabbiness of the vicarage, but I feel our home is so much more of a real home than where Elizabeth lives. Tom's mother and his two sisters also came today, and it was good to see them. His mother, Hannah, is a small, stout woman with a big heart. Her home is always clean and shining, and she has a keen sense of humor. She is also known in our village as a "healer" because of her knowledge of herbs and roots and their healing powers. Tom's sister Emily is the oldest of his brothers and sisters and is quiet and shy. She loves music, however, and plays the organ for our Sunday services. Abigail is fifteen years of age and has beautiful blonde hair and brown eyes. She is so full of life and fun and loves pretty things. She always adds an extra touch to her appearance, such as a flower or a piece of pretty ribbon. Abigail says she is going to marry someone with money so she can have a fine house and many servants.

The conversation during tea was, as usual, all about local happenings. Mother tries to keep the discussions on a positive note so that negative comments about people won't occur in our home. Eventually, one of the women mentioned she had seen the Mormon missionaries preaching in the square and had stopped to listen. Tom's mother seemed quiet and thoughtful as we talked about the strangeness of their message and their appearance in our small town. Finally, she mentioned that she and her family had attended a meeting and found it very interesting. She said that a few other families scattered throughout the valley had also been there and expressed that the missionaries seemed very sincere in their beliefs. I could tell Mother and several other ladies were not comfortable with Mrs. Fisher's comments because Mother quickly changed the subject to the cold weather we are having and how tired she is of winter by the end of January. I felt an unreasonable fear listening to Mrs. Fisher and hope they will not go again. These missionaries are surely going to bring discord into our village, and I don't want anything to happen to the way Tom's family is respected in our valley. I hope these religious zealots won't influence Tom. Why can't things stay the same?

Chapter 5

The next few days flew by quickly as Abby tackled her grandfather's office. It was obvious that her grandmother had not sorted through his papers since his death. Her grandfather had kept all the banking and household accounting sheets for the last ten years of his life, and they filled an entire filing cabinet. She carefully boxed the papers her father would need to go through. In addition, she found quite a few documents from much earlier years. She found Tom and Dorothy Fisher's citizenship papers, along with a copy of the original deed to the house. In one drawer of the filing cabinet, she found a packet of letters carefully tied together with string. She opened one and found they were letters her grandmother had sent to her grandfather while he was on his mission. It touched Abby to see that he had kept them through the years. She read a few of the letters and then tied them back together and placed them in another box for her mother. The words of the letters certainly painted a picture of a grandmother she had never known—one so young and newly in love.

In the bottom drawer of one of the filing cabinets, Abby found her grandmother's genealogy book and records. She opened the book with interest, slowly reading through the pedigree and family group sheets. Somehow it made these ancestors seem more real to her as she read the names of parents and children, their birth dates and deaths. A section in the book was dedicated to life histories, and several hours flew by as she read the stories, bringing to life these precious predecessors. Abby chuckled as she read the life story of one of her fourth great-grandfathers and how he had proposed to her great grandmother. He was a sea captain and lived in Sunderland, England. One day he stopped for lunch at an English pub located near the ocean front. He took a seat in the section reserved for naval officers, and when the waitress came to take his order, he noticed that she was a very pretty woman and so he started talking to her. Before he left the pub, he was so captivated by her that he asked her to marry him. She thought he was joking but said yes anyway. "In three days' time I'll be back for you," he told her.

On the third day she was outside washing the steps in front of the pub when she saw a beautiful carriage drawn by two white horses come down the street. It stopped at the pub, and the sea captain got out. He noticed her standing on the steps and told her he had come to take her to get married. She pondered for a few minutes then got in the coach and left to marry her sea captain.

It reads like a fairy tale, Abby thought. *How different from my romance with Scott.* She wanted to wait until she was completely sure before she married him, and this great-grandmother was willing to face an unknown future with a man she had only met once.

Her grandparents' histories were thick, and Abby set those books aside to read later; the rest she placed in the box for her mother. Along with the personal records, she found a box of old photographs. There were many pictures of her mother with her parents, and Abby gazed carefully at each one. How young her grandmother and grandfather looked! There were also several old photographs without names written on the back to identify who the individuals were, and she spent several more minutes carefully looking at each picture. She felt herself drawn toward one photograph of a young girl dressed in the style of more than a hundred years ago. Holding it in her hands, she carefully studied the face in the picture. Something in the eyes and mouth of the young girl reminded Abby of her grandmother, and she examined it for several minutes before turning the picture over. The name "Catherine" was printed in small black letters, the ink faded with time. She looked at the face a few more seconds then, unwilling to put it in the box with the other unknown pictures, set it aside. The resemblance to her grandmother was so evident that she wanted to ask her mother if she knew who the girl was. There had to be a family connection somewhere; maybe she was Tom and Dorothy Fisher's daughter. However, she had never heard her grandmother talk about a Catherine in the family, and another quick glance through her grandmother's pedigree sheets revealed no one by that name. As she placed the stack of unknown pictures in a box, she shook her head sadly. Without names to identify them, no one would ever know who these people were.

Each night she called her mother and updated her on the progress she was making. Her mother was interested in what she had found and reminded her that she and Abby's father would come as soon as they could. Abby could tell her mother was anxious to see the records and genealogy she had set aside for her to read. Abby also looked forward to talking to Scott. She found she missed him more each day. She had managed to schedule her real estate closing around the night of Scott's formal dinner party so she could attend with him, so at least she would see him for a few days next month.

Thursday, she worked late into the evening, sorting the last of the material in the filing cabinets. As she was preparing to turn the lights off in the room, her cell phone rang. Wiping dusty hands on her jeans, she reached across the desk and picked up her phone.

"Abby, it's Scott," the voice said on the other end of the line. "I've just gotten home from the office and knew after the hectic day I've had that what I needed was to hear your voice. Honey, I wish you were here and I could hold you in my arms for a few minutes, but I guess this will have to do." Scott's voice sounded tired and discouraged. "Your father and I have been working late every night this week on the Chapman case. I go home for a few hours of sleep, and then I'm back at the office early the next morning. Jury selection begins on Monday, so I'm sure we'll be working through the weekend."

Lowering herself into her grandfather's chair, Abby pushed a stray lock of hair behind her ear. "Mom has commented on the fact that Dad is never home either. You sound tired, but knowing you, you also thrive on the pressure; in the end, it's what keeps you going. You would never survive in a no-stress, routine job."

Abby heard him chuckle. "You're right," he said, "I wouldn't really have it any other way. What about you, what have you been doing today?"

"I've been missing you as well, but you'd be proud of me for all the work I'm getting done here. Today I've been cleaning out my grandfather's office, and you wouldn't believe all the paperwork and things I've had to sort through. I found my grandmother's genealogy book and enjoyed reading the life histories of my great-grandparents. It's been a different feeling, Scott. Being an only child with no cousins, I've felt alone and in many ways disconnected. Looking at the pedigree charts and family group sheets has made me feel more linked to family, like I'm an important part of a large family." She sighed. "Oh well, I hope that makes sense to you because it's difficult to explain." She paused for a few seconds then changed the subject.

"The highlight of my social calendar so far this week was Tuesday when I met my childhood friend Megan Fellows for lunch. It was fun to talk about old times, when I was here for the summers and holidays. I think I told you about her when we talked Tuesday evening. I can't remember if I told you she's invited me to dinner tomorrow night, but I'm looking forward to going. All in all, it's been a very long week. How about you, any plans for the weekend—besides working?"

Scott chuckled again. "You know your dad. I'll be lucky to find time to eat. If I do get a break on Saturday or Sunday, I'm going to the club for some golf—that is, if the weather cooperates. I'm glad, though, that you have something fun to do Friday evening. Let me know how it turns out."

They talked for a few more minutes then said good-bye and hung up. Abby sighed as she turned out the lights and started downstairs. She really did miss him.

* * *

She awoke early Friday morning and lay in bed listening to the busy chatter of the birds in the large cottonwood tree outside her bedroom window. Stretching her arms lazily over her head, she watched the soft whisper of breeze lift the lace curtains at her window. It had rained during the night, and the fresh, washed smells of damp earth and flowers floated in with the breeze. Through the window, she could see the pink and gold of the sunrise, promising another beautiful day. Giving a last stretch, she rose from her bed and headed to the bathroom for her morning routine.

Splashing her face with cool water, she mentally organized her day. She'd go for a quick run and then make herself a real breakfast. She felt the anticipation of doing something different today because she planned to take the morning off from all the packing and make a special dessert for Megan's dinner.

After her run and breakfast, she searched through her grandmother's cookbooks, looking for a good dessert recipe. It would have to be something with lots of chocolate for Megan. She debated for a few minutes about buying a chocolate cake, but she loved to cook and usually didn't have the time to do much baking. Besides, she had shared many happy memories in this kitchen, cooking alongside her grandmother. As she thumbed through her grandmother's cookbooks, she came across a recipe for a double chocolate cheesecake. Surely this recipe would fill all of Megan's chocolate expectations. She scanned the recipe and quickly made a list of the items she would need at the store.

When she returned to the house after buying the things she needed, she set the ingredients on the countertop. Tying one of her grandmother's aprons around her waist, she began the process of assembling the cheesecake. Soon the decadent smell of melting chocolate filled the kitchen, and Abby hummed to herself as she mixed and measured ingredients, relishing the look of the rich batter. Placing the pan carefully in the oven, she closed the door and set the timer, hoping it would turn out perfectly. After cleaning the kitchen, she gave herself up to the pleasure of going through more of her grandmother's cookbooks, making a list of the ones she wanted. When she returned home, she would prepare a gourmet, home-cooked meal for Scott.

As soon as the timer sounded, she took the cheesecake from the oven and spread a sour cream chocolate mixture over the top of the cake and set it back in the oven. When the timer buzzed again, she took the cheesecake from the oven and placed it on a cooling rack. For the finish, she melted a cup of chocolate chips and used a spoon to drizzle the chocolate in thin lines across the top of the cheesecake. To avoid cracking, the cheesecake needed to be cooled thoroughly before placing it in the refrigerator.

Abby spent the afternoon doing a final cleaning of her grandfather's office. It seemed so different now, with the boxes neatly taped, labeled, and stacked at one end of the room. *How empty and sad it looks*, she thought, *without the family pictures and photographs displayed on the desk and around the room.* She had felt close to her grandfather as she had lovingly touched and packed the things he had used and treasured. He had died when she was fourteen, twelve years ago, but it seemed longer than that to her. She could see herself as a child, her arms full of coloring books and crayons, reaching up to place them carefully on the desk across from her grandfather. She would sit and color patiently while he finished his work, and then he would let her pick out a storybook from the crowded bookshelves. Taking her on his lap, he would read the chosen story, making the voices of all the characters in the book. As she grew older, she wrote letters home or to friends while he worked. As she surveyed the room one more time, she felt almost as if she was saying a final good-bye to him again, and she felt her heart tighten with sadness.

After showering and blow-drying her hair, she contemplated her wardrobe, trying to decide just what to wear for her evening out, and finally settled on a pair of tweed dress slacks with a deep cream silk blouse. She added pearl drop earrings then lightly dusted her cheekbones with a soft coral blush and smoothed a glossy, soft lipstick on her lips. After spraying on the lightly scented perfume she loved, she gave a final check in the mirror before picking up her matching jacket and purse and going downstairs.

In the kitchen, she took the cheesecake from the refrigerator. Running a knife around the edge, she placed the cake on a platter, unlatched the edges of the pan, and carefully removed the cake. She placed a few leaves of fresh mint she had picked earlier from her grandmother's herb garden on the center of the cheesecake and carefully wrapped the dessert.

Megan and Ryan's new home was in the small town of Hurricane, located about sixteen miles northeast of St. George. Ryan's father owned the land for the new housing development and was also the builder of the homes in the subdivision. For their wedding gift, Mr. and Mrs. Fellows had given the young couple their choice of building lots, and they had selected a site high on the hillside, overlooking the beautiful Hurricane valley. Megan had told Abby that Ryan had helped his father build their home, and they had moved into it just six months ago. After ringing the doorbell, Abby stood on the wide front porch and looked around her, impressed with the spectacular views. Looking to the east, she could see the rock mountains of Zion National Park in the distance, as well as the small town of Hurricane itself. Directly in front of her loomed Pine Valley Mountain, with its red bluffs and hills at its base. To the west, she could see the waters of Quail Creek State Park. The views were breathtakingly beautiful from every direction.

Megan answered the door with a smile of welcome. She took the cheesecake from Abby's hands, exclaiming, "Oh Abby, this looks so luscious, and I'm so glad you came." As Megan led her into the entry hall, she called out, "Ryan, she's here," just as a pleasant-faced young man entered the hall. Abby barely recognized him; it had been so long since she'd seen him. She remembered him as a somewhat short, stocky boy with unruly brown hair. The man who greeted her now had grown several inches and had lost the slight weight of his youth. His hair had darkened to a deep brown and was neatly cut. One thing that had not changed was the friendly smile he gave her as he reached out and took her hand.

"Welcome to our home, Abby. Megan is excited that you are here for a while." He released her hand, adding, "I'm sorry about your grandmother. It can't be easy for you to be the one going through her things, and anything we can do to help, you only need to ask."

Abby returned his smile. "Thanks, Ryan, I appreciate your offer and may take you up on that." She looked around as she followed him into the living room. "What a beautiful home. I love the view from your front porch, and the inside of the house is every bit as wonderful." They'd built the home with the desert in mind: cool sand-colored tiles covered the floors, and the high walls were painted a light sage green. A fountain on one wall in the entry with its musical sounds of splashing water enhanced the feeling of coolness and peace. The living room had floor-to-ceiling rounded windows that looked out on Pine Valley Mountain, and the evening shadows drifted lazily over its face as well as on the red hills and bluffs below. The view took Abby's breath away, and she walked directly to the windows. She was so entranced that she failed to notice the man who rose from a chair to greet her.

"The view is magnificent, isn't it," Blake Matthews said, coming to stand beside her. Abby turned, surprised to see him there, but gathered her wits enough to answer, "It's breathtaking! I would probably spend all my time in this room looking out the windows."

He smiled at her surprised expression. "Megan and Ryan are special friends of mine. Ryan and I have been friends since my family moved into their ward when I was a kid."

Ryan spoke from behind them. "We used to get into all kinds of trouble when we were younger. My mother said that what I didn't think up to do on my own, Blake would! We both left on missions about the same time. I went to the New York Manhattan mission and Blake went to England." He gave Blake a friendly pat on his back. "It's nice when friendship endures and strengthens with the years."

"Oh, good," Megan said as she came into the room. "You've introduced her to Blake. I don't know if you remember, Abby, but he used to be in our ward, and he and Ryan were always together." She laughed and gave Blake a smile before continuing, "We invited another couple to come tonight as well, but they called earlier this afternoon to say they have a sick baby, so it's going to be just the four of us for the evening." As she walked by Ryan, she reached out and took his hand. "If you men will excuse me, I have some last minute things to do in the kitchen. Abby, come talk with me while I finish."

Abby smiled at her friend. "I'd love to, but I think I'll help, too, instead of watch you bustle around while we talk. Besides, I'm dying to see more of your home."

She followed Megan into a large kitchen, the aroma of garlic and onion scenting the air. Megan gestured toward the stove where a rich tomato sauce simmered. "I hope you don't mind if it's only spaghetti and meatballs for dinner. It's the one thing I can cook without burning! Ryan and I take turns cooking, and I hate to admit it, but he's better than I am. I'm learning, though," she finished with a smile.

"You should remember," Abby retorted, "that pasta is my very favorite food. I love it with anything and everything." She leaned her head over the sauce and sniffed appreciatively. "This smells wonderful. What do you want me to do?"

Megan handed her an apron. "You better put this on; your clothes are so nice. Me, I have a hard time reminding myself to wear an apron, and it seems I always spill something on what I'm wearing." She motioned down at her neat khaki maternity pants and navy blue sweater. "Do you mind tossing the salad? I have tomatoes and avocados to add, as well as the dressing, there on the counter behind you." Megan lifted the lid on a large pot on the stove and peered inside. "Finally! I thought this water would never come to a boil." She placed the spaghetti in the pan, stirring it carefully until the strands were covered in the boiling water. Abby had located a knife and was busy dicing tomatoes and avocados for the salad.

Taking a plate of cheese and crackers from the refrigerator, Megan turned to look at Abby, a mischievous twinkle in her eyes. "I hope you don't think I was trying to line you up with Blake—not that I think it's a bad idea. And if I think far enough back, I vaguely remember you having a crush on him at the same time I was starting to fall madly in love with Ryan." She laughingly added, "Actually, I think it would be a terrific idea for you to fall madly in love with someone here in St. George and stay here forever!" Balancing the plate in her hands and heading toward the living room, she asked, "Abby, would you please bring the napkins and those small plates for me, and we'll take this in to the men."

Abby picked up the stack of napkins and small plates and followed Megan out of the kitchen. "I think you're looking for a miracle, Megan. Remember, I told you Tuesday how happy I am with my life in Denver and that Scott and I are talking marriage."

They entered the living room to find the men chatting about the final college basketball games at Dixie State College. Ryan quickly rose, took the plate from Megan, and placed it on the coffee table, glancing at the contents skeptically. "This will only keep us from starving for a few minutes, so how long before the real food is done?"

Megan grinned at him. "Only another ten minutes, so I think you'll live."

Abby placed the napkins and plates on the table beside the dish of cheese and crackers and returned to the kitchen with Megan.

Working together, they quickly finished putting the meal together. Abby carried the bowl of salad into the dining room and placed it on the table. This room also had large windows and faced Zion Canyon. She paused a minute to gaze at the view, fondly remembering the trips she'd taken to the national park with her grandparents, and decided she would make time to go there again before she left for home.

Megan interrupted Abby's memories as she called to the men, "Come and get it!" Abby quickly returned to the kitchen to help bring in the last of the food. As she carried in the last dish, the four took their places around the table, with Abby and Blake sitting across from one another. Ryan offered a blessing on the food, and then they loaded their plates. Conversation was easy and relaxed as they discussed the events going on in St. George. The city was growing at an astonishing rate. The sleepy little town had existed at the same pace for many years but was now changing rapidly. The housing market was fairly active with prices on land and homes changing constantly. Construction on a larger airport was also in the beginning stages, and this would connect the expanding community more closely with the rest of the world.

Blake served on the city council and was involved in the important decisions being made. He related that many people who had lived in St. George for several years expressed how they felt the town was losing the quality of life and beauty that had existed for so many years as new homes and businesses spread outward through the agriculture fields. Huge homes were also going up rapidly on the bluffs overlooking the city. As Abby listened to the discussion, she was impressed with both Blake's ability to analyze the situation and his desire to see only the best happen to his city. She also realized from the conversation that her grandparents' home would be worth more on the market than she originally thought. She found herself for a few minutes wanting to be part of this new growth, excited at the thought of opening an office here and selling the homes that were going up overnight. Just as quickly, she subdued the idea. She could not imagine either Scott or herself being content to live here in a small town, even one growing so rapidly. She also reminded herself how much she loved Denver and how she would miss her life there if she were to move.

After dinner, Abby started to gather up plates, but Megan quickly took them from her hands. "You and Blake go into the living room and relax. Ryan will help me clear things up." She glanced at Ryan and added with a laugh, "Besides, it's his turn to do the dishes tonight, so he's getting off easy."

Ryan shrugged his shoulders. "See, Abby, how she keeps me in line?"

Abby and Blake smiled and walked together to the living room. Abby sat down on the sofa, and Blake took the seat across from her. "Okay Abby," Blake said, "you were pretty quiet during dinner. Tell me about yourself and your life in Denver."

Abby leaned back and crossed her legs. Giving a small laugh, she said, "That's a short story. I work for a large brokerage firm in Denver and sell real estate. I really love my job, but I confess, as I listened to the discussion during dinner, I thought how exciting the market is here and how fun and challenging it would be to be part of it." She continued thoughtfully, "This area has meant so much to me through my life. I spent my summer vacations here and a lot of the holidays as well, so I have plenty of good memories. When I was little I hoped Mom and Dad would want to live in St. George, but I adjusted to big city life many years ago. Besides, I love all the cultural events and shopping that big cities offer. I don't think I could really feel comfortable living here all year round. I've become a big-city girl! Now, how about you? What made you decide to settle in St. George?"

Abby couldn't help studying Blake as he took time to answer. Tonight he had dressed in well-pressed casual navy blue pants with a sky-blue shirt, which he left open at the collar. The blue of the shirt intensified the deep blue of his eyes, and his thick, light-brown hair just brushed the edge of his collar. Glancing at his feet, she noticed he wore a different pair of boots tonight. Blake noticed her looking at his boots and laughed. "I enjoy the comfort that boots offer; besides, I guess they partly fit my lifestyle. I have a couple of horses and enjoy riding when I have the time."

She smiled at his answer. "I've only been horseback riding a few times in my life, but I enjoyed it. It's been long enough now, though, that I'd probably be a little nervous around a horse. You didn't answer my question, Blake; what made you decide to go into practice here?"

Blake settled himself back in his seat. "After I graduated from medical school, I served my internship at a large hospital in California. I considered staying on to become a cardiologist when I finished, but my plans changed when I came back to St. George for a visit just before I was through. I noticed that my father, who was also a doctor, was overworked and tired; he really needed someone to help him. He never asked me to move home, but I could see both he and my mother needed me. After finishing my internship in internal medicine, I decided to come back here and work with my father and have never regretted that decision. He died a few years later, and I took over the full practice." Blake shook his head. "At first I was so busy it was hard to find time to eat or sleep. In addition to the new workload, my mother's health was steadily declining. She passed away two years ago, and I was grateful I'd been here to help her. A year ago I expanded the practice to include two additional doctors, and it has made my life easier. I really needed the help with all the growth we are experiencing." Blake looked at Abby and smiled. "End of story. Now, Abby, I was serious Sunday when I offered to help you with the house. When would you like me to come? I have Monday afternoons free, so I could come this next Monday."

Abby nodded her head and smiled. "I really do need some help outside with pruning and trimming. Monday afternoon would be fine, if you're sure you have time." Her expression became serious as she continued. "Blake, I'm so sorry about your parents. I barely remember them. I know how hard it's been for me to lose my grandparents, and I can't imagine how it would be to lose parents that you love so much. It must have been so comforting for them to have you home. I seem to remember that you had a sister. Does she live here in St. George?"

Blake smiled and shook his head. "I do have a sister, but she and her husband and their two little girls live in Salt Lake City. However, she comes to visit when she can. I kept the old family home, so to her it's still like coming home. We both decided we just didn't want to sell for a while."

"I always wished I had brothers and sisters," Abby reflected, "but it never happened. It took ten years for my parents to get me, and after that, they weren't able have any more. I'm lucky, though—my parents are terrific, and I'm very close to them. Now, what time would be good for you on Monday, if you're sure you want to come?"

Blake laughed, "You bet I do. I never offer unless I can make good. How about I come around two o'clock Monday afternoon? And I'll bring my truck so I can haul things away after we're finished. Will that fit in with your schedule?"

Abby was just saying, "That would be perfect!" when Megan and Ryan entered the room, carrying the plates of dessert. "Abby, I remember this cheesecake," Megan exclaimed. "This was your grandmother's most requested recipe. She always brought it for special occasions. Each time I ate it, I'd tell myself to ask for the recipe, but then I'd forget. You have to give it to me!"

"I'll make sure you get the recipe," Abby replied. "I haven't done any baking for quite a while, so I hope it's all right. I had such a good time this morning going through all her old recipe books. There are some I would really like to have, but I'll have to wait and see if Mom wants them, too."

After dessert, they chatted for a while; then Abby rose. "I should probably get going," she said, a little regretfully. "Tomorrow is going to be another full day!"

When Blake said he needed to get back as well, they all stood and walked to the door together.

"It was a wonderful evening, and the meal was fantastic," said Abby, giving Megan a big hug and shaking Ryan's hand, "and I insist you keep the rest of the cheesecake. Let's get together again soon."

"I'll walk Abby to her car," Blake said, taking Abby's arm. "Thanks for the dinner and evening."

Abby walked down the front steps carefully, aware of Blake's touch on her arm. He opened the car door for her, and she slid into the seat. "I'll see you Monday afternoon at two. And thanks, Blake, for your offer," she said.

"I'll be there. See you then, Abby." He closed the car door and watched as she backed carefully out of the driveway and drove away.

***

15 February 1845

Today has been a quiet day at home. Our parish is holding its winter bazaar and bake sale next week, and I have been busy knitting three sets of caps and mittens. I have finished two sets and a third cap and am now working on the mittens. I enjoy knitting, letting my thoughts journey in different directions while my fingers are busy with yarn and needles. Lately, I will confess, my thoughts usually dwell on Tom and our future together. I will soon be eighteen years of age, and Father has said that Tom and I can then be officially engaged. I am so excited at the thought of being with Tom all the time and starting our own home in this valley that I love.

In the afternoon I took a walk to the village with Elizabeth. It was good to be outside with the cold north wind blowing the fluffy clouds across the blue sky. I love the brisk air with its tang of smoke from the chimneys. On the way home I passed through the Village Square, and again the Mormons were preaching, their cheeks and noses red from the cold winter air. As I stopped and looked at them, I thought they surely could use the mittens and caps that I am knitting, for one of the men did not have mittens to warm his hands, and they were raw and red from the cold. I will also confess that I stopped to listen, for I was curious about the remarks Mrs. Fisher had made at tea last week. As I listened to their simple words of love and hope, my heart and mind felt the sincerity of their faith. Their words awoke deep within my soul a feeling of intense yearning toward something. My thoughts were so centered on what was being said that I did not hear Elizabeth at my side until she nudged me and asked why I was wasting time standing there in the cold. I flushed and hurried away with her, but tonight as I said my prayers, I tried to understand what I'd felt as I'd listened.

Chapter 6

The doorbell rang Saturday afternoon as Abby was dusting the living room. Placing the can of Pledge and the dust cloth on a table, she hurried to the door. Mrs. Givens was standing on the porch. "I haven't had the heart to disturb you these past few days, as I know how busy you must be," she said with a smile, "but I thought this would be a good time to see how you are coming along."

Abby smiled and held the door open wide. "Please come in. I've been meaning to come over and see you, too, but I have been busy." As they entered the living room, Abby motioned toward the sofa, inviting the older woman to sit down. Abby seated herself in a wingback chair opposite Mrs. Givens and looked around the room. "As you can see, I've been dusting, and I'm glad for a break. This old furniture has so much wood that cleaning it takes quite a bit of time."

Mrs. Givens also looked around the room, noticing that the knickknacks and pictures had been removed and that a neat row of boxes was lined up under the window. "I see you are making progress," she said, pointing to the stack of boxes, and then sadly shook her head. "It's a very lonely and sad feeling for me to see this room looking so empty." She sighed softly. "There are so many memories for me as well in this home, and I have to admit, I hate seeing it sold. It's the end of a long line of Fisher descendants living here. My husband and I moved into our home next door shortly after we were married, and we soon became such good friends with your grandparents. We've shared many heartaches and happy times together over the years."

Abby nodded her head in agreement. "It's been slow work packing, partly because so many things bring up memories, and I find myself reflecting and remembering all the good times I've had here. It took me three days to go through Grandfather's office. I found their family history books and spent quite a while reading the stories and looking at the pedigree charts." Abby looked seriously at Mrs. Givens. "Deep down, I'm hoping Mom and Dad will reconsider about selling. The more I read the histories, the more I realize how much this home is tied to my family. I want it to be here for my children as well. I get the feeling when I'm talking with Mom that she, too, is having second thoughts about selling this old home." Abby held up crossed fingers and smiled. "Wish me luck. I'm a Realtor, and I'm going to do a 'hard sell' on my parents to keep the house. But, regardless, I do need to go through and get things in order."

Mrs. Givens looked around the room again. "I hope you can convince them, dear." She paused then asked, "Abby, I wondered if I could ask for another ride to church tomorrow. My car is still having problems, and I enjoyed going with you so much last week; would you mind picking me up again?"

Abby hesitated, thinking of another Sunday morning lost, but then answered with a smile, "I'd be happy to take you, Mrs. Givens. I haven't attended church regularly for years, and, I'll admit, it felt good to go last week. Shall I pick you up at the same time?"

Mrs. Givens gave a sigh of relief. "Please call me Agnes, and, yes, the same time would be fine. And Abby, I would really enjoy your having dinner with me after church." As Abby started to protest, Mrs. Givens went on in a firm voice. "You have to eat, and I have a feeling you're just getting by with whatever is handy. I know you have things you want to get done tomorrow, but just come over long enough to eat."

Abby laughed, knowing she would give in. "Thank you. I'll be glad to have dinner with you. You're right, I usually just grab a sandwich or something quick, and a home-cooked meal sounds wonderful. Can I bring something for dinner?"

Agnes stood up and smoothed the skirt of her housedress. "No, my dear; it won't be fancy. I'll just enjoy having someone to share a meal with me."

Abby followed her to the entry hall and opened the door for her. "Well, I'll see you in the morning, and thanks for looking out for me." As she was closing the door, Abby heard her phone ringing in the kitchen, and she hurried to answer it.

"Abby, it's Megan. Can you get away for a few hours this afternoon? Ryan is helping his dad for the day, and I need to go shopping. Come with me."

Abby thought over the list of things she had planned on doing then decided it could wait. Besides, she had only brought the one suit with her that could be worn to church, and she didn't want to wear it again tomorrow. And it would be nice to take a break and look around the shops. "I'd enjoy that, Megan. I need to buy something to wear tomorrow to church. Where and what time shall I meet you?"

"How about in front of Dillard's department store in an hour? There's a bench just outside the store entrance inside the mall. See you in an hour."

Abby hurried through the dusting then took a quick shower and changed her clothes. As she entered the parking lot for the mall, she smiled to herself, thinking of the large malls and shopping centers near her home in Denver. The Red Cliffs Mall was small compared to where she usually shopped, but it did offer a selection of stores. She also knew there were other retail stores scattered around town. As she neared the appointed meeting place, she saw Megan already seated on the bench. Abby glanced at her watch and noticed that she was a few minutes late.

She hurried up to her friend. "Sorry, Megan! Have you been waiting long?"

Megan shook her head. "Actually, I just got here. I'm just happy you were able to get away, because I know you must be very busy." Megan put a hand on the back of the bench for support as she stood. "Abby, do you remember when we used to come shopping here? We always had so much fun trying on clothes."

Abby chuckled. "I do, but the way I remember it is that we were always hoping a couple of cute boys would be wandering through the mall at the same time."

Megan's eyes sparkled. "That's really the way I remember it, too. We did do quite a bit of scouting for boys, didn't we?" She looked down at her expanding stomach. "Oh well, those days are definitely over. Today I want to find something I can wear for work. I just keep getting bigger and bigger, and nothing fits anymore. Shall we look in Dillard's? They're having a big clearance sale right now. What are you looking for, Abby?"

"Something for church, I guess. I can't wear the same suit every week," Abby replied. "And if Agnes Givens has her way, I'll be going every week."

Entering the store, they made their way toward the clothing section. Abby stopped to look at skirts and tops. "I'm going over to maternity to see if I can find something there," Megan told her, "then let's meet and try our selections on at the same time."

Abby nodded. "Sounds good to me," she responded, holding up a blue skirt for inspection. "See you in a few minutes." Megan hurried toward maternity, and Abby continued her search through the racks of clothing, selecting several different outfits to try. With her arms full, she started off to find Megan, only to see her coming toward her, her arms full of clothing as well. Laughing at the piles they each carried, the two women walked toward the dressing rooms.

"I guess some things never change. This really is just like old times," Megan laughed. "Although the clothes I'm trying on are certainly different."

As Abby zipped up a skirt, she thought how fun it was to spend an afternoon shopping with Megan. She chuckled as she thought of the difference between the huge two-story malls in Denver and the small one here in St. George. *I'm always in such a hurry at home that it's just a rush from one store to the next; plus, I usually just go by myself.* She pulled on a soft yellow knit shirt that matched the green and yellow floral print in the skirt she had on then stood back to look at her reflection in the mirror.

"No fair changing before you show me how it looks, Abby," Megan called from the adjoining dressing room. "I'm just pulling on a top and then I'll be out."

After trying on several outfits, Abby, with Megan's help, settled on the yellow shirt and matching skirt and a deep violet dress. Megan had found two pairs of pants and matching tops. Armed with their purchases, they walked to the food court for ice cream.

"I don't know why my body seems to crave chocolate so much," Megan said as she licked the sides of her ice cream cone. "I just never seem to get enough of it. Ryan finally froze the last of the cheesecake so I wouldn't eat it all at once." She sighed blissfully. "It was my idea of chocolate heaven." Then she looked over at her friend doubtfully. "Um, Abby, I hope you didn't think I had ulterior motives with just you and Blake as our guests last night. We really did invite another couple for the evening."

Abby laughed. "For just a moment I wondered if you were playing matchmaker, but I really enjoyed the evening, and Blake seems to be a very nice man. I know Grandmother always thought he was special. He's coming Monday afternoon to help me with some of the heavier yard work. He offered in church and again last night, so I took him up on it." Abby took several licks of her ice cream cone before continuing. "I was impressed when he told me he had given up an opportunity to become a cardiologist to come back here and help his father." She took a bite of the cone. "He seems content living here in St. George."

"He's a good doctor." Megan finished her cone and wiped her mouth on the napkin. "He had a difficult time after his father died, trying to juggle his father's patients as well as his own. I'm glad things are easier for him now."

"I'm surprised he's not married," Abby said. "I thought the Church encouraged young men to marry, and he's a very attractive man."

"Well, he was engaged about three years ago, before Ryan and I were married," Megan told her. "Her name was Emily Evans, and her family lived in our ward."

"I think I vaguely remember her," Abby said thoughtfully. "She was our same age, wasn't she?"

"Yes. She was a small girl with long blond hair, and I always liked her. Ryan and I used to double-date with them quite a bit." At Abby's questioning look, Megan continued. "Blake was devastated when she broke off the engagement, and eventually she married someone else and moved away. I think the problem was that Blake was just too busy. His father died a couple of days after they became engaged, and between helping his mother and working long hours—I think Emily felt he never had time for her. He dates occasionally now but hasn't had a serious relationship since Emily. Ryan and I keep hoping he'll find someone. He's such a good man."

Noticing that Abby had finished her ice cream, Megan added, with a glance at her watch, "I guess I should be getting back so I can get a few things done before Ryan gets home. I've had such a good time, Abby; we'll have to make this a practice."

"I agree," Abby said as she and Megan gathered up their packages and walked toward the parking lot.

Abby drove home relaxed and happy. Living in a small town had some definite benefits. She loved the "no stress" traffic and the friendliness of the people.

When she arrived at home, she carried her packages up to her room and hung her new clothes in the closet. Notebook and pencil in hand, Abby directed her steps to the backyard to make a list of things she wanted to accomplish on Monday with Blake's help. Selecting a chair that faced the late afternoon sun, she sat back and closed her eyes for a few minutes, basking in the warmth of the sun on her face, the silence broken only by the occasional chirping of a bird. *What a peaceful day this has been,* Abby reflected. *I can't remember the last time I took time to go shopping with a friend or took a few minutes to just lie in the sun. And,* she opened her eyes in wonder, *I'm actually looking forward to going to church tomorrow!* With a blissful sigh, she sat up, opened her notebook, and began taking inventory of needed tasks. She had just started to write when her cell phone rang and, leaning forward, she picked it up from the small table in front of her.

"Hi, honey," Scott's voice came over the line. "How are things going in Dullsville? I bet you're ready to come home by now."

"Not really," Abby answered. "I took part of today off and went shopping with Megan, and it was a nice break. Agnes Givens— remember she's the neighbor next door—asked me to take her to church again tomorrow, and I needed something to wear."

"So tomorrow is going to be another wasted day? Can't you just tell her that you have more important things to do than go to church?" Scott sounded upset.

"It won't be a wasted day, Scott," Abby said soothingly. "I'll have the afternoon and evening to pack. I've finished the living room and

Grandfather's office, so I'm making good progress. I also have someone coming Monday afternoon to help with the heavier outside work." At the thought of Blake, Abby quickly changed the topic of conversation. "What about your case? Have you worked all day or did you get a chance to play some golf?"

"We worked all day, and even if I'd had the time, the weather's been lousy," Scott complained. "Your mother has been pressuring your dad to go to church with her in the morning, so I won't be able to work with him at the office until after two in the afternoon. I was hoping to finish by noon so I could be free to do something else, but it seems your whole family is set on going to church tomorrow," he finished.

It was news to Abby that her parents were going to church together, and a feeling of gladness entered her heart. She smiled into the phone. "I'm glad they're going, and actually, Scott, I'm glad I'm going, too. We've been away from it too long. But I'd better get busy now so you won't be so upset with me the next time you call," she said a little teasingly.

"I'm sorry, Abby." Scott still sounded frustrated. "But I miss you and want you back soon. It seems as if you are using excuses not to hurry. I think you should just do what needs to be done."

Abby felt hurt and a little rebellious at his hasty judgment. After telling him she needed to start working, she ended the call. She sat for a few minutes longer, finishing her list, then stood up and walked back inside the house. Scott had managed to take away the pleasure of sitting in the sun.

***

24 February 1845

Today is Sunday. As I attended church this morning, I listened with all my heart to the sermon Father gave and tried to recapture the feelings I had experienced as I'd listened to the Mormons. But although Father did his usual beautiful job of delivering his speech, it did not stir my spirit in the same way.

I had been invited to Sunday dinner at Tom's home after services, and had been looking forward to going all week. His family is always fun to be with, as there is much laughter and peace within their home. I rode home with Tom and his youngest sister, Susan, as he had brought the small trap with him to church. Susan is five years of age and has fine brown hair and soft blue eyes, and Tom and I laughed all the way home at her stories. His home is nestled in a small valley with rolling hills surrounding it. The fields around Tom's home show the careful management that Mr. Fisher and his sons give to their land. Even during wintertime, the fields are cleared and ready for the early spring planting. This same cleanliness and organization is also present inside the Fisher home; the rooms sparkle and shine with the efforts of Mrs. Fisher and her daughters. Dinner was a cheerful meal, with much laughter and good conversation. Having no brothers of my own, I am always amazed at how much food Tom's brothers, Carl and Jonathan, eat. Mr. Fisher teased Carl that he is sure one of his legs is hollow.

After dinner, Emily and I did the dishes, and then Tom and I took a walk around the farm. I feel so secure with Tom and love listening to his ambitious plans for the future. He has been saving the monies he makes doing cabinetry and carpentry work for Mr. Jones in the hopes he can lease and manage a small piece of ground for farming. I love his gentleness and kindness to others and the way his eyes reflect his feelings. He is truly a good man and a good friend.

I mentioned to Tom that I had listened to the missionaries yesterday and the strange feelings that had entered my heart as they talked. He said that he too has felt a stirring within him and that he and his family are going to attend their next meeting. He has asked me to go with him.

Tonight, after Bible reading and prayers, I asked Father if I could go with Tom and his family, but Father has said I cannot go. He said he does not understand why Tom's family is interested in attending the meeting. I tried to explain to Father the feelings I had as I listened to the missionaries, but he said that it was just the allurement of something new and different. I must get a message to Tom that I cannot go with him. I cannot disobey Father.

Chapter 7

Sunday morning Abby woke to the sound of thunder and the smell of rain in the air. She jumped out of bed and ran to the window, pulling it closed quickly. Thick gray clouds hung low in the sky, and as she walked back to bed, she heard the first drops of rain patter against the closed window. She looked at the clock on the bedside table. It was a few minutes after seven; not enough time to go back to sleep, though she looked longingly at the bed. It had been after two in the morning before she had finally fallen asleep. Scott's phone call had upset her, and as she lay in bed her mind kept going over their conversation. She disliked arguing with him and felt that his accusations of stalling were unjust. *Why can't he understand that I can't just walk in here and clinically pack everything up? Is he even trying to see my side of this?* Abby sighed. *Maybe I am taking a little longer on some things, but each box that is packed is also filled with memories for me. I feel close to my grandparents here, especially Grandmother, and when the house is empty of their possessions, it becomes just another empty house.* It was a good thing that she would be going back early next month for the Towers' closing and they would have a chance to spend some time together then.

Abby pulled on her robe, slid her feet into slippers, and headed downstairs for breakfast. While eating her cereal and fruit, she gazed at the storm through the windows. The rain had intensified, falling in noisy sheets, and puddles were beginning to form on the uncovered portion of the patio. *Why is it,* she thought, *that things always seem worse during the night and on a dark, stormy day?* Today she would be glad to go to church instead of staying home with her thoughts. She finished her breakfast and rinsed her bowl quickly before placing it in the dishwasher and hurrying upstairs to get ready.

After doing her hair and makeup, Abby carefully slipped the new deep violet dress over her head and settled it around her hips. Looking at herself in the mirror, she noticed the color brought out the rich highlights in her hair. The vibrant color of the dress also lifted her spirits. She fastened small gold earrings in her ears before gathering up her grandmother's scriptures and going downstairs.

Today Abby drove next door to pick up Agnes. She carefully unfurled an umbrella as she stepped out of the car and walked to the front door. Before she had a chance to ring the bell, Agnes opened the door and stepped onto the porch. Abby held the umbrella over both their heads as they walked back to the car.

"We really need all the rain we can get, living in a desert as we do," Agnes said as they drove to the meetinghouse. "Spring rains are really important if we are to have the amount of water required for the rest of the year."

Once again, Agnes, with Abby following behind, led the way to the front of the chapel before sitting down. As Abby listened to the peaceful prelude music, she felt herself relaxing. She enjoyed the talks given during sacrament meeting and found herself smiling as she walked with the older woman down the hall to the Relief Society room for the Gospel Doctrine class. She was pleased to find she remembered the names of people that had introduced themselves to her the previous week. When she entered the classroom, her eyes met Blake's, and as he smiled at her a shiver ran through her body. Giving herself a mental shake, she sat down and opened her scriptures to the study material listed on the board. This week the lesson was taken from the books of Enos, Jarom, and Omni in the Book of Mormon. As they read, she was impressed by Enos's faith in praying all through the day and into the night to receive a remission of his sins and an answer to his prayers. She pondered the words of Enos: *And my soul hungered.* From within her came the answering cry that her soul had been spiritually hungry for too long a time. She yearned to feel the comfort and direction of the Spirit in her life.

At the conclusion of the lesson, Blake bore his testimony that prayers are answered and that joy can be found in living a Christ-centered life. Tears misted Abby's eyes as the Spirit bore witness to her that this lesson was true.

On his way out of the room, Blake stopped to shake her hand, and she thanked him for the lesson he had given.

"I'm glad you enjoyed it," he responded. "The Book of Mormon is close to my heart." He smiled down at her, still holding her hand. "I'm still planning on coming tomorrow, unless your plans have changed. Is two o'clock still a good time?"

"You bet! I'm grateful for the help," Abby replied, aware of the warmth of his hand holding hers. Releasing her hand, he gave her another quick smile. "See you tomorrow afternoon, then," he said.

At the end of Relief Society, Sister Richardson caught Abby just as she was leaving. "Sister Peters, I know you are only here for a short while, but I was wondering if we could enlist your help at our Relief Society activity next month. We've chosen the theme of temples for our lesson. Sister James was going to give a presentation on the background of the building of the St. George temple, but her husband called this morning to tell me she won't be able to give her part." Sister Richardson shook her head sadly. "She is expecting a baby in two months and is threatening to miscarry, so her doctor has ordered her to bed for a while. I know your ancestors helped build our beautiful temple, so could you fill in for her?"

Abby thought of all the reasons she had for declining and had every intention of doing so. She had so much to get done, and Scott was already frustrated with her. But as she opened her mouth to answer, she found herself saying, "Yes, I can do that; I think I'll still be here at that time."

"Oh, thank you," Sister Richardson gushed, shaking her hand enthusiastically. "I just knew you would help us. Your grandmother was so proud of her heritage, and I know it would have pleased her so much to have you tell some of your family stories. The activity is on the second Wednesday of the month."

As they left the building, Abby looked up. The rain had stopped, and the sun was trying to shine through the thin white clouds that lingered in the sky. The air smelled fresh and clean, and she felt uplifted. After turning the car into Agnes's driveway, Abby helped the older woman from the car.

"Thank you, Abby, for the ride. Dinner will be ready at two, so I will see you then," Agnes said, giving Abby's hand a quick squeeze. "My dear, I'm so glad you're coming, as Sundays are always a little lonely for me."

"Are you sure I can't bring anything?" Abby asked as she walked back to her car.

"No thanks, I have everything organized. It's just going to be a simple meal," Agnes replied and gave a final wave before entering her house.

Abby waved back and moved the car into her own driveway. Upstairs she changed into a pair of slacks and a knit top. She did a few odd jobs around the house, then looking at her watch, decided she had time to call her mother before walking next door. She punched in the numbers on her cell phone and heard her mother's voice after the second ring.

"Mom, it's me. I just couldn't wait to find out how Dad handled going to church this morning. Scott told me when he called last night that you had talked Dad into going with you. So, how was it?"

Abby could hear the laughter in her mother's voice as she replied. "I think he was in shock, poor dear. But after he got through complaining about all the things he needed to do at work and was dressed, I think he was glad to be going. If you thought Bishop Anderson was surprised to see me last week, you should have seen his face when we both walked into the chapel. He made a point of coming off the stand to shake your father's hand and welcome him." Mary's voice became serious as she continued. "Abby, it felt so good and right to be there together. I realized how much I've missed it without being aware of that fact. It brought back all the memories of the years we went faithfully, and I felt a deep sense of loss because we'd let so many things become more important in our lives than the gospel. We both got so busy with our social lives and work that we just drifted away from what should have been more important to us—our activity in the Church. So we're both determined now to do better. Your father hasn't left yet; do you want to talk to him?"

"Oh Mom, I really would. I've missed him, and it seems ages since I last talked to him." Abby heard her mother call her father to the phone and in a minute heard his familiar voice on the line.

"Abby, I'm glad you called before I left for work. I've missed my girl. How are things going there?"

"I've really missed you too, Dad. I'm making headway here, but it's slow work, and it's going to be a while before I'm through. I have to be honest with you and Mom—I'm having second thoughts about selling this home. I hadn't realized all the good memories I would feel as I went through things."

She heard her father chuckle in agreement. "Your mother and I have also started to question if we really want to sell. But either way, what you're doing has to be done, so we can decide later."

"Dad, Scott told me last night that you were going to church this morning with Mom, and she confirmed it. What did you think? Did it seem good to be there?" she questioned.

David Peters chuckled again. "Yes, it did. I think I ruined Scott's morning plans, but I'm glad I went with your mother. I wish you could have seen the look on Bishop Anderson's face; I'm sure he thought the roof would fall in on us all. Seriously, Abby, your mother is determined to become active again, and I'll admit that it felt wonderful to be sitting next to my sweetheart in church. We both wish you had been there to go with us. We've also done quite a bit of talking about things this morning, and we both want to start doing what we should. It's time we change our priorities to spiritual goals rather than temporal ones."

Abby's voice was solemn as she replied. "Well, Dad, I have gone to church the last two weeks here, and today I felt a real desire within myself to be more spiritually active. I guess Grandmother and Grandfather Brown are working on us even though they aren't here." Changing the subject, Abby asked, "Are you prepared for your upcoming trial?"

"I think we're ready, and I guess I'd better head into the office. Scott is supposed to meet me in an hour, and there are a couple of things I want to have ready before he gets there. As I took the sacrament today, I made a personal commitment to eliminate using Sundays to catch up on my work, so I'll just have to do better planning from now on. You take good care of yourself, Abby, and we'll come as soon as we can."

"Thanks, Dad. I love you. Let me talk some more to Mom." She heard him say good-bye to her mother before Mary's voice came on the line.

"Mom, after Relief Society today Sister Richardson, the president, asked me to give a presentation on the building of the St. George temple. Do you have anything I can use, or should I just use the material I found in Grandmother's genealogy? I remember over the years the stories she told about Tom Fisher and wondered if you would be willing to write down any that you recall being told."

"My grandmother Walker told me a lot of stories, so I'll try to put together a few and e-mail them to you," Mary answered.

Abby looked at her watch and gasped, "Mom, I've got to go. Agnes Givens invited me for dinner, and I'm supposed to be there in about one minute. I'll call you tomorrow."

After a quick good-bye, Abby grabbed her purse and walked next door. Agnes answered the door as soon as Abby rang the bell. The delicious smell of roast beef assailed her as she entered the house, and she felt her mouth water with anticipation. It also brought memories back of Sunday dinners at her grandparents' home. Grandmother Brown had always put a roast in the oven to cook while they were at church. Agnes led Abby into the dining room. Most of the food had already been placed on the table. Pointing to a chair and place setting of china, she gestured Abby toward it.

"Why don't you sit here? I'll just bring in the gravy, and I think we're ready to eat." As Abby sat down, Agnes bustled back into the kitchen, emerging a few seconds later carrying a bowl of brown gravy. Placing it on the table, she sat down. "I'll just say a blessing on the food before we get started," she said. Bowing her head, Agnes offered a humble prayer of thanksgiving.

"Agnes, you've gone to so much work," Abby exclaimed as she helped herself to mashed potatoes and surveyed the feast in front of her.

"It was nice to have someone to cook for," Mrs. Givens rejoined.

Abby enjoyed the meal more than she had anticipated. Agnes kept her entertained and laughing as she related some of her experiences with Abby's grandmother.

After helping with the dishes, Abby hugged Agnes. "I'm so glad I came. This has been one of the nicest Sundays I've had in a long time. Thanks for inviting me to share your wonderful meal."

Agnes linked her arm through Abby's as she walked her to the front door. "It's been nice for me, as well. My daughters live far enough away that I don't get much company. Usually on Sundays your grandmother and I would take turns fixing the meal and eating together. I've missed that."

Abby walked home slowly. The clouds had cleared completely, and the late afternoon sun beamed its warmth down on her. Instead of turning in at her grandmother's home, she kept walking, enjoying the feel of the warm sun. The Relief Society president's request prompted Abby to think about the history of the houses as she passed. This part of St. George was one of the first areas to be settled and, from her background as a Realtor, Abby knew that many of the old homes were listed on the National Register of Historic Homes. The pride of ownership was shown in the neat flowerbeds and the large trees casting their afternoon shadows across the well-manicured green lawns. She walked several blocks before turning around and starting back home. It had been a long time since she had felt the peace and quiet of the Sabbath as she had today. Her Sundays at home were usually busy days spent catching up on the chores she had neglected the rest of the week. Many Sundays found her in her office, busy with paperwork or at the country club with Scott. Abby found herself thinking about Blake and the deep spirituality he radiated, and she reflected on what a comforting feeling that was. She could not imagine Scott being willing to give up his practice in the city and settle in a small town, regardless of the circumstances. Nor could she imagine him, at this point, being interested in going to church. After their discussion last night, she realized more than ever there were important differences they would have to resolve before committing to marriage, her desire for more church activity being one of them. She knew she was still feeling hurt. If she was honest with herself, she was sure Scott was also hurt that she was unable to see his view as well.

When she arrived at home, Abby headed upstairs to her room. After putting her purse in the closet, she noticed her grandmother's scriptures on the bedside table where she had placed them after church that morning. Picking them up, she sat down in the rocking chair by the window. She fingered the gold lettering of her grandmother's name on the leather cover then, with a wistful sigh, opened the Book of Mormon and thumbed through the pages until she reached the book of Enos. She started reading the scriptures they had covered in Gospel Doctrine and was soon lost in the beauty of the verses. After reading the books of Enos, Jarom, and Omni, Abby flipped back to the beginning of First Nephi; she wanted to start over at the beginning. As she read, she studied the notes her grandmother had made to clarify different scriptures. Abby read through several chapters before realizing she was having a hard time seeing the print in the book. Looking up, she became aware of the gathering darkness and the setting sun, and a startled glance at the clock confirmed that several hours had gone by. She placed the scriptures again on the bedside table and hurried downstairs. Grabbing an apple from the bowl on the counter, she reached for her list of jobs that needed Blake's help.

Later, as she was preparing to get into bed, she found herself on her knees. Prayer was something else she had not done for a long time, and for a while she simply stayed on her knees and thought about the blessings and problems in her life. Abby soon found herself pouring out her heart to her Heavenly Father. When she arose, she felt more at peace within herself. As she climbed into bed she remembered the family prayers she had shared with her parents in her childhood, as well as here at her grandparents' home, and thought of the secure and happy feeling they had given her. Again she felt that Grandmother Brown would have been pleased to see that she was beginning to make the needed changes in her life.

***

10 March 1845

Two weeks have passed since I wrote in my journal, and much has happened. Mother has been very sick with a bad cold and fever, and we have been much worried it would affect her lungs. I have kept busy taking over the house duties as well as caring for her. She has been so sick with fever and cough that the doctor bled her yesterday. It must have helped because her fever broke during the night. Father has stayed at her bedside as much as he could, and I can see how much Mother means to him. This past week I have been afraid Mother might die but am relieved now that she seems to be recovering. Still, she is so pale and gaunt that when I hold her hand as I sit by her bedside, it lies weak and thin within my own. But God has heard my prayers, and she is starting to get well.

Elizabeth stopped by yesterday to tell me her news. She is going to London to visit her aunt and uncle and will be leaving next week. She has had several new dresses made to take with her, and I enjoyed hearing her describe them in detail. She looked so beautiful with the flush of the fresh air on her cheeks and her new blue cape that I felt even more tired and unsightly, but it was good to see her, and I will miss her when she is gone.

Mrs. Fisher has been by several times to bring herb teas and plasters for Mother. She is such a kind woman. She gave us the news of the village and said that Mr. Jones has been so sick that he has been near death. She said the Mormon missionaries performed a miracle for him. Evidently the Jones family has been attending the meetings. When Mr. Jones became so sick the doctor did not give much hope for him, Mrs. Jones called for the missionaries, and they laid their hands on his head and gave him a blessing that has healed him. She said that when he is well, the family will be baptized. On the way out, Mrs. Fisher confided in me that she and her family have been attending the meetings when they can and have found them to be full of hope and truth.

Chapter 8

After breakfast Monday morning, Abby opened the back door and went outside. Gathering her grandmother's gardening tools from the garage, she set out for the backyard. She looked sadly at the tangled mass of flowers bravely trying to survive the surrounding weeds determined to quench their new growth. The lawn desperately needed cutting, and she decided this should be the first order of priority. Returning to the garage, she found the mower in the back, though when Abby checked the gas level she saw it was empty. A few minutes' search revealed a gas can, but it was also empty. After a quick trip to the service station for gas, she was ready to start. After several exasperating pulls on the lawn mower's ignition line, the engine started then slowly increased in speed as it warmed up. Abby steadily guided the lawnmower row after row until she'd finished the front and back lawns. Then she wiped the perspiration from her forehead and put the mower back inside the garage.

Dusting her hands on her jeans, she looked through the other gardening tools until she found the weed eater. Thankfully, this was electric and easier to start. Abby carefully cleared the long grass around the trees in the yard and then tried her hand at edging the lawn. After she had gone a few feet, the line broke, and she had to stop and rethread it. This happened several more times before she was through, and each time her patience was more difficult to recover. By the time she finished, she was ready to throw the weed eater in the garbage. Edging was definitely not that easy, she decided grumpily, looking at the jagged borders of the lawn. She certainly wouldn't plan on trying that again; next time she'd hire someone else to do it.

By this time it was noon, and she was more than ready to take a break. Inside, Abby splashed cold water on her face and peered at her image in the mirror. Her face was red and flushed from the morning's exertion. After patting her face dry, she brushed through her hair. She smiled at the thought of Scott seeing her now. He was proud that she was always well-groomed. Well, she certainly didn't look too polished at the moment in her dusty jeans and tee-shirt. Holding her hands out, she noticed a couple of fingernails that had broken thanks to her efforts that morning. As she was walking downstairs, the doorbell rang. She opened the door and found herself facing a deliveryman holding a large bouquet of spring flowers. Smiling, she thanked him and closed the door. Abby pulled out the card as she carried the flowers into the living room and placed them in an empty vase on an end table. Opening it, she read the message,

Abby,
I'm sorry. I didn't mean to argue with you. I know that we
are both under a lot of stress right now. I'll call as soon as I can.
All my love,
Scott

Abby felt some of the tension inside of her release as she placed the card on the table and took a deep breath. Burying her face in the flowers, she breathed deeply of their sweet perfume, picturing Scott and the fun times they had together, his arms around her. She smiled. The flowers had certainly brightened her day and lightened her heart. Glancing at her watch, she hurried to the kitchen. Blake would be here before too long, and she needed to eat lunch before he came.

Abby made herself a sandwich and poured a glass of milk then walked outside to the patio. The chair facing the backyard was quickly becoming her favorite place to eat. She munched her sandwich and examined her handiwork, mentally reviewing the list of afternoon projects that needed Blake's help. After eating her lunch and straightening the kitchen, she again walked outside and sank into a lounge chair. Closing her eyes, Abby savored the warmth of the spring sun filtering through the latticed roof of the patio, the rich smells of lilacs and newly mowed grass heavy in the air. She could hear the buzzing of bees as they busily explored the flowers close to where she lay.

"Abby, are you out here?"

Startled, she quickly opened her eyes. She must have fallen asleep for a few minutes. Her watch said it was just after two.

"I'm out in back, Blake," she called and quickly stood up just as he came around the corner of the house.

He grinned at her. "I rang the doorbell, but when no one answered I figured you might be in back." Looking around, he continued. "It looks as if you have already put in a full day's work this morning. The lawns look wonderful, but I bet you're tired."

Abby smiled back at him. "Thanks for that, but if you look at the lawn borders, you can see that I'm certainly not used to doing this kind of work, and I'm not good at it. But I've enjoyed being outside. I really enjoy working with flowers more than mowing lawns. And I've had my nap in the sun, so I'm ready to go again."

Blake nodded his head in agreement. "I agree with you about enjoying being outside in the fresh air. There's just something about working with nature and getting your hands dirty that puts things in the right perspective." He surveyed the yard and shook his head sadly. "Your grandmother also loved working in her yard, and I often had to remind her not to push herself so hard. She loved her flowers, and they seemed to know it; they just bloomed and flourished under her care. I know that she hired someone to mow her lawns and do the heavy work, but the flowerbeds were her kingdom."

Abby laughed. "I decided this morning that I'm going to hire a neighbor boy to do those jobs as well. I'm certainly no expert on edging."

This afternoon Blake had come ready to work. He was dressed in jeans and a sport shirt, his arms already suntanned. His blue eyes echoed his smile, and for a second Abby's breath caught in her throat. Just over an hour ago she was smiling over Scott's flowers and imagining him here with her, so she surely couldn't be feeling an attraction for Blake. She wasn't a schoolgirl anymore, and she needed to remember that Scott was her type of man.

Briskly she said, "I thought we could start with the pruning, if you're sure you don't mind using your truck to haul the debris to the dump." Then she pointed toward the rose bushes and asked, "Is it too late to prune the roses for spring? They're already leafing out, and I've noticed quite a few buds starting to form."

Blake walked across the lawn to the flowerbeds, and Abby followed him.

"Usually they are pruned in February, but it looks like they really need it now," Abby said.

Blake studied the bushes before replying. "They should be fine, Abby, and they'll catch up." He stepped back to survey the trees. "We need to prune some of the limbs off a few of the trees as well. And I'm glad to take all the loads we need to the dump. My truck is constantly used for hauling, so don't worry about that." He started back across the lawn, calling over his shoulder, "I brought some sharp clippers with me, and I'll just get them from the truck."

He was back in a few minutes, carrying the clippers under his arm and pulling on his gloves. Abby followed him, pulling on her gloves as well. "Do we need to bag the branches?" she asked as he walked to the nearest rose bush.

"No, we'll just toss everything in the back of the truck. We'll use your grandmother's wheelbarrow to carry it there. Have you seen it anywhere? It should be in the garage."

"I think I saw it in there this morning," Abby replied, already on her way to look. She located it at the back of the garage and wheeled it to where Blake was busy clipping branches from one of the rose bushes. He was cutting them quite short, and she caught her breath at seeing the branches with the thick green leaf buds and small new leaves being trimmed off the bush. Glancing up, Blake noticed the expression on her face. He stopped clipping and looked at her. "This really does make the plant healthier, and soon they will be full of new green buds and leaves again. Do you remember how beautiful your grandmother's roses were?" At her nod, he continued. "She was very careful to prune them each spring, and that is one reason they were always so healthy."

"I know. I just have a hard time throwing away anything that is growing. When I have a vase of fresh flowers, each flower has to be dead before I can bring myself to throw it away." Abby bent over and began picking up the branches off the lawn and placing them in the wheelbarrow. They worked together quietly for a while, and she thought again how good it felt to be working outdoors. Blake was an easy man to be around, and she was enjoying his company.

When the wheelbarrow was full, Blake put down the clippers and started pushing the load through the gate to the front yard. "I need to put a tarp down on the floor of the truck. Then we can just toss these in," he said.

Abby followed him around to the front. The green Dodge truck that stood in her driveway was an older model, but its finish was clean and shiny. Moving the wheelbarrow to the back of the truck, Blake let down the tailgate and jumped up inside. He opened the folded black tarp and carefully laid it on the truck bed. Abby reached in to help him, and together they laid it on the floor of the truck. "Thanks, Abby," Blake said as he jumped down. They tossed the branches from the wheelbarrow into the truck. By the time they were finished, both Abby and Blake had scratches on their arms.

By late afternoon, the backyard roses were trimmed, several trees had been pruned, and the truck was full. Abby helped Blake fold the edges of the tarp over the top of the trash and tie it down. Although her body ached with the strain of unused muscles, she felt a deep sense of satisfaction as she thought of the freshly mowed lawns and trimmed bushes. Watching Blake tie the last knot on the rope over the tarp, Abby said impulsively, "Blake, please come back for dinner. It won't be anything special, but I did thaw a couple of hamburger patties for grilling. It's small thanks for all your work, but I really would like you to have dinner with me."

He gave the rope one final tug, making sure it was fastened tight, and then turned toward her, giving her a quick grin. "I'd like that. All that's facing me at my house for dinner is a bowl of cold cereal. I'll take this to the dump. What time shall I be back here?"

She brushed her hair back from her face and, looking at her watch, saw that it was a few minutes after five. "Around six fifteen would be a good time, if that's all right with you."

"That's perfect," he said as he climbed into the cab and shut the door. "I'll see you then." She watched as he started the engine and, with a final wave, backed out of the driveway and drove off.

"What have you done? You're not thinking straight," she said aloud as she entered the house. She knew Scott would be upset to know that she had invited Blake for dinner, but she rationalized it was her way of thanking him. Besides, Abby knew that she would probably be enlisting Blake's help again in the near future; they still had the front yard to do, and there were a few other projects that would probably need his help. And anyway, he was turning out to be just a good friend. Shoving the doubts to the back of her mind, Abby raced upstairs. She wanted to take a quick shower and change clothes before seeing about dinner.

Once again Abby was thankful for her short hair. As she was applying a light gloss to her lips, she noticed that her arms and face were sunburned. She bent over to pull sandals on her feet and felt her muscles painfully comply. Tomorrow morning she would be stiff.

In the kitchen, Abby tied an apron around her waist before starting to prepare dinner. Next she turned on the patio grill, thankful that it still had propane gas. She tossed red potatoes, fresh garlic, green onions, and fresh rosemary with salt and pepper and drizzled olive oil over the top. Placing the potato mixture on heavy-duty foil, she sealed it tight and placed the packet on the back of the grill. Inside, she arranged plates of fresh fruit and vegetables and then set the table in the kitchen, placing Scott's flowers in the center. She had just seasoned the hamburger patties when the doorbell rang. Taking off her apron, she hung it on the inside door of the pantry. Abby paused before the front door and took a deep breath before opening it.

Blake had taken time to shower as well, and his hair was still damp. He had changed his clothes to a pair of khaki slacks and a green sport shirt. His eyes smiled at her as she opened the door. "It's not very often I get invited to dinner, and I'm hungry enough that I'm glad to forego the cold cereal," he said.

Abby ushered him inside and closed the door behind her. "We're just going to eat in the kitchen, if that's all right. And you can make yourself useful by cooking the hamburgers. As hard as you worked today, I wish it were steak—you earned it."

As she led the way to the kitchen, Blake followed, remembering his impression of her at the funeral. He remembered seeing her at church when they were both kids and had thought she was cute, but as she was a few years younger than he, Blake had not gotten to know her very well. When he returned home for good, her grandmother had talked to him so much about Abby that he had been interested in seeing her again. At the funeral, however, she had been dressed in an expensive black suit with a silk blouse, her hair carefully styled. Everything about her spoke of money and sophistication, and he had thought she was now definitely out of his league—a rich career woman. However, tonight she was dressed casually, and her skin was lightly burned from the sun. A few red scratches from thorns were on her arms, and her hair was clean and shiny. She had worked hard and uncomplainingly today. Blake had offered to help because he had cared so much for her grandmother, but suddenly he felt a desire to get to know the real Abby. He realized, with a start, that he was becoming interested in her.

"I hope you don't mind being the chef," Abby said with a smile, handing him a plate of burgers. "The grill is on the patio, and it's good and hot."

He carried the plate outside, and as he lifted the lid on the barbecue, the smell of roasting potatoes and garlic surrounded him. He placed the hamburgers on the grill then closed the lid and looked around the yard. He always loved this time of day, the sun giving its final blessing as its light swept the earth one last time before disappearing, the shadows lengthening and deepening. The hush of the evening filled him with peace, and he breathed deeply of the fresh spring air. He glanced through the glass on the French doors and could see Abby inside filling glasses with ice water. A deep contentment washed over him. When Emily had given him back his ring, he had been heartbroken and had pushed himself even more in his work. It had been a hard loss, following closely on his father's death and his mother's failing health, and he realized he had used his busy practice as an excuse for not seeking a new relationship. Oh, he had dated occasionally since then but had never allowed himself to become emotionally close to someone else. Maybe it was finally time to put the past behind him and move forward. The smell of cooking meat brought him out of his thoughts, and he lifted the lid and turned the patties. The door opened, and Abby stepped outside carrying a plate with hamburger buns.

"How is the meat coming?" she asked, handing the plate to Blake. "I didn't know if you liked your buns toasted or just warmed, so I'll let you do what you want with them. I like mine either way."

"I like mine toasted," he said, "and the meat should be done in about three minutes." Again he glanced around the yard. "I love this time of day. It's so peaceful and quiet out here."

Abby walked over and stood by his side, looking at the newly mowed grass and the neatly trimmed roses. "I really enjoyed working outside today," she said softly then added with a grin, "but I bet by tomorrow I'll be stiff in muscles I never knew I had."

He threw back his head and laughed at her remark. "I'll probably discover a few sore muscles myself." He walked over to check the meat again. "I think these are done. Shall I put them on the same plate that you used for the buns?"

"That's fine. I'll run inside and get another plate for the potatoes if you want to turn off the grill."

Inside, Blake held the chair for Abby before seating himself across from her. "Abby, everything looks and smells so good," he said. "The flowers are really beautiful."

"They are beautiful." She smiled over at him. "Scott Shafer, a man I'm dating from home, sent them to me this morning."

Blake felt an unexpected jolt go through him. He had heard from Ryan that Abby was dating someone but had forgotten that fact. He just hoped that it was not as serious of a relationship as Ryan had implied.

"Blake, would you mind blessing the food?" Abby asked. He nodded at her and bowed his head. She listened as he blessed the food and asked a blessing to be on the home as well as on her. Abby felt a feeling of contentment inside her, and as she raised her head and met his eyes, a shiver ran through her body, a connection of spirit touching spirit. "Thank you," her voice and eyes told him.

During the meal, Abby found herself relaxing and enjoying Blake's company, their conversation easy and comfortable. After dinner, they took their dessert and sat outside on the patio. It was almost dark; a few pale stars were starting to wink in the sky, and cheerful crickets added their voices to the night. The two of them sat in companionable silence for several minutes before Abby, in a reverent voice, said, "It's been a long time since I've felt so at peace. I remember as a child sitting here in this same spot with my grandfather. We would wait while the stars appeared in the sky and then he would patiently point out the constellations. He had such a love of the night sky. Grandfather would tell me stories about the stars and how they had given light and guidance to people through the ages. He would say that just as the stars stayed the same, so the gospel was the same plan that it had always been, and that I could always count on it if I followed it as my guide, much as the ancient sailors used the stars to navigate uncharted seas."

"I remember your grandfather very well, Abby," Blake said. "He was a good and kind man, and many people in this town owe their present financial security to him. He helped when they had hard times, making loans available to see them through their crises. Many times when they were turned down at other places, he would give them a loan. My father told me once he thought your grandfather used his own money a few times to provide those loans. He was a man of integrity, and you can be proud of your heritage."

Abby wiped tears from her eyes. "I miss them both so much, Blake. Life always seemed so simple here, the pace so much slower and richer. The last time I came was just after graduating from college, and I only stayed for the weekend. I was so full of ambition, so determined to set the world on fire, that I couldn't wait to get back to Denver and get started. I know Grandmother was hoping I'd stay longer and was disappointed when I left." She shook her head. "What I wouldn't give to have her here now." With a catch in her voice, she added sadly, "I wish I had come last winter when I'd planned. I'm sure she was disappointed, and I never had the chance to see her again and tell her how much I loved her." She finished speaking with a sob in her voice.

The tears were coming faster now, and Blake reached over and put his arm around her, letting her cry on his shoulder. He held her close, savoring the feeling of her in his arms. He was surprised that it felt so right, so natural to be holding her. It was with reluctance that he let her go as she raised her head and scooted away. With a shaky laugh, she said, "I haven't done that since I was a little girl." She reached in her pocket for a tissue and wiped her eyes.

"Your grandmother knew you loved her, Abby. She was proud of your accomplishments, and she would want you to remember and treasure your relationship with her." Blake gently continued. "Remember, this life is not the end. Someday you will have a chance to be with her again."

"I'm trying to remind myself of that, Blake, but I feel almost like a kid again as I try to catch up spiritually. My family became totally inactive when I was a teenager, and except when I was here with my grandparents, I haven't attended church regularly for quite a while. When I came here a few weeks ago, Agnes Givens asked me to take her to church, or I wouldn't have gone. But when I entered the chapel, it felt right to me. I can't explain it, but it felt like—like returning to a beloved home. Even if Agnes didn't continue asking me to take her, I would go on my own now. I've realized these past few weeks that my life has been missing something, something important. I've started reading Grandmother's scriptures and saying my prayers again. But I'll admit, I feel like I'm just learning how to swim in spiritual waters." She ended with a weak laugh.

Blake laughed softly as well. "We have all gone through times like those; it's the way we gain our testimonies. The scriptures say we learn 'line upon line, precept upon precept.' I remember feeling much the same way when I left for my mission. Oh, not that I didn't have a testimony and a real desire to serve, but I felt so inadequate. I can promise you, Abby, that if you will continue to study and sincerely seek Heavenly Father's help, you'll have a richness added to your life you never dreamed was possible."

Abby wiped her eyes again at Blake's words. "Maybe this will be the best of the treasures Grandmother left to me—the chance to put myself back on track again. I'm sorry that it's taken her death to make me realize what's important in my life. I just wish she were here to see the changes I'm making." She stood up. "And I'm sorry I cried all over you after all the work you did for me today. I didn't mean to turn the evening into one of sadness and tears."

Blake reached for her hand and drew her close to him again, looking deeply into her eyes. "I'm honored that you would share your feelings with me. I've really enjoyed working with you today and getting to know you better. I remember as a kid I always thought you were pretty well in control of your life."

Abby laughed. "I remember you, too; those summers and holidays here were always pretty special for me. I hope this evening and my tears won't frighten you away from helping me some more." Then in a serious tone she added, "But thanks for letting me share my thoughts with you. I feel better now. Maybe I needed to finally shed the tears I've felt in my heart."

"My pleasure," he said with a smile. "I guess I'd better go. I have a pretty big day tomorrow."

Abby walked him to the door, and after closing and locking the door after him, went back to the kitchen to clean up. She was afraid to analyze her feelings too deeply. But in her heart she could not visualize sharing the thoughts with Scott that she had shared with Blake.

***

15 March 1845

Today is my eighteenth birthday, and it has been a happy, happy day. This morning Father and Mother gave me a brooch that contains strands of their hair twisted together with a lock of mine. The combination of Mother's black and gray hair, Father's light brown, and my dark black is a symbol of the closeness and love we share as a family. They are very dear to me, and I have truly been blessed with noble parents.

This afternoon Tom came to see Father and asked for my hand in marriage. I was so nervous as I waited while Tom met with Father. Mother and I sat in the kitchen trying to knit, and she assured me they both loved Tom as a son. Father did give his blessing, and then Tom and I took a walk along the river. I felt as if my feet and body were floating, and only his hand in mine kept me on the ground. The day was truly beautiful. Light, fluffy clouds floated like a ship's sails across the clear blue sky. The smells and signs of the coming season were in the air, the damp earth of fields was plowed and planted for spring, primroses were pushing their way through the winter grasses, and daffodils were shooting their green sprouts upward. I know that I will remember this day always, my own life being reborn as well as the world around me. I am so happy and excited for all that lies ahead of us.

Tom has given me a small carved oak box as an engagement present. He made the box while working for Mr. Jones. The sides of the box are carved with intertwined hearts and surrounded by oak leaves. Tom said the hearts symbolize the joining together of our lives. I think Tom is much like the oak tree as well; he is strong and willingly lends his strength to those who need it. Tom, I know, will be someone that will always choose right over wrong, and I will be able to depend on him. He is so pure and kind. I will try to be a good wife to him. I will cherish this box as the first symbol of his love for me. When we went back to the house, Mother and Father joined us in celebrating our engagement with a small glass of sherry. We will wait until fall to marry.

After tea we rode over to see Tom's family and give them our news. I was received with love and rejoicing. Abigail says I should have a wedding with a white silk dress, but it matters not what I wear as long as Tom is standing beside me. The Fishers have truly welcomed me to their family. I am doubly blessed to have such wonderful parents and now to be part of Tom's family as well.

Tonight as I lie in bed and look out my window at the stars in the heavens, I feel so much joy in my heart that I cannot find the words to express what I feel. I hope God can read the thankfulness in my heart for all that He has given me. My cup of happiness truly runneth over.

Chapter 9

Abby spent the next few days weeding the front flowerbeds and cleaning out the garage. Scott called each evening, but he was so busy with the trial that he didn't have much time to talk. She also talked to her mother a couple of times, but even those calls were not long, as both she and Mary were busy. Abby had called Mr. Arbogast, her client involved with the Boulder Towers' purchase, and confirmed that everything was on schedule for the closing of the sale. Megan had also phoned one evening to talk. During the quiet evenings, Abby often pondered on her discussion with Blake. It had been so comforting to have someone really listen to her. She was sure that the losses he had suffered in his own life helped him to understand what she was feeling. She had also appreciated his spiritual insight into her grief and tried to remember his reassuring words as she continued her work in the old home. With frequent, albeit brief, phone calls and so many other tasks on her plate, Abby had little reason to feel lonely. Still, she found herself at odd moments of the day thinking a little longingly of her busy life in Denver. When she looked at herself in the mirror each morning after pulling on jeans and a tee-shirt for her work in the yard, she thought of her challenging days in the city. Abby missed the fervor and excitement of her job and her busy social schedule. And she realized she missed Scott and the excitement he added to her life.

***

Thursday, Abby spent the day working in the front flower beds. The beds were thick with weeds, and she figured it would not be an easy process.

The sun was becoming warmer now as the days became longer, and frequently she stopped to wipe her forehead dry. By late afternoon, she was hot and tired and decided to call it quits for the day. Abby had just come into the house and was starting up the stairs for a shower when the doorbell rang. When she opened the door, she was surprised to see Blake standing on the porch.

"Hi, Abby. Just thought I'd stop by on my way home and see how you're coming with the packing and if you need any help. I had a couple of last-minute cancellations, so I'm off early today."

Blake looked so neat and clean that Abby blushed as she looked down at her own dirt-smudged jeans. "Uh, come on in, Blake," she stammered. He entered, closing the door after him, and followed her into the living room.

"Thanks for your offer, Blake, but I'm not going to do anymore heavy work today," Abby said tiredly. "I haven't decided yet who won the battle today, me or the weeds."

Blake laughed and leaned forward to wipe a smudge of dirt from her cheek. "Well, it looks to me like you put up a good fight."

Abby laughed too, looking down at her dirty clothes. "I tried, but seriously, Blake, I really am not going to work anymore tonight. I just want to shower and change then curl up with a good book and a large bowl of popcorn."

Blake thought for a minute, noticing how tired and discouraged she looked. "Okay, Abby, I'll go and let you shower, but I'll be back in about thirty minutes to pick you up. I think this is a good time for you to meet a couple of four-legged friends of mine. There's even enough time before it gets dark that we can take a short ride, if you want. I think you need a complete change of scene."

Abby shook her head. "I don't know, Blake, maybe we should wait for another day."

Blake looked at her for a few seconds. "Abby, I really think you need to do something different. You know what they say: a change is as good as a rest. I promise you'll enjoy this, Abby, and it will refresh you as well."

Abby thought about the solitary evening ahead. "Well, I guess a change would be nice, but you have to give me some time to clean up."

Blake walked to the door and opened it. "Good, I'm glad you're coming. See you in thirty minutes."

Exactly thirty minutes later, Blake's pickup pulled into the driveway. Abby opened the door and met him before he had a chance to ring the bell. The shower had relieved some of her tiredness, and Abby found that she was looking forward to getting away from the house for a few hours.

Blake helped her into the truck and then walked around to the driver's side. After he buckled his seatbelt, they started off.

"I board my horses at a farm about ten miles from my house, so it's not too far of a drive." Glancing over at her, Blake added, "I'm glad that you decided to come. I wasn't sure when I arrived if you would want to come."

She laughed. "I wasn't sure either but then decided I really did need some time away. But I have to warn you, I haven't been around horses in a long time, and I'm more than a little frightened of them. I don't know if I'm ready to climb up on one of their backs and let them take me for a ride."

Blake grinned. "I have the perfect horse for you. I've had her for a long time. Her name is Marshmallow, and her name says everything about her. She's getting up there in years, but I just haven't had the heart to sell her."

"Well," Abby said, smiling, "with a name like that, she definitely will be my kind of a horse."

When they arrived, Blake helped Abby from the truck, and they walked the short distance to the stables. On the way, he handed her an apple. Abby held up the apple questioningly. "What is this? A snack for us to eat on our ride?"

Blake threw back his head and laughed. "That's for you to feed Marshmallow to help you become acquainted."

Inside the stables, Blake took a pail and put a little grain in it. Then he grabbed a couple leads and halters before leading Abby outside and over to the fence. Abby held the pail while he opened the gate to the pasture and gestured for her to follow him in.

"Shake the pail a little, Abby," Blake said as he shut the gate. "The horses will hear the grain rustle and come running."

Abby complied and watched as two horses on the far side of the pasture lifted their heads from where they had been quietly eating grass. Blake took the pail from Abby as the horses trotted to where they stood. The larger of the two was a deep brown and held his head aloft proudly, his nostrils flaring, while the smaller horse trotted up behind him. She was a beautiful horse, too, with black and white patches and four white socks. Blake turned to Abby, scratching the neck of the large bay.

"Abby, I'd like you to meet Blaze. He's a four-year-old gelding, and I've owned him for about two years." While Blake spoke he was busy putting the lead around the neck of the horse and slipping on the halter. He quickly did the same on the smaller horse then turned to Abby. "And this is Marshmallow," he said, reaching out to stroke the smaller horse. "She's as gentle as a kitten, and you'll have a nice easy ride on her." Taking the apple in his hand, he cut it into two pieces and handed them to Abby; then he cut another apple for his horse.

Abby, trying to calm her fears, reached out her hand timidly to stroke Marshmallow as she had seen Blake do. The mare moved closer to her. Abby held her breath and extended her other hand. She laid one of the apple pieces on the palm of her hand and offered it to Marshmallow. The mare stretched her neck forward and Abby felt warm lips nuzzle her hand to take the piece into her mouth. Marshmallow chewed it and lowered her head for more. Abby offered her the other half and again felt the warm, soft lips on the palm of her hand and felt her tense muscles begin to relax.

Blake smiled then offered Blaze his pieces of apple as well. Turning to Abby, he asked, "So, shall we go for a ride? There's a riding trail leading from here that isn't too long."

She looked over at Marshmallow one more time and took a deep breath. "Okay, I'll try it. But I'm not making any promises on how long I'll last, and she'd better be as gentle as you say she is."

Blake grinned and handed Marshmallow's lead to Abby. "Well, I'll get their saddles on and we'll get started on that ride."

Abby took the rope hesitantly, whispering softly to the horse as she followed Blake and Blaze back to the stable. "Okay, here's the deal, Marshmallow. I'm somehow going to get the courage to climb up on your back so you can take me for a ride. But these are the rules: no bucking or fussing, just have pity on me, and don't do any galloping or running."

Back in the stable, Blake quickly saddled both horses, making sure to tighten the cinch on Marshmallow extra tight so the saddle wouldn't slip while Abby was riding, then led the horses out of the stables. He helped her up on Marshmallow and handed her the reins. Nervously adjusting her seat on the horse, Abby breathed deeply and tried to calm her beating heart. Marshmallow looked a lot bigger and stronger from the view on top. Blake swung into his saddle and, giving her an encouraging smile, started slowly down the trail. As her horse stepped forward to follow, she forced herself to relax as much as possible and tried to adjust her body to the swaying of the horse, telling herself she would not fall off if she just stayed focused.

As they left the pasture behind, Abby felt the tension inside her begin to ease as she found herself remembering the times she had ridden when she was younger. She sat up straighter and raised her eyes to look around. She could see so much more from this higher vantage point! Watching Blake riding in front of her, she noticed how comfortably he rode; he and his horse seemed to be one, whereas she seemed to jostle and bump with Marshmallow's every movement.

They rode for about thirty minutes before Blake brought his horse to a stop. Abby rode up beside him, pulling on the reins and feeling surprised when Marshmallow actually stopped. They had ridden to the top of a small ridge, and Blake pointed to the view in front of them.

"Isn't this spectacular?" he asked.

Abby looked at the scene below her. The trail moved through the brush and spring wildflowers before starting up again on another ridge; the setting sun reflected golden rays onto the plants, magnifying their color and beauty. A lizard watched them carefully from a rock a few feet away. Abby caught her breath and felt the thick silence surrounding her. The air itself seemed to breathe peace and calm the soul. She turned to Blake. "It's beautiful," she whispered, not wanting to dispel the mood.

"We'll go farther next time, but I think we'd better turn around now," Blake said quietly. "The sun's getting low, and we need to get back before it's dark."

Abby nodded her head in reluctant agreement, surprised at how much she had enjoyed her ride and being with Blake. When they reached the stables, Abby sat on her horse until Blake reached up to help her down. She felt his arms tighten for a few seconds. "Did you enjoy your ride?" he asked hopefully.

"You were right. This is what I needed," she answered, aware of Blake standing close to her, his hands still resting lightly on her waist. "And I feel a little less terrified of Marshmallow now."

Blake grinned. "I'm glad. We'll go again sometime," he said, releasing her.

Abby reached down and rubbed the top of her legs, shaking her head. "I'm sure tomorrow I'll be stiff and sore, but it was definitely worth it."

Blake was busy unsaddling the horses and nodded his head. "It takes a while to get your muscles used to riding for long periods of time."

They led the horses back to the pasture and locked the gate behind them. As they pulled out of the driveway, Blake glanced over at her. He had really enjoyed the time with her and how easy she was to be around.

After pulling into her driveway, he got out and walked with Abby to the door. She turned to face him with a smile. "Thanks, Blake, for a wonderful afternoon. The terror seems to have rejuvenated me, so I suppose it really was the break I needed. I guess I'll see you on Sunday."

"You will, and don't forget that I'm coming Monday afternoon around two so we can tackle more of the pruning and trimming."

Blake walked slowly back to his truck and got in. *I haven't enjoyed being with a woman this much since Emily left.* He was startled to find the thought entering his mind and recognized that the barriers around his heart were truly falling.

***

Sunday afternoon after church, Abby dropped Agnes off and hurried home. She had invited Agnes to have dinner with her this week and still had some last-minute preparations to do before Agnes arrived. She quickly changed clothes and then rushed to the kitchen. Last night she had set the table before going to bed as well as made a cold chicken salad. She quickly prepared a fruit platter and had just taken the refrigerator rolls out of the oven when the doorbell rang. Abby opened the door for Agnes and helped her inside.

"Is there anything I can help with?" Agnes asked, walking into the kitchen.

Abby smiled. "No, everything is just about ready. I hope you don't mind if I've set the table in the kitchen instead of the dining room. This is my favorite room in the house. I just love the sunshine coming in and being able to look out into the backyard."

"Oh my, no," Agnes gushed. "Everything looks so nice and smells so good."

Abby helped her sit down and then brought the food to the table. She hesitated for a minutes, and then, surprising herself, told Agnes that she would say the prayer today. After dinner they walked out to the back patio and sat down.

"Oh my dear, you have been busy," Agnes said, looking around the yard.

Abby laughed. "You can certainly say that again. Blake came Monday afternoon and helped me with the trimming. I don't know how I would have managed to do it without his help. He's a good man. He also took me horseback riding Thursday evening. I really needed that break, although I'm not too comfortable around horses."

"Yes, he's certainly a good man." Agnes nodded her head in agreement. "Your grandmother thought the world of him; he often stopped by to help her as well."

"He didn't tell me that. He said that Grandmother invited him for dinner once in a while and that he loved coming here."

Agnes was quiet for a few minutes. "You know, Abby, I think one of the reasons he wanted to help was that your grandmother was such a good friend to his mother. He had a hard time of it after his father died. His mother never did fully recover from the loss and eventually had a breakdown. Blake was caught between taking care of his father's patients and his own large practice as well as caring for his mother. His sister was married by that time and had moved away, so he was the only one here to care for Sister Matthews. Your grandmother made a point to visit her at least twice a week, and that really helped Blake."

Abby thought of what Megan had told her of Emily breaking off the engagement during that time as well, and she thought of all the losses Blake had suffered at the same time. It was no wonder why she felt so comfortable around him; he understood so well the grief she was experiencing.

After Agnes left, Abby wandered to the piano and opened the bench. Her grandmother's hymn book lay on top of the sheet music. She picked it up then closed the bench and opened the cover of the piano before sitting down. She leafed through the pages of the songbook and, when she came to "I Am a Child of God," placed her hands on the keyboard and started playing, improvising the simple hymn as she went. She found herself quietly singing the words, remembering how as a child in Primary she had loved this song. She recalled how proud her grandparents had been when she had learned the song well enough to play it for them. Abby played one hymn after another, letting the music speak to her spirit. After a while, a feeling of deep peace again filled her heart. *The hymns really are musical prayers to Heavenly Father*, she thought.

Later that evening she sat outside on the patio with her laptop computer. At Relief Society that morning, Sister Richardson had reminded her of the special upcoming Relief Society evening. Abby began writing down the stories she remembered her grandmother telling her of Tom and Dorothy Fisher and his participation in building the temple. She had opened one of the boxes of books from her grandfather's study, remembering that she had seen one on the temple. She was impressed as she read of how the foundation of the temple was formed. A natural limestone ledge was used for the base on one side of the temple, but the other three sides had underground springs that formed a bog. To solve the problem, loads of lava rock had been hauled from the ridges above the town to the temple site and then dumped on the marshy bog. The rock also had to be crushed, and this was done by pounding down the foundation footings with the town cannon. The cannon had its own remarkable history; it had been made in France, and Napoleon had taken the cannon with him into battle against Moscow, leaving it behind when he fled the city. It was then taken to Siberia, then Alaska, and finally ended up in Fort Ross, California. The Mormon Battalion had found the cannon and hauled it to St. George. The pioneers had devised a method of using pulleys rigged to horse teams attached to the cannon. They had filled the cannon with lead and then used it to pound the lava rock for the footings of the temple foundation.

Wow, Abby thought. *I don't remember Grandmother telling me about that.* She made a few more notes before putting her work away and getting ready for bed.

***

30 March 1845

This afternoon I disobeyed Father. I went with Tom and his family to a meeting the Mormons held at Mr. Jones's home. Father does not know that I went to a missionary meeting; he just knew that I was with Tom. I felt so remorseful within my heart for deceiving him, but Tom has said that he and his family have felt the conviction of truth in the message they have heard, and he wants me to hear the gospel message for myself. I also was sorry for letting Tom think Father knew where we were going.

The Jones family lives at the other end of the village. Their small house is above the carpentry shop. Mr. and Mrs. Jones greeted me with smiles and said how pleased they are with my engagement to Tom and how skilled he is becoming as a carpenter's apprentice to Mr. Jones. The Paynes, Fishers, Joneses, and I were the only ones in attendance.

The missionaries greeted me most warmly. They are humble men but have a kindness and goodness that radiates from their eyes and smiles. We sang a song, and Mr. Jones gave the opening prayer. Elder Winter, one of the missionaries, gave a lesson on the restoration of the priesthood of God on the earth. Elder Winter declared that with this authority restored, all the covenants and blessings of Christ's original Church are here again upon the earth. Elder Durham, the other missionary, read from the Book of Mormon of Christ's birth and how the people in the Americas were aware of the signs of that birth. Both missionaries bore testimony of the truthfulness of the words they spoke, and once again my heart and spirit felt an answering cry and a desire to learn more. After the meeting I was given a copy of the Book of Mormon to read and was promised that if I read it prayerfully and asked God if it were true, my prayer would be answered. We then sang another song and closed the meeting with prayer.

On the way home, I told Tom I had not let Father know I was going to attend a Mormon meeting. Tom said I must be honest with Father and Mother, especially if I truly felt there might be some worth to the message I had heard tonight. I have promised to do so, but I will admit to being nervous at the thought of telling Father where I have been. Tom also wants me to meet with the missionaries when they come to his home next Tuesday.

Chapter 10

Monday morning Abby was up early, pulling on her exercise pants and tee-shirt. She tied the laces of her running shoes and let herself out of the house, taking a deep breath of the clean fresh air before she did a few stretches. Abby started her run off slowly, picking up her speed as her muscles and breathing adapted. After her reading last evening she wanted to take a closer look at the temple, so she turned her steps in that direction Abby slowed her stride as she came to the fence surrounding the grounds. She looked at the temple's clean white walls with new appreciation, feeling a sense of wonder at the graceful and beautiful building that had been erected in the middle of the desert. After what she had read and heard from her grandparents, it was almost overwhelming to think of the work and sacrifices that had been made so this temple could be a beacon and light to those seeking spiritual advancement. As she circled the temple one final time, a deep desire rose inside Abby to be one of those able to enter its doors, to obtain the blessings and covenants that Heavenly Father promised to His faithful children. *Well,* she thought, *at least I can go through the visitors' center.*

Back at the house, she was finishing her quick breakfast of juice and toast when her cell phone rang.

"Abby, it's Scott," said the deep voice on the line. "It seems all I do is apologize when I call. I'm sorry I've been so busy lately that our calls have been short. This trial has been all that's on my mind and has taken pretty well all my time. But so far all the preparation and work have paid off; things are going well. How are you coming along on your end?"

"All right, Scott," Abby replied. "I'm doing fine, but I've really missed talking with you and being home this past week. Believe it or not, I've been homesick. Instead of getting up in the morning and thinking through all the challenges of my job and getting excited for the day, I get up and dress for another day of cleaning and sorting." As Scott started to respond, she quickly went on. "Not that I'm sorry to be here doing this; I've just been missing my life there this past week." She paused and drew a breath before continuing. "As I remember all the good times I've had here in the past, it's been difficult to be alone. And Scott," she paused again, "you know I've been going to church each week, and now I find myself wanting to put a spiritual balance in my life as well."

"I'm sorry you're alone, too," Scott said understandingly. "And I think it's great if being at church helps and you want to continue going. I'm busy most Sunday mornings anyway. Frankly, it might be a good place for you to meet people that can help you grow your business."

Abby gave an exasperated sigh. "Scott, you don't have the least understanding of what I'm talking about. What I'm saying is that I need to make some changes in my life, to become active again, not for what I can use to advance myself in my career, but for what it can help me become." Taking a deep breath she asked hesitantly, "Are you ever going to be interested in having the missionary discussions or going to church with me?"

"Hey, slow down," Scott jumped in. "I'm not sure at this point just what I want to do. I'll go to church with you occasionally, but I certainly don't feel any great spiritual need in my life right now. Come on, Abby, remember all the things we've talked about, what we both want in our lives? I don't remember religion playing that big a part in our discussions when we talked about our goals and dreams. You were happy and excited with your life before going to Utah."

"I know, and I wish I had the words to tell you just what is going on inside me, but I'm not sure how to express it to you. I just want you to think about taking the missionary discussions." As he started to respond, Abby quickly changed the subject. "Can you come for a visit soon? Maybe I just need to see you again and things will smooth out in my mind as well."

"I'm not exactly sure when I can get away for a weekend right now, especially with the trial, but I'll come as soon as I get a break from work," Scott answered.

"Well," Abby responded, "at least I'll be coming home a week from this next Friday and we can see each other then."

"Thanks for scheduling the Towers' closing over the same weekend as the Rosses' dinner, Abby," Scott replied, eagerness sounding in his voice. "I'm just glad you're going to be here to go with me. Honey, just remember how much I care for you. I'm still anxious to put that ring on your finger and talk about setting a date for our wedding. We both need to be looking ahead, getting excited for our life together. And Abby, I'm sorry if I'm rushing you to come home; I'll try to be more patient."

They talked a few minutes longer as Scott told her about the trial, then they said their good-byes. After ending the call and pocketing her phone, Abby walked slowly around the house, her mind going over her conversation with Scott. She realized she had not told him about her evening horseback ride with Blake. Abby knew that she was starting down a path where she might have to make some difficult choices, and she was not sure she wanted to place herself in that position. Life had certainly seemed easier in Denver.

That afternoon, Abby was putting away her ironing when the doorbell rang. Glancing at her watch, she saw it was just two o'clock and hurried downstairs to answer the door.

"So, where do we start today?" Blake asked with a smile as she let him in.

Abby felt her mood lift as she returned his smile. "I thought we could prune the last of the trees, and if there's time maybe you could look at the sprinkler system. When I turned it on yesterday, I noticed a couple of the heads must be broken. Water went everywhere!"

"All right, captain, lead the way," Blake laughingly replied. "Shall we start with the pruning first? It looks like you finished the flowerbeds in the front. They look terrific, but I bet they were a lot of work."

Abby opened the back door, and Blake followed her outside. "It took me most of the week to get them really weeded and organized, and now I can't wait to buy flowers to plant." She looked around the yard and shook her head. "I hope I can get someone in to maintain the yard, as I really should be working inside, but each morning the sunshine calls me and, before I know it, I'm busy outside. Scott thinks I should be winding up here, but there has been so much to do."

At Scott's name, Blake felt another jolt go through him. He had enjoyed the evening they had gone horseback riding together so much that he had totally forgotten that she was supposed to be seriously involved with someone from Denver. He was just beginning to care for her and didn't want to think of her with someone else. Looking over at Abby, the realization hit him that when she finished packing up the house, she would be leaving. He knew he should be careful not to let his emotions go too far, but in his heart, he knew it was already too late. With her coming, the protective shell he had placed around his heart had finally dissolved.

Abby gestured toward the trees. "Do we need a ladder, or is it just the smaller branches at the bottom we trim?" she asked.

Blake walked around, looking at each tree carefully. "I think we can just reshape them without a ladder. I seem to remember your grandmother having a large pruning pole she kept in the garage, and that should work just fine." He walked back to the garage, emerging a few minutes later with a shout of triumph and carrying a large pruning pole with a rope attached to the cutter.

They worked together for a couple of hours until Abby, sinking wearily into a lawn chair, said, "I think we need a break. Let's rest a few minutes and have a glass of lemonade. I made a pitcher this morning."

Blake wiped his forehead on his sleeve. "I think that's a good idea. Can I help?"

"No, I'll get it. Why don't you move those two chairs and that small table into the shade, and I'll be right back." With a small groan, Abby hauled herself up from the lawn chair. She walked inside and took the cold pitcher of lemonade from the refrigerator. She added ice to the glasses and pitcher and then set them on a tray. Opening a bag of cookies, she put several on a plate along with napkins. Then, carrying the tray carefully, she opened the back door and walked to where Blake had set the chairs and table. He stood up and took the tray from her and set it down on the table.

"I think it's getting hotter each day," Abby exclaimed as she sat down gratefully on a chair. She poured the lemonade into the glasses and handed one to Blake. Taking a sip of the cold drink, she looked at the newly pruned trees. "I'm glad we are about through with the pruning." Flushing, she added, "But here I am complaining, and you're the one doing most of the work."

He laughed. "And here I thought we were sharing the work." Holding up a cookie, he said, "Besides, I'm getting well paid. This is the best lemonade I've had since my mother died." He turned and smiled at her again. "And besides, I'm enjoying the company."

Abby felt the impact of his eyes as he looked into hers and blushed. *Really,* she told herself, *not again. You need to stop doing that every time he looks at you. You never blush with Scott.*

It was early evening by the time they finished. Blake had fixed the sprinklers and set them on a timer so Abby wouldn't have to worry about watering. When they were finished putting away the tools in the garage, Abby felt tired and hungry, and she was sure that he felt the same. She was too tired tonight to fix dinner, but she could order a pizza and share it with him. Besides, she was tired of eating dinner by herself.

"Blake, after you dump this load, how about coming back and sharing a pizza with me? I'm sure you're as hungry as I am, and I'm starved! What do you want on your pizza?" Not giving him a chance to refuse, she went on. "I'll order it delivered at seven, which gives you an hour. Will that be enough time?"

"Seven is great," he answered enthusiastically. "Anything you want is fine with me, with the exception of anchovies."

"I don't like anchovies either, so you're safe." Abby helped him tie the tarp over the load in the back of the pickup then watched him drive away before hurrying inside the house and running upstairs to shower and change. As she stood under the steaming flow of water, she thought of Tom and Dorothy Fisher and their trip across the plains before settling here in Dixie. At that time water was scarce and had to be carried for baths; now it was so easy to just turn on the faucet. She did not think she would have made a very good pioneer; she needed her shower every day. Today's world certainly offered a lot of blessings with its myriad of conveniences.

Abby dressed quickly and hurried back downstairs, humming to herself as she went. She ordered a large combination pizza and a salad then wandered to the back door and stepped outside. Gazing at the beauty of the evening, she felt the light breeze gently lift her hair and whisper against her skin. At this moment she felt completely at peace and forgot her loneliness and frustrations of last week. The ringing of the doorbell brought Abby out of her thoughts, and she hurried back inside. Opening the door, she found Blake holding a pizza box and a salad.

"Thank you, Blake, but I ordered one for us, and it should be here any time."

"I know; this is the one you ordered. The deliveryman was just getting ready to ring the bell when I got here, so I took the pizza from him."

"But I was going to buy it and treat you to dinner! Please let me pay you back."

"No way! It's *my* turn this week. Just tell me where you want this," Blake said as he followed her to the kitchen and placed the box on the countertop.

"I thought we'd eat in the kitchen again, if that's all right with you. Either that, or we can fix a plate and take it outside, but it's starting to get dark."

"The kitchen is fine with me," Blake said as he glanced around. "I really like this room. It's a blending of the old and new."

"I do too," Abby returned. "Every time I sit here I think of Dorothy Fisher, my fourth great-grandmother, setting this table, and find myself running my hands over the wood and thinking of her and Tom. The things he made in this house are so old yet still so beautiful. It seems strange that our possessions live on after we die." She paused then added with conviction, "But isn't it wonderful they do? To me, they become links to family. Each time we look at something that was used and prized, our ancestors' names and stories surface, and they are remembered. It's a way of feeling a connection to them and an appreciation for their sacrifices." She flushed as she finished speaking. "I guess I'm too sentimental."

Blake felt his heart respond to her words as she talked. He found new dimensions in her each time they were together. She was well worth getting to know.

They chatted easily during dinner. Afterward, they moved into the living room. Blake, looking around, felt the emptiness of the room. "This room looks so impersonal now," he stated, pointing to the row of stacked boxes.

"I know. This and Grandfather's study are the only rooms I've finished. Tomorrow, regardless of how appealing the sunshine is, I'm going to work inside. But if I'm honest with myself, I'll admit I've been putting off the sorting and packing because it's so difficult going through my grandparents' belongings, especially their personal letters and journals. It feels like a violation of their privacy." At his look, she grinned, "Oh, I know they won't be coming back, but there are too many years ingrained in me of respecting other people's possessions. But I guess the biggest reason I'm dragging my feet is that I'm not enjoying getting this home ready to be sold." Her eyes lovingly scanned the room. "It seems wrong, somehow, to sell a home that has been in our family for generations."

Blake nodded his head in agreement.

Abby continued. "But the good news is that I think Mom and Dad are having second thoughts about selling as well."

He looked at her for a few minutes before answering. "I hope they won't sell, either. It would make a wonderful place to come to during the cold months of winter. Of course, I love living here year-round. So many times friends from out of state will call me during the summer and ask how I can stand living here during July and August when temperatures soar between 105 and 110 degrees. But I've found the desert has a charm all its own. The air is so clear, and there is a beauty in the wildflowers that bloom in the spring and the smell of the sagebrush on hot summer nights that doesn't exist in the city. Plus, I love seeing the glitter of the night sky. I remember when I was doing my internship in Los Angeles, there were so many lights from homes and the big city, plus the thickness of the air with humidity, that the sky was never as crystal clear and beautiful as it is here in the desert."

"I know," Abby acknowledged, thinking of her horseback ride. "Although many times this past week I've found myself feeling really lonely, and I'll admit I've missed the excitement of my work and being with family. I don't remember a time in my life when cleaning the entire house and taking care of the yard has been completely my responsibility. Mom's always had someone come in to clean twice a week, and Dad has a gardening team to maintain our huge yard. I've been living on my own these past two years, but my small condo is easy for me to keep up, and I just hire someone to do the major work."

He chuckled and looked over at her thoughtfully. "As a doctor, I'm going to prescribe your taking another fun break." As she started to protest, he went on. "Now, now," he said with a laugh, "Remember, the doctor is always right, and think how good it felt Thursday night to get away. But seriously, Abby, I was going to invite you to go with Megan, Ryan and me to Zion National Park this Saturday. When I talked with Ryan last night we decided this was a good weekend to go. Megan mentioned she was going to call and ask you, but I told Ryan I would be seeing you this afternoon and would ask you to go with us." At the thoughtful look she gave him, he plunged ahead. "How long has it been since you were there?"

Abby paused to think a minute before answering. "Not since I was about eleven. It's actually on my list of things I want to do before going home, but," she said with a sigh, "I'm not making much headway with this packing."

Blake waited, noticing she had a habit of biting her lower lip when she was thinking hard.

"Oh well, I'm sure it will be much more fun to go with friends than all by myself." She paused a minute more before breaking out with a huge smile. "Okay, count me in. If it's as much fun as the horseback ride, it will be a good break. Also, I have to go back to Denver on business the following weekend."

He hadn't realized he was holding his breath until she gave her answer, and he gave her a pleased smile. "I'm glad you're coming. I'll pick you up at nine Saturday morning, and be sure to wear comfortable shoes for hiking. But I'm sure I'll talk to you during the week."

Blake stood up. "Well, I should probably go. We've worked hard, but I've really enjoyed these Monday afternoons."

"I have too. Thanks, Blake, for all the help you've given me. And," she said, "I'm excited to see Zion's. Thanks for thinking of me."

She walked him to the door and opened it. He took her hand and held it for a minute; again she felt her skin tingle at his touch and withdrew her hand quickly. "I'll see you Saturday morning, then," Blake said as he walked to his truck.

She watched him as he got in his truck, then she slowly closed the door. As she was walking back to the kitchen, her phone rang.

Glancing at the caller ID she noticed it was Scott and felt an alarm go off inside her. This was his second call today, and she hoped nothing had happened. Taking a deep breath, she said, "Hello, Scott. Is anything wrong?"

"Hi, honey," he said, "No, nothing's wrong. I just wanted to talk to you again before heading off to bed. We didn't end on a very positive note this morning, did we?"

Abby looked at her watch with a start. She had enjoyed visiting so much with Blake that she had not realized it was after ten. "I'm just getting ready to go to bed myself," she said. "How is the trial coming?"

"It's going faster than we expected, and there's a good chance it will go to the jury by the middle of next week. So far I think it's going well, and your dad seems pleased. How are things at your end? Are you making progress? Think how nice it would be if when you came home next weekend you could be all finished."

Carrying her phone with her, Abby walked over to the table, pulled out a chair, and sat down. "Now Scott," she said impatiently, "I told you this morning that it's going to be a while yet. Blake—I mean, Dr. Matthews—came by again this afternoon and helped with the last of the heavy yard work, so I should be able to hire someone now to just maintain it. Honestly, Scott, I don't know how I could have finished the outside so fast without his help."

There was a pause on the other end of the line, and Abby could picture him thinking through how to phrase his next question. "So, Abby, how old is this Dr. Matthews? It seems as if he's looking for excuses to hang around you."

"Don't go there, Scott," Abby warned. "He's someone I knew briefly when I came to visit my grandparents years ago, and now he's become a good friend. Blake's a doctor with a very busy practice, and he's given up his free time to help me. Right now, I'm grateful for all the help I can get." She added the last statement with firmness, still aware that she had not told Scott about spending Thursday evening with Blake.

"You didn't answer my question, Abby. How old is he, and are you sure he's not interested in you as more than a friend?"

"He's probably around thirty, and *he is just a friend—a good friend.*" Abby said, emphasizing her words. "Now let's talk about something else, shall we?"

Scott chuckled reluctantly, "Okay, Abby, we won't talk about Blake Matthews. I've just missed you and sometimes it seems you are enjoying being back there so much that I worry you won't want to come back."

"I am enjoying being here and reconnecting with old friends, and it has helped to heal the grief I've had over Grandmother's death. But as far as not coming back, that's one thing you don't need to worry about, Scott. You know my life is there, and I'll be back soon. Are you going to be through early enough that Friday night that we can do something?" she asked.

"I'll make sure that I am," he told her. "I thought it would be nice to go to dinner at our favorite restaurant, if that's all right with you. Or is there somewhere else you would rather go?"

"Anything you plan will be fine with me," she returned. For the next few minutes they talked of other things, until Abby yawned. "Scott, I really am tired and need to go to bed. Let's talk again tomorrow about next weekend, all right?"

"All right, Abby, I'll let you go. Just be careful not to spend too much time with Dr. Matthews. I guess I'm pretty possessive about you, after all."

Terminating the call, Abby thought to herself, *But I'm still my own person and have a right to make my own decisions.*

***

15 April 1845

Tonight my heart is full of joy and deep sorrow. I completed my reading of the Book of Mormon today. It has touched my soul and heart in a way I have not the words to express. As I read, I truly felt the truth of this book, and its people and prophets have touched my life. I have wanted to read every minute that I could. When I knelt in prayer to ask Heavenly Father if it is true, my body was flooded with a warmth and love that I have never experienced. I cannot doubt the book's truthfulness. This is the great joy I feel tonight: a new sense of my Heavenly Father's love for me and a new awareness of the Savior's sacrifice on my behalf. Even as I write, my eyes are dim with tears. I know I want to be baptized with Tom and his family this Friday.

The deep sadness I feel is because Father has been so upset and angry that I have been listening to the missionaries. He has also forbidden Mother to listen. I have pleaded with him to hear their message and judge for himself, but he has refused. He has said I cannot be baptized, nor can I speak of their doctrine in our home. He would also like me to break off my engagement with Tom, but this I will not do. He has pointed out that since Mr. and Mrs. Jones and their family were baptized, no one in the village will do business or talk with them and that if I marry Tom, my friends will not have anything more to do with me, either, and I will find myself leading a lonely life.

The only peace I feel is when saying my prayers. I pray for the strength to do the right thing, both for my parents as well as for Tom and me. I will lay my burden at my Savior's feet and trust that He will guide and comfort me in the difficult decisions that I have to make in the days ahead.

Chapter 11

When Saturday morning dawned bright and clear, Abby gave a sigh of relief. Thunderstorms had pretty much been the order for the previous two days. The change in the weather had forced her to make good on her promise to work inside, even if it was a few days late, so she had begun boxing and sorting in her grandmother's bedroom. It had been every bit as difficult going through her things as Abby thought it would be, so she was glad that the good weather would permit her friends' trip to Zion National Park—she needed a day away from the memories. All in all, Abby was looking forward to the day. After showering, she pulled on a pair of tan pants and a green oxford shirt. She tied the laces of her running shoes and gave a final glance in the mirror. Reflected back at her was the suntanned face of a young woman, her short hair shining with new highlights from the hours spent in the sun, and her green eyes bright and clear. She smiled at her reflection then turned and ran quickly downstairs.

Megan had called Wednesday morning to plan the food for the picnic. She and Megan had decided that Megan would provide hoagie buns, meat, and cheese, and Abby would take care of the side dishes and dessert. Last night Abby had made chocolate chip cookies and placed them in a plastic container with a lid. Now Abby divided celery sticks, baby carrots, grape tomatoes, and cucumbers into plastic bags and set them on the counter next to the container of cookies. One more trip to the refrigerator for apples and grapes, and she had her share of the picnic food set out. Just then the doorbell rang, and her heart lifted in anticipation. Opening the door, she saw Blake standing on the porch and found herself feeling shy as she invited him in.

"Ready to go, Abby?" he asked, stepping inside the house.

"You bet. I just need to put the food in a bag and then I'll be ready."

He followed her to the kitchen, and she took a large bag from the pantry and carefully set in the cookies, vegetables, and fruit. She looked around the kitchen a final time, making sure she had collected everything.

"There," she said, handing him the bag. "If you don't mind carrying this, I'll grab my jacket."

Blake took the bag from her. "I can't remember the last time I've been on a picnic; good food, good company—what more could any man want?"

Abby laughed as she picked up her jacket and purse and followed Blake outside. He placed the bag in the back of his Ford Explorer then hurried around to open the passenger door for her.

Abby smiled up at him as she slid into the car. "I'm excited for the day as well," she said, meeting his eyes. His eyes held hers for a minute, then smiling and whistling softly, he closed the door and walked around to the driver's side.

At the Fellows' home, they transferred everything to a cooler. "I'm so glad to have the day with you, Abby," Megan said as they finished packing the food. "I was afraid you would decide not to come."

"I thought about canceling, but each time the thought surfaced, I realized how much I really wanted to go. I used to love Zion National Park, and I haven't been there for years. This was just too good an opportunity to miss." Giving Megan a quick hug, she added, "Besides, I wanted more time with you before I go home."

"Are you two ready?" Ryan called. "Blake and I are anxious to be on the road. The longer we wait, the warmer it's going to get."

"We're ready," Megan answered. "Come and get this cooler for me while I get our jackets."

It took only a few minutes to load the food in the car, and they were on their way. Abby took a deep breath and relaxed in her seat next to Blake. He and Ryan were talking about the upcoming NBA semi-finals, and she enjoyed watching the scenery pass before her eyes.

As they entered the small town of Springdale, located just outside the park, she sat up straighter in her seat. This was another town that had certainly grown since she had come as a child with her grandparents. Small shops and boutiques catering to tourists were abundant, and already the sidewalks were crowded with spring visitors. Soon they passed through the park entrance gates, and the vista of towering white, red, and golden rock formations was before her. At the road level, the Virgin River flowed swiftly, already swollen from the spring rains and snow runoff from the nearby mountains. Pine and cottonwood trees crowded against each other, and the ground was covered in lush green grass, bending in the gentle wind. A burst of color from wildflowers dotted the view here and there.

Blake turned and smiled at her. "Pretty impressive, isn't it? As often as I come, I never tire of the beauty of this park. If you look closely, you might see deer or wild turkeys."

Abby leaned closer to the window. "I had forgotten about the wild turkeys, but I remember seeing deer. I had also forgotten how beautiful this is." They drove farther into the park before she announced excitedly, pointing out her window, "Oh look, there are two deer behind those trees."

Blake slowed the car so they could better see the deer.

As they continued their drive, Ryan asked from the backseat. "Is it all right with everyone if we hike the Emerald Pools trail? I don't want Megan hiking anything more strenuous than that."

"I'm fine," Megan protested. "In fact, the walk will do me good. I sit far too much at my job."

"Actually, the Emerald Pools trail is a good choice," Blake said. "With all the rain we've had this past week, the waterfalls around the pools should really be something to see. Is that trail all right with you, Abby?"

"Anything is fine with me," she answered. "You're the experts."

Within minutes they arrived at the canyon junction and turned toward the lodge and the Emerald Pools trail. "This is the last week we can drive through this end of the park until November," Blake told them. "The park shuttles start next week, and this road will be off limits for cars, except for those people staying at the lodge."

He drove the car into the parking lot for the trailhead. When Abby stepped out of the car, she took a deep breath of the pine-scented air and sighed with satisfaction. Clutching water bottles, the group started off. They stopped on top of the walkway bridge that spanned the Virgin River to look at the view. The scene in front of them was fantastic. The deep red of a majestic rock mountain loomed in front, and the sky overhead was a deep, deep blue with fluffy white clouds floating lazily along. The Virgin River flowed swiftly just below the bridge, the sound of the rushing water soothing to hear, and the sun sprayed golden sparkles on the water.

"Isn't it staggering," Megan said in an awed voice, standing next to Abby. "I'm so glad we came today."

Abby turned and smiled at her friend. "It's so beautiful; I feel like I'm on vacation."

Megan and Abby started up the trail together, with Ryan and Blake following close behind. "You set the pace, honey," Ryan called, "and we'll follow. That way if you have problems, I'll know. Just don't overdo it, and stop to rest if you get tired."

Megan and Abby exchanged smiles and continued walking. The trail went straight for a short distance then angled away from the river before climbing upward. The smell of pine grew heavier, and they heard the musical bubbling of water as they passed several small springs surrounded by ferns.

Abby, taking another deep breath of the sweet air, uttered in a reverent voice. "I don't remember Zion's being this beautiful, or maybe I just appreciate it more now."

Megan grinned at her friend. "I know. It's been a while since I've been here as well."

As they started up another incline, she slowed and patted her stomach. "I'll be glad when this baby arrives and I can move about easier. Oh well, I can last another two months." Looking over at Abby, she asked, "So tell me, how are you coming with the work at your grandmother's?"

Abby sighed. "Slowly. Blake helped me do the major cleanup in the yard, but I should be farther ahead in the house. I probably should have stayed home today and worked, but I really needed this outing. Oh, Megan, this last week I've been discouraged and a little depressed. The one bright spot is remembering how much fun it was when Blake had pity on me and took me horseback riding last week. But when I'm packing things up at the house, so many memories keep surfacing, and I find myself becoming dispirited, which isn't like me. I miss the excitement of my work and life in Denver, but on the other hand, I find myself being drawn to life here. So my mind is in continual conflict." She gave another sigh. "Plus, I miss Scott, but when I talk to him, we often find ourselves arguing. I know he misses me, too, but I wish he could understand how much is involved in getting Grandmother's house ready to be put on the market. Plus, he's defensive about Blake helping me. It's a good thing that I have to go back to Denver next weekend on business. We need some time together, and maybe that will help me sort out my feelings."

Megan looked at her friend with sympathy. "I'm sure it must be hard on you both. I didn't know you were going home next weekend, Abby. How long are you going to be gone?"

"Only for the weekend. I leave early Friday morning and will be back Sunday afternoon, so it's a short trip," Abby said with a laugh. "I have a real estate closing Friday afternoon and some other loose ends to check on at my office. I'm spending Saturday morning shopping with my mother, and then I'm going to spend the rest of the day with Scott. That night I'm going with him to a formal dinner party that a client of his is giving."

"Is Scott going to come here for a weekend before you're finished?" Megan asked. "I'd like to meet him."

"I don't know. He says he is, but right now he's tied up with a case that has gone to trial. I just hope being together next weekend will help us." She hesitated for a few minutes. "Megan, if I'm honest with myself, there's more to our differences right now than my not being finished here." Again she paused. "I'm beginning to analyze my life in several areas." Megan looked at Abby thoughtfully as she continued. "I've been going to church each week."

At this, Megan put her arm around her friend and gave her a huge smile. "So what's wrong with that? I think it's wonderful."

Abby chuckled. "I'm glad you do!" Her expression grew serious. "This brings up more problems, though. The more involved I become with the Church, the further away Scott and my life with him seem.

I've asked him about taking the missionary lessons, but he just doesn't feel the need for religion in his life right now, and then I find myself wondering if I'm really prepared to make all the changes in my life that being fully active requires. I felt content with my life and choices before coming to St. George. Things are starting to change—*I'm* starting to change. And I have to ask myself, if I marry Scott and want to continue my activity in the church, am I willing to live my life without being able to share that part of it with him?"

Megan linked her arm through Abby's. "I don't know if you want my advice, but I love you enough to tell you that a marriage based on a gospel-centered life is the closest we can come to the celestial kingdom here on earth. As a married couple, your beliefs govern everything you do and every decision you make. Married life requires compromises in so many areas—religion should not be one of them. Plus, I can't imagine being married to Ryan for this life only, that with death our marriage bonds would be severed." She paused to catch her breath. "And Abby, there is a special sweetness and a deepening of love when Christ is allowed to be part of the marriage. Just be prayerful and seek Heavenly Father's help before making your decision on marriage." She smiled. "End of lecture, but I wanted you to hear this from the lips of a happily married but very pregnant woman."

"Thanks, Megan. I'm just experiencing a lot of different and new feelings lately. Did I tell you that Mom and Dad have started going back to church, and it looks as if they are committing themselves for the long haul? Mom has accepted a call to work in the Relief Society, and Dad has agreed to go home teaching. Who would have thought that Grandmother's death would have brought about so many changes?" She stopped walking and stood still for a minute. "Listen, I think I hear the falls up ahead, so we can't be too far away."

"Good thing—I'm out of breath," puffed Megan as they started on the downward slope of the trail, the sound of the waterfalls growing louder with each step. Turning around, she motioned to Ryan and Blake, who were behind them. "We're almost there."

Together the four of them approached the falls and pools. A high red ledge surrounded the pools on one side with water plunging over the top into several waterfalls that cascaded into green pools at the bottom. Abby noticed that the emerald color was due to the moss growing in the bottom of the pools.

The trail continued on under the ledge of waterfalls and up the other side, the red dirt of southern Utah forming a muddy path. As they stopped to look, Abby felt the coolness of the spray of water on her flushed face. How beautiful it was. She was aware of Blake standing beside her, gazing at the falls as well. "I think this is the first time I've hiked this trail," she said. "I'm sure I would have remembered this."

He smiled at her. "This is one of my favorite hikes in the canyon." They gazed silently at the beauty of the scene for a few minutes before hearing Megan and Ryan's laughter just behind them.

"Ready to start back, you two?" Ryan asked. "Megan swears if she doesn't get something to eat soon she'll die of hunger."

"We're ready," Blake answered. "You two start down, and we'll follow in a minute. I want to take Abby a few feet along the trail under the falls. It's really something to see with the screen of water in front."

They continued the climb down until they were standing directly under the falls. Impulsively, Abby reached for Blake's hand. "Thanks for asking me to come today," she said, trying to speak over the noise of the water. "You seem to know when I need something extra to put me back on track. This has been just what I needed; all this beauty feeds my spirit."

Blake gave Abby a smile, enjoying the feel of her hand in his. "I needed the day away as well."

Abby released his hand, and they moved farther back under the ledge to let a young family pass by them. They stood for a few more minutes before turning their steps back the way they had come.

"How is Marshmallow?" Abby asked with a grin as the roaring of the falls receded. "I still have a few sore places on my body from that Thursday night, and Friday morning when I got out of bed, I thought my body would refuse to obey, my legs were that sore."

Blake laughed. "Marshmallow's fine and hoping you'll let her take you for another ride sometime. I'm just glad you enjoyed it after my almost forcing you to go. That reminds me, what are you planning to do on Monday?" he questioned. "Anything that needs my help?"

"I started packing in Grandmother's room yesterday, and it's slow going. But I think I should be fine without tying up another of your Monday afternoons. And then Friday morning I'm leaving to go back to Denver for the weekend. I have a closing scheduled for one of my real estate contracts and some other business contacts to catch up on. It will be good to be home for a few days. "

Blake looked at her, disappointed that she didn't need his help. He also hadn't remembered that she was going home on the weekend. "Actually, Abby, I'll miss spending Monday afternoon with you." As he said it, he thought of just how much he would miss being with her. There was so much he liked about her, and she never ceased to amaze him. He also felt a stab of dismay as he realized that she would be spending time with Scott.

"Do you need me to take you to the airport on Friday?" he asked, aware that he would miss seeing her at church as well.

"Thanks for offering, Blake, but I plan on leaving my car at the airport while I'm gone."

They turned a bend in the trail, their steps evenly matched. "I would think you'd be glad for a Monday off, Blake. I've worked you pretty hard." Abby glanced over at Blake, and the thought came to her that she would miss their Monday work session as well. "I remember Ryan mentioning that you didn't always live here. Where were you born?" Abby asked.

Blake looked over at her and smiled. "I was born in a little town outside Atlanta, Georgia, called Lawrenceville. We lived there until I was ten. When I was nine, my parents joined the Church, and a year later a friend of my father's from medical school contacted him. He had a practice here in St. George and needed a partner. It was quite a decision for my parents, but I think they decided to come partly because it would mean living nearer the center of the Church. I remember as a kid what a difference living here was from being in the South. Our home in Lawrenceville was very large and completely surrounded by trees and vegetation, plus I had grandparents and cousins that lived nearby. I remember when we first arrived here I thought there must have been some terrible mistake. St. George seemed so bare and ugly after the lush, deep green of the South." He smiled at Abby's astonishment. "But it did not take long for me to learn to love the desert. Ryan's family lived just a couple of doors down from us, and we became best friends. The Fellows family had a large home and kept horses as well. I found I really enjoyed horseback riding, and they made me feel welcome to ride anytime I wanted."

"So that's how long you've been riding," Abby replied. "You looked so experienced when we went the other evening and seemed to know exactly what to do. You must have done a lot of exploring on horseback over the years."

"There are some pretty unique areas to see here," Blake nodded his head. "Ryan's family also loved to camp, and they often invited me to go with them. Much as I loved my dad, he and Mom were definitely not campers. Their idea of camping was a good hotel with room service."

Abby laughed at his story. "Your parents sound just like mine. However, I don't think I've ever been on a camping trip. Our vacations were always to some holiday resort."

Blake joined in her laughter. "Ryan's family introduced me to the joys of nature and camping, and I have loved it ever since. I love watching the early morning sunrise in the middle of a forest of trees, or watching the brilliance of the night sky, or sitting around a campfire with good friends. When I'm exploring nature, I always feel a special closeness to my Heavenly Father and thankfulness for this world. I don't see how anyone can witness the beauty of God's creations and be an atheist."

Abby looked around her and acknowledged the truth of his words. "I understand what you are saying, Blake. There is such an order and perfection in His creations, and I love the outdoors too. But I'm not sure just what type of camper I'd make. Cooking dinner over an open campfire sounds like hard work to me."

Blake laughed then studied her for a minute before answering. "There are easier ways to cook dinner when camping than over an open campfire. But, Abby, I think you would enjoy it very much. From what I've been able to see, you're a very adaptable person, and you seem to appreciate the beauty in the world around you."

Rounding another bend, they saw Megan and Ryan waiting for them at the end of the trail. "About time you two got back; I'm ready to head for the picnic tables," Megan called out to them.

The drive to the picnic area was just a few minutes away from Emerald Pools. After parking the car, they carried the cooler and picnic basket to a table. Abby spread the tablecloth out while Megan opened the cooler and began setting out the food. As they blessed the food and began eating, Abby looked around at her friends, and a deep feeling of contentment rose inside her. *Nothing could be better than this,* she thought. Maybe she would enjoy camping after all. However, she couldn't picture Scott sleeping in a tent and cooking over a fire; the thought made her laugh softly to herself.

After lunch they rested for a few minutes before getting in the car and driving through to the end of the park. The Riverside trail was an easy one, and Blake thought Abby would enjoy the walk along the river. He pulled into the parking area and opened her door.

"If you don't mind, I think Megan and I will sit here on a bench in the sun while you two go ahead," Ryan said, helping his wife from the car.

"We don't need to go," Abby protested. "I don't want to leave you here."

"Please, Abby, go ahead. I'm happy to just sit here with Ryan," Megan told her.

Blake looked anxiously at Megan. "Are you sure you're feeling all right? Maybe we should head for home."

"No, I'm all right. Just a little tired. I really would enjoy sitting here for a few minutes. Ryan and I may catch up with you later."

Blake looked over at Ryan, who nodded his head. "Yes, take Abby along the trail for a little ways, at least. It really is something she will enjoy."

"OK, but we'll hurry." Blake took Abby's hand and pulled her to her feet.

"I don't think we should be long, Blake," Abby said. They had only gone a short distance down the trail when they heard Ryan shout after them.

Abby and Blake looked at each other in alarm then turned around and ran back.

Ryan was holding Megan in his arms. Her face was white, and she was holding back tears. As they reached her side, she doubled over with pain.

"What happened?" Blake asked quickly, dropping to his knees beside Megan.

"She was on her way to the restroom and tripped over a rock," Ryan said, worry showing in his voice. "She went down pretty hard and instantly felt pain in her stomach."

"I'm worried for my baby," Megan cried as new pain made her clutch her stomach. "It's too early for her to come. Oh, Blake, can't you do something?"

Abby felt her heart wrench as she looked at Megan and Ryan. Ryan had Megan in his arms and was trying to soothe her.

"Let's get her back to the car and have her stretch out on the backseat," Blake said. "Then I can examine her. I have my bag in the trunk."

Ryan picked Megan up as if she were a child and carried her quickly to the car. Abby ran ahead to open the doors and make sure that the backseat was clear. As Blake opened the trunk to get his medical bag, Abby noticed a blanket in the corner and carried it, along with her jacket, to the backseat. She folded her jacket to make a pillow for Megan then placed the blanket where Blake could use it if needed.

Blake quickly examined Megan then called Ryan aside. "I'm sorry, Ryan, but the fall has triggered contractions, and she has started labor. We need to get her to the hospital as quickly as possible."

Ryan's face blanched at the news, and he nodded his head. He and Blake returned to Megan, where Abby was holding her hand as another pain overtook her. "Blake, am I going to lose my baby? It's too early for her to come."

Abby held her breath as Blake answered in a calm voice. "We just need to get you to the hospital. I'll call ahead so your obstetrician can meet us there. Don't panic, Megan. It will be all right."

"Ryan, before we go, would you and Blake give me and the baby a blessing?" Megan whispered, reaching for Ryan's hand.

"Of course—I was going to suggest it," Ryan said. "Blake, do you have any oil?"

Blake reached into his bag and withdrew a small vial of consecrated oil.

Abby watched as Blake anointed Megan's head with the oil. Then he and Ryan, leaning into the car, placed their hands on her head. Abby closed her eyes and listened as Ryan blessed Megan that her contractions would stabilize until they could get to the hospital and reminded her of Heavenly Father's love for her and their baby, promising that He would strengthen and comfort her. He then blessed the baby in her womb that she would be all right and would live to bless their lives. As he finished, Abby's eyes were full of tears, and she looked at Megan, who now seemed to be calmer.

Ryan got into the backseat, cradling Megan's head in his lap. "How are you doing, honey?" he asked.

"I'm feeling a little better, and I'll be all right now," she replied.

Blake put his bag back in the trunk, and he and Abby got in the car. He backed slowly onto the road, and they started the drive back to St. George. Abby noticed that Blake drove slowly enough to avoid the rough bumps in the road but that he was trying to get Megan to the hospital as fast as he could.

***

29 April 1845

Tom and his family were baptized today. In respect for Father's wishes, I was not baptized with them, but I did go to watch. They were baptized in a shallow spot in the River Tas. The day was cold with rain and wind, but their faces radiated the joy they felt in the new commitment and covenants they had made. Tom's face glowed with an inner glory, and I loved him all the more. I wanted so much to be baptized with them.

The Fishers are talking about going to America with the Jones family and living with the Saints in Nauvoo. Tom wants me to go with them. But how do I leave my family here, knowing I will never see them again? How can I bear not being near my parents, not feeling their love, and never seeing their dear faces again in this life? But I cannot think, either, of life without Tom and my new religion. I think of Nephi and his family as they left their friends and their way of life to follow what the Lord had commanded. They were small in number, but the Lord has always blessed the righteous that desire to follow His commandments obediently. I will continue to pray and fast until I feel the confirmation of what I should do.

Chapter 12

The ride to the hospital seemed long to Abby, and she kept glancing back to see how Megan was doing. She often looked over at Blake as well, seeing him in a different way. She thought of the conversation she'd had with Megan on the walk to Emerald Pools and now understood more of what Megan had tried to tell her. This was what it would mean for a husband and wife to be spiritually equal, to be able to find strength and comfort in their faith together. How glorious it was to witness how the two young men's worthy lives enabled them to seek a blessing from Heavenly Father on behalf of someone else. How wonderful it would be to have that power in one's home, to be able to ask a blessing from a husband or father when needed. Even though she still worried for Megan, Abby marveled at the peace she had felt as Blake and Ryan had given her a blessing.

Megan's obstetrician, Dr. Baker, met them as they entered the emergency room at the hospital. A nurse helped Megan into a wheelchair and pushed the chair toward the women's center as Ryan followed anxiously. Dr. Baker stayed behind to confer with Blake. Abby took a seat in the waiting area, and a few minutes later Blake sat down beside her.

"She's been taken to a labor room in the women's center, where they will do a thorough check of both her and the baby. There's a waiting room in the center, so let's head over there."

Abby stood and followed him. "Blake, what if she loses this baby? She and Ryan want her so much."

Blake put his arm around Abby. "It will be all right. Megan's only two months away from her due date, so even if the baby is born now there is a good chance of survival. As Ryan and I gave her the blessing, I felt confirmation from the Spirit that both she and her baby will be all right. Megan is a fighter, and if the baby is like her mother, she'll be a fighter, too."

Abby smiled up at him, grateful that he was here with her. Entering the women's center, they found seats in the waiting room and sat down. Almost half an hour went by before Ryan came out. He drew a chair forward so he could face them before sitting down. Tiredness and worry showed in his voice as he spoke. "So far everything is all right. They have given Megan something to slow the contractions, so it's too early to tell just what's going to happen. The baby seems all right, and her heartbeat is strong." He smiled at them both. "I'm so grateful you are here with us. Can you stay a while?"

"We're here until we know just what's happening," Blake answered, gripping his friend's shoulder. "Now you go back and be with your wife, and try not to worry too much. We'll be fine; just let us know if there are any changes."

Ryan replaced his chair, giving them a small smile before returning to Megan, and Blake leaned back in his chair. "Too bad this had to happen, that such a perfect day should end with this," he said.

"It was a wonderful morning, Blake," Abby said quietly. "I loved the hike and being with good friends. It's something I'll remember when I get discouraged." She leaned back in her chair. "I'm sorry Megan fell, but I was glad to be there, and now here—to be part of what has happened. Megan was always a close friend to me when I was here visiting my grandparents, and I missed her during the years we didn't see each other. I've never had another girlfriend I felt so close to." As Blake looked at her doubtfully, she hastened to add, "Oh, I've had lots of friends, but Megan was special. I like Ryan, too, very much. Megan had such a crush on him when she was younger. I'm glad they married and have each other."

Blake's eyes looked into hers as they talked, and Abby again felt herself being drawn toward him, and she felt even stronger the desire to be with him. She blushed at her thoughts and reached over to the table, randomly picking up a magazine and pretending to read as she thumbed through the pages, all the while trying to quell that line of thinking. Blake was so different from any man she had known. She thought over the afternoon's events and tried to picture Scott's reaction if he had been there. She knew that he would be concerned, but she could not visualize him sitting in the hospital with her, waiting for news. He was not comfortable being around sickness or signs of discomfort. He would have shaken Ryan's hand, asked him to call when he had news, then left. She glanced out of the corner of her eye at Blake, who was also thumbing through a magazine. She knew he would not leave until the danger was over. He would be there to offer help regardless of what happened. She closed her eyes and sank back in her chair, suddenly feeling very tired.

When Blake glanced over at Abby, he saw that she was slowly dozing off. He put his arm around her and drew her head to his shoulder. He felt a need to protect and care for her completely and was surprised at how quickly this feeling had developed. He had dated Emily for a year before he'd had feelings this strong. Abby's light perfume drifted toward him, and he found himself studying her as she slept. He enjoyed being with her more each time he saw her. When they had arrived back and found Megan in trouble, she had been calm and helpful, noticing and doing things without being asked. Abby sighed softly in her sleep, and he held her a little tighter. What was going to come of this situation, he didn't know. He knew he was just a heartbeat away from falling deeply in love with her. And if he was honest with himself, he'd have to admit that he already was in love with her and wanted her as his wife, someone to share his life. He also knew that if he told her how he was feeling he would scare her away. He smiled and thought of the time that John, his roommate from medical school, had come home from a second date and announced that he had found the girl he was going to marry. Blake remembered that he had doubted that it was possible to fall in love so quickly, and now here he was in the same position. He frowned as he recalled that Abby was involved, for the time being, with someone else. But his heart told him that she also cared somewhat for him. From what she had told him of Scott, he knew she was struggling with some issues about the relationship and that he could not interfere. However, he was going to do everything in his power to win her.

Abby flushed when she woke and realized Blake was holding her, and instantly he released her. "I can't believe I dozed off," she said as she sat up straighter in the chair. "Has there been any more news?"

"Ryan hasn't come back yet, so everything must still be all right. Try not to worry. I'm sure in this case no news is good news." At her look of concern, he asked, "Would you like me to try and find out what's happening?"

She nodded.

He stood and walked through the doors to the labor rooms. Abby reflected on the day while she waited for Blake to return. It had started out so well; then Megan's fall and pain. Standing up, Abby stretched then tried to find a comfortable position in her chair. From time to time she glanced anxiously at her watch; more than two hours had passed since their arrival at the hospital. She picked up another magazine then put it back on the table, unable to concentrate. A few minutes later Blake was back beside her, a smile on his face.

"Everything is all right. The contractions have stopped, and Megan is resting. They will keep her overnight, and in the morning if she's still okay, they'll let her go home. She'll need to take it easy, but Dr. Baker is optimistic that she'll be able to carry the baby for a few more weeks."

Abby gave a sigh of relief. "Oh, Blake, I'm so glad. May I see her before we leave?"

"You bet. Megan has been asking for you. I'll take you in to see her, and then I think we should leave. There's nothing more we can do now by staying."

Megan had her eyes closed when they entered the room, and Ryan sat in a chair next to the bed, holding her hand. They entered quietly, but even so, Megan stirred and opened her eyes. She smiled when she saw Abby.

"Abby, everything's going to be all right. I can't believe I tripped and fell. I guess I still haven't outgrown being clumsy!"

Abby reached down and gave her friend a hug. "I'm glad they're keeping you overnight. Blake says you will have to rest for the next few weeks, so what can I do to help? I'll bring dinner over tomorrow night for you and Ryan. I can also do washing and ironing, cleaning, whatever you need."

Megan laughed. "I know you would help, but we've just called our parents. We didn't want to worry them until we knew just what was happening. My mother insisted Ryan and I stay with them for the next few weeks so she can take care of me. Aren't mothers wonderful! Ryan has also called my boss, and he placed me instantly on maternity leave, so that's taken care of as well. The best thing you can do is come visit me often."

"I will. It will be good to see your parents again! I really like them. You just do what you've been told. Megan, I'm so glad everything turned out all right." Giving Megan's hand a last squeeze, she walked to where Blake and Ryan were standing by the door. "Please call, Ryan, and let me know if you think of anything I can do."

Ryan gave her a hug. "I'm just grateful Megan has such a good friend. I'll give you a call tomorrow and let you know how things are."

Abby nodded, and she and Blake left the room. She peeked at her watch as they walked out of the hospital, noticing it was after seven in the evening. It had been a long day.

In the car, Blake looked over at her. "Abby, let me buy you dinner before taking you home. I know you must be tired, but it would give us a chance to unwind a little now that we know Megan's all right."

She looked back at him, noticing how tired he looked. "I'm not very hungry, but I could enjoy something light to eat."

They stopped at a small Italian restaurant so they could get a variation of salads and pastas. As they entered, the mouth-watering smell of garlic beset them and Abby's stomach rumbled. Laughing, she said, "I guess I'm hungrier than I thought. And pasta is one of my favorite comfort foods."

They both ordered the specialty of the house: Spaghetti Bolognese. As they ate, they talked easily together about the day. When Abby looked at her watch, she was surprised at how late it was.

"I think we'd better go, Blake. I have a million things I need to do tomorrow."

Blake stood up, chuckling at her remark. "I hope it really isn't a million, but you're right, it's getting late. I guess we'd better go."

She laughed as well and stood up. "I'm glad you suggested stopping. The dinner was what I needed."

As they walked out the door of the restaurant, Abby saw it had become dark, the rising moon golden in color as it began its nightly ride across the sky. When they arrived at her home, Blake got out of the car and opened the car door for her. They walked to the front porch, and Abby opened her purse to find her house key. She fumbled through her purse until, exasperated, she started taking out items and placing them on the porch rail. Finally, jubilantly, she felt the key in the bottom of her purse.

"Ah-ha, I knew it was somewhere in there!" she said triumphantly, holding the key up for him to see. As he put out his hand to take the key from her, it slipped through her fingers and dropped to the ground. They both stooped to pick it up, and Abby found herself gazing into Blake's eyes, just inches from her face. He picked up the key, his eyes never leaving her, and they both slowly stood up. She felt the breath catch in her throat as he put his arms around her and gently drew her forward. Placing his hand under her chin, he turned her face upward to meet his. Abby held her breath with anticipation, aware of her body leaning toward him, and as his face bent toward her, she closed her eyes. His lips touched hers hesitantly at first, then he gathered her close to him, enfolding her in his arms. When he raised his head, she opened her eyes wonderingly and stepped back, breathless. The kiss had affected her deeply, and she knew she should not have allowed it to happen.

She gave a shaky laugh. "I had a marvelous day, Blake. Even with all the worry about Megan, it's been wonderful."

Blake leaned forward and inserted the key in the door. He opened it for her then handed the key back to Abby. "It has been a perfect day for me too, Abby. I'll see you in church tomorrow."

She stepped inside and watched him walk back to his car and drive off before she closed the door. Abby turned the lock slowly, her mind full of guilt and confusion as she acknowledged the growing attraction she felt for Blake.

***

5 May 1845

I have made my decision. I know I need to be baptized and go with Tom and his family to America. Tom has arranged for the missionaries to baptize me early tomorrow morning, and then we will leave immediately with his family for Liverpool to board a ship for America. I am feeling such sorrow over Mother and Father tonight that I can hardly bear it. I told them of my decision early this morning, after wrestling through the night in prayer over what I should do. Toward morning a peace came into my heart, along with the knowledge that I will be blessed with the strength to handle the choice I have made. But it has broken my heart to see their tearful faces.

Mother wept openly as she helped me pack, and she has given me the quilt that she and I completed this last winter. I know that as I lay this quilt over my bed and finger the stitches her worn hands have made, I will feel a loss in my life and remember all I have left. I will miss her all the remaining days of my life.

I know that Father does not understand what has made me join a church that would take me away from family, friends, and country to join a small group of people in faraway America. Ordinarily he is a kind and tolerant man, and I cannot visualize life without his gentle wisdom and love. Each night of my life he has brought out the worn and much-loved Bible and read to Mother and me. Sitting at his knee, I would visualize the young David with his slingshot marching forth to meet the giant Goliath; I could hear the mother of Moses crying as she laid her baby in his cradle of reeds and placed him in the river; and I felt awe at the baby Jesus' birth in the stable. I shed tears as Father read of Christ carrying His cross to the hill where He would be crucified. He has told me often how Jesus loves us, and his stories of Bible heroes prepared me to receive the gospel when it was preached to me. He has guided me with his wisdom and patience throughout my life, and I know he truly loves Christ. But his heart has been hardened against the missionaries. These past few days he has pleaded with me for hours to forsake these new beliefs and stay with them. Today, however, Father has not argued with me to change my mind, but the slump of his shoulders and his reddened eyes have told of the tremendous heartbreak I have caused in his life. But I am of age, and I must follow the confirmation and burning testimony within me even though it breaks my heart to leave all that is dear to me. I know not what is in front of me, but it is the prayer of my heart that someday these two dear people who gave me life and love will listen to the beauty of the gospel message and we will be reunited.

Just before closing my trunk tonight, I laid the small box that Tom gave me for my birthday on top. What a happy day that was, and now it seems so far away. Inside the chest is the brooch my parents gave me of our combined hair. As I look at it, I hope so much that one day our lives can be intertwined eternally as a family.

Chapter 13

Abby was awakened early Sunday morning by the strident ringing of her cell phone. Sleepily she opened her eyes and reached for the phone on the night table.

"Abby, it's me," Scott said.

"Hi, Scott . . . what time is it?" she asked drowsily, pulling herself up in bed and trying to wake up more fully.

"It's a little before six. I tried calling you several times yesterday, but your cell phone must have been turned off. The last time I tried was after nine. Where were you?" he asked suspiciously.

Abby sat up straighter in bed and sighed irritably. "I'm sorry, Scott. I wasn't aware I had to clear my schedule with you. As it happens, I had a chance to go with friends to Zion National Park. I wanted to see it before going home, so I went."

"I was hoping you would be able to finish this week so when you come back Friday you would be through there," Scott said, frustration showing in his voice.

"Scott, it's just not possible to get everything done before I come home this weekend," Abby responded firmly. "There's still too much left to do. Even if I hadn't taken yesterday off I would still have to come back to finish packing up and cleaning the house. Besides, Mom mentioned that she and Dad are coming to St. George for Easter, and they can help with some of the final sorting. It shouldn't be long now until I'm home for good. But for now, let's just enjoy the thought of having the weekend together. I'm really looking forward to being with you."

"It just seems as if you're not putting in the time that's needed to get the job done," he replied wearily.

"Believe it or not, I *do* have a schedule," Abby emphasized, slightly annoyed at Scott and herself for everything that had been going on. "However, I am enjoying seeing people I haven't seen in a long time and rediscovering a place that has meant a lot to me in my life." Although she tried to shrug it off, Abby felt the sting of truth in Scott's words.

"I'm trying to understand, Abby, and I'm sorry," Scott said, softness entering his voice. "I just want you back so we can start planning our own future together. I hope you had a nice time. Did you go with just Megan and her husband yesterday or with a group?"

Abby took another deep breath before answering. "I went with Megan, her husband, and Blake Matthews." As he started to interrupt, she added, "I know what you're thinking, but I didn't go with Blake as his date. They are all just good friends. Ryan and Blake have been friends since childhood, and I've told you before how much time I spent with Megan when I was staying with my grandparents."

Exasperation surfaced again in Scott's voice. "Maybe you didn't think of it as a date, but I bet that Blake did. I thought you weren't going to see him anymore."

"Scott, he's a friend, and he's been a big help to me. This work is going much faster with him than it would without him. And if I need more help, I'll probably call him. I'm sure he didn't think of it as a date, either." As she spoke these last words, however, Abby remembered how close she had felt to Blake the day before, how her spirit and body had responded to his kiss. She blushed and felt a twinge of guilt.

"I'm sorry again, Abby," Scott apologized, trying to sound more calm. "I worry that your trip is putting more than just physical distance between us, and it's been a long time since I've seen you. I'm so glad you're coming home this weekend; we really need the time to talk things through."

"I'm sorry too, Scott." Abby told him. "I just need you to be patient with me. Since being here, I've started questioning several things in my life. I've told you about the feelings I'm having about being active in my church again. On our hike yesterday, Megan, who is a little more than seven months pregnant, fell and started going into labor. Things were pretty scary for a time. Ryan, Megan's husband, gave her a blessing, and soon after the contractions stopped. Oh, Scott, as I listened to Ryan's blessing and saw the peace it gave Megan, it made me realize all the more that I want to be entitled to receive spiritual blessings in my life as well. Megan is going to have to stay in bed now until she has the baby. I will be taking time out to visit her as I'm sure it's going to be hard for her to stay down."

Scott replied gently, "I'm glad your friend Megan is doing all right, Abby, and you do need to visit her. Just don't let it consume you. On a more positive note," Abby could hear a forced brightness in Scott's tone as he changed the subject, "our case has gone to the jury, and hopefully it won't be too long before a verdict is given. I feel confident they are going to decide for our client."

"I'm glad." Abby tried to sound encouraging. "You've certainly worked long and hard on this case. I'm glad that I'll be home this Friday." Abby looked over at the bedside clock and swung her legs over the side of the bed. "I guess I'd better get up and get going. I'll call you soon. And Scott, I really am looking forward to spending the weekend with you."

"Me too," Scott said, "I'll make reservations at our favorite restaurant for Friday night. I love you, Abby."

After saying good-bye, Abby placed her phone back on the night table and looked at it for a few minutes before picking it up again. She climbed back in bed and pulled up the covers. Punching in the numbers for her parents' home, Abby waited while it rang. After the third ring, she heard her mother's sleepy voice on the line.

"Mom, I'm sorry to call so early, but I just needed to talk to someone."

"Abby, is everything all right? You sound a little upset," her mother asked anxiously.

"Everything's fine, really. I'm just a little confused—and who better to talk to than my mother? I'm so glad I'll be able to see you on Saturday."

On the other end of the line, Mary smiled. Abby had always been such a self-reliant child that it pleased her when she asked for help.

Abby started by telling her mother about going to Zion's and the wonderful day it had been. She related in detail Megan's accident and the priesthood blessing that Ryan and Blake had given her. "It was so humbling and touching to me to witness it, to see the comfort and peace it gave Megan. Ryan and Megan are excited for this baby, and he's so tender with her. It's made me rethink some of the goals Scott and I have discussed. When we started talking about getting married, we decided we wouldn't have a baby for a few years. That way we could both get ahead professionally and financially. But I'm starting to question whether I want to put off having a baby for that long. Plus, the more I read and pray and attend church, the more I want to participate."

"Abby, have you talked to Scott about your feelings?" questioned her mother.

"He knows I'm getting serious about the Church, but he has expressed no interest in it at the moment. But, Mom, I haven't told you all that's happened." She was silent for a minute, gathering the words she wanted to say. "You know Blake Matthews has been helping me with the yard work, and he took me horseback riding one evening. Well, I find myself feeling attracted to him in many ways. I keep telling myself that he is just a really good friend and that I am drawn to him because of the spiritual comfort I receive when I'm with him. Our discussions have helped me feel more peaceful with Grandmother's death. He's the exact opposite of Scott in the way he looks at life, and he has made me question many of the things I thought were important to do and achieve. When he brought me home last night, he kissed me, and I felt something I've never experienced." When she finished speaking she waited for her mother's reply.

Mary answered gently. "You know, Abby, your father and I have complete confidence in you. You've always been able to analyze a situation and make good choices based on what you know. But I can tell you this: a good marriage has to be founded on common goals and desires in order for it to work and to endure. You should never marry Scott with the idea that he is going to change and become what you want him to be. That's not fair to you or him. You need to be sure you and Scott are both walking down the same path, that you want the same things from life. If you are growing spiritually and Scott feels no need for the Church in his life now, are you willing to take the chance that he will someday? After you're married, will he be supportive of you and your children's activity in the Church? As for Blake Matthews, I know my mother thought the world of him. But only you can determine why you're feeling this attraction to him. But Abby, this is something you need to resolve before committing yourself to Scott."

Listening to her mother's words, Abby felt comforted. Granted, it raised a lot of questions about her relationships with Scott and Blake, but it had been good to talk it through with someone.

Abby sighed. "Thanks for letting me talk, Mom. It has helped. Not that I know what I'm going to do, but at least I don't feel quite so overwhelmed with everything. I can't wait to see you—I just wish Dad didn't have to be out of town."

Mary laughed. "I can't wait to see you either. Give me a call Friday after you arrive and let me know what time Saturday you want to meet. And Abby, try not to worry too much over your feelings for Blake and Scott—you have time to work things out. Just keep saying your prayers and listening to the Spirit."

"Thanks, Mom. I'll see you Saturday."

Abby hung up the phone. A glance at the clock had her hurrying out of bed. She only had an hour before picking Agnes up for church.

After showering, Abby sorted through her closet for something to wear. She was nervous about seeing Blake again, not sure how comfortable the situation would be. She finally settled on the green suit, knowing it brought out the green in her eyes. Somehow it was important this morning to look her best.

When she and Agnes entered the chapel, she followed Agnes to the front where they always sat. She noticed Blake sitting near the front and gave a start when Agnes gestured Abby into the same row. She smiled hesitantly at Blake as he beamed at her and rose to shake their hands.

"I thought this was about where you always sat," he whispered, smiling at her as she sat down. "When I talked with Ryan this morning, he said Megan will be going home later today and that everything is fine. I thought you'd like to know."

"I'm so glad," she whispered back, returning his smile. "Thanks for telling me."

During sacrament meeting, Abby was aware of Blake sitting close to her. When it was time to sing the opening song, he offered to share his hymn book, and she noticed he had a nice baritone voice. She had a difficult time concentrating on the speakers with him sitting so close to her, and she knew his effect on her was growing each time she saw him.

After the closing prayer, Blake gathered up his lesson materials for Sunday School. "I need to write some information on the board, so I'll see you in class," he said with a smile as he exited the row.

She was not aware that she was staring after him until Agnes took hold of her arm. "Are you ready to go, dear?"

Abby nodded her head, and they hurried to the Relief Society room for Sunday School. During class, she glanced often at Blake, and her confusion grew every time their eyes met. It was a good thing she was going home on Friday. She needed to see Scott again, and hopefully that would clarify her feelings.

After Relief Society, Abby told Sister Richardson that she would not be at church next Sunday but assured her she would be there for the upcoming activity. She dropped Agnes off at her home, promising she would eat dinner with her another time, then entered her own home. With a deep sigh, she laid her purse on the entry table and walked out to the patio to sit down. Abby looked around at the neatly trimmed trees and bushes and the new green leaves and flower buds sprouting on the rose branches and remembered the afternoons she and Blake had spent working together. She also thought of Scott and the last time she had seen him. *It's a good thing we didn't become engaged. We really do have some issues that need to be resolved before taking that big of a step. If we are both expecting different things from each other, neither one of us would be happy. But I still feel love and a connection to him.* She sat for several more minutes, reveling in the warm sun, before glancing at her watch. Then she arose and went back inside the house.

***

Tuesday evening Blake stopped in to see if Abby needed his help, but within a few minutes of his arrival he received an emergency phone call and had to leave for the hospital. As she watched his car pull away, she wasn't sure if she was relieved or sad.

Abby spent a busy morning Wednesday going over the papers for the Towers' real estate closing scheduled for Friday afternoon. Checking the file, she found the title papers had not been sent. She made a quick call to the title company and received the promise that they had been mailed by Fed Ex yesterday and would be arriving by noon that day. Another call was made to her client, Mr. Arbogast, to assure him that everything was still scheduled as planned and to make sure that there were no problems on his end. By one o'clock, the title papers had arrived, and after making a final review of the file, Abby placed it in her briefcase and sat back. What a satisfying morning it had been! She had briefly forgotten how she loved her job and the feeling of gratification it gave her.

That afternoon Abby drove to Megan's parents' home. When she arrived, she grabbed the flowers she'd bought for Megan out of the backseat of her car and went up to ring the doorbell.

Megan's mother, a neat, trim woman dressed in jeans and a checked shirt, answered the door. "Well, for goodness' sakes, come in, Abby," she said, pulling Abby inside and shutting the door.

"Thanks, Mrs. Morris. Is Megan asleep or can I see her?" she asked.

Mrs. Morris shook her head fondly. "It's all I can do to keep her down. She's like a kid that has to be entertained every minute, and I'm just glad you're here. Abby, Frank and I are sorry about your grandmother; she was a special person. Megan said you're here for a while packing up the old home, and I'm sure that must be hard on you."

"Thanks, Mrs. Morris. It has been difficult, but I'm getting things done. Is Megan in her old room?"

Mrs. Morris put her hands on her hips. "Yes, she is. You remember the way, don't you?" Just then a bell sounded, and Mrs. Morris gave a start. "That means I have a cake I need to take out of the oven. Excuse me, Abby."

Abby nodded her head and gave her another smile before going down the hall and into Megan's room. Megan was sitting up in bed, a book in her hand, but was obviously not reading. As Abby entered, she looked up. "Oh, Abby, I'm so glad to see you! I get so bored staying in bed day and night. I'm too used to being busy. Remember, I've always had a hard time sitting or standing still."

Abby laughed. "I remember, but you just do what you've been told to do. Your poor mother looks more tired than you do, trying to keep you down."

"I know, but it is hard," she said with a slight grimace. "What beautiful flowers, Abby," she said as Abby placed the vase of flowers on the table by the bed.

"I thought I would bring a little of the outdoors inside for you," she said. "Seriously, Megan, how are you feeling, besides bored?"

"I'm doing well, and the contractions have stopped. I just need to carry this baby a little longer if I can." She rubbed her stomach affectionately. "I can't wait to hold her in my arms. Abby, this has been such a wonderful experience, carrying her. I feel her move inside, and I remind myself that a new life will be ours to raise. I can't believe how protective and loving toward her I feel already."

Abby watched the emotions flit across Megan's face as she talked and felt a little envious. If she married Scott and they followed their schedule, it would be several years before she experienced what Megan was feeling now.

Mrs. Morris entered the room carrying a tray of cold punch and chocolate cake. Abby stood and took the tray from Mrs. Morris. "Where shall I put this?" she asked.

"I'll just move this little table closer to the bed," Mrs. Morris said as she moved a small table on wheels. Abby set the tray down, looking at the size of the slices of chocolate cake. If she ate desserts this size all the time, she soon wouldn't fit in her clothes.

"Mom," Megan said, reaching for a plate. "You made my favorite chocolate cake." Taking a big bite, she licked the fork clean. "I never get enough chocolate. Thanks, Mom."

"You're welcome, dear," Mrs. Morris said on her way out of the room. "If you want more, Abby, there's plenty."

Abby smiled her thanks. *I'll do well to eat this,* she thought.

"So how is Ryan doing, living with his in-laws?" she asked.

"He's doing well. You know my mother; she fusses and spoils him. He probably will want to stay here even after the baby is born." Looking at the expression on Abby's face, she laughed and added, "Okay, not really, but he's not complaining."

After finishing the cake and visiting a little longer with Megan, Abby stood and leaned over to give Megan a squeeze. "Just keep me posted on what's happening, and I'll try to stop in again when I can. Remember, I'm going home this weekend, so I'll check with you when I get back. But, Megan, please do as you're told. It won't be long now. And don't wear your mother out."

Giggling, Megan replied. "I'll try, but come and see me again if you can. It has been so good to have you back."

***

Thursday morning Abby walked over to Agnes's house and rang the doorbell. Agnes answered the door, a smile of welcome on her face. "Come in, Abby, and sit down. I'm glad to take a break."

Abby followed Agnes into the living room. "I couldn't remember if I told you I was going home to Denver for the weekend, and I didn't want you to worry when you didn't see me around."

"No, you didn't, dear, so I'm glad you've let me know. I probably would have worried. Did you say you would only be gone for the weekend? That's not a very long visit."

Abby laughed. "I know, but I'm anxious to finish here, and there still seems like there's quite a lot to do. On the other hand, I'm really looking forward to being home for a few days. Mom and Dad are coming here the following weekend for Easter, and I know Mom will want to see you then."

Agnes's look was contemplative. "Is it coming up on Easter already? My, the days go by so fast. I hadn't realized that it was that close."

Abby laughed again and stood up. "You sound like me! Time slips by so fast I can't keep up. I'll give you a call when I get back. Will you have a way to church on Sunday without my being here to take you?"

Agnes nodded her head. "Don't you worry, dear. If I need a ride, I can always call Sister Neilson. You just let me know when you get back, and enjoy your time away. It's not been easy for you here alone, I'm sure."

Reaching home, Abby made a final call to her client to confirm the closing time and then packed for her weekend trip home.

Just before going to bed, Blake called to make sure she had everything she needed and to see if she still wanted to drive her own car to the airport. Hanging up from the call, she finished packing her small case and went to bed.

***

6 May 1845

As I write in my journal tonight, I am in a small wayside inn on the way to Liverpool. I was baptized this morning in the River Tas, just as the sun was breaking over the hills. The air was cold, but with the rising sun, warmth seemed to flood my spirit with the promise of new life and new joy to replace the deep sadness I feel at leaving my home. As I was lowered in the cold water, I felt cleansed and reborn and filled with the love of my Heavenly Father and Savior. I know I am doing the right thing. Tom's dear face was the first I saw as I came out of the water. I felt a peace enter my heart at knowing that he would be by my side through all the days ahead. Mrs. Fisher took me in her arms and held me close, crying softly, and promised her love and support in the years to come.

When we went back to the house to load my trunk, Father and Mother silently bid me good-bye, holding me close as I kissed them one final time. With my heart breaking, I turned on the wagon seat, and my last vision was of them standing by the door of our home, Father bent over with grief, his arm protectively around Mother's shoulders. She had tears pouring down her face, her handkerchief over her mouth. I could feel tears streaming from my eyes as well, and I thought my heart would break in two. I was so overwhelmed with sadness at leaving them that I almost had Tom stop the wagon, but he laid his hand on mine, giving me strength. I turned on the seat and willed myself to look forward to the future instead of to the past.

Tomorrow will be a long day of traveling before we arrive in Liverpool. Tom and I wanted to marry before leaving our village, but Father refused to read the banns or perform the ceremony, so we will be married aboard ship. The Fishers have sold everything they could for the cost of passage for their family, and Tom has saved enough for his and mine as well. The Fishers are starting over with only the few belongings they are bringing, but they, too, are looking ahead.

Chapter 14

Abby leaned forward in her seat and looked out the small window as the plane rapidly began its ascent into the air. The city of St. George lay spread beneath her and looked more and more like a child's village as the plane rose higher in the sky. As the city disappeared, the earth below reflected the red and brown of the desert landscape. When the Fasten Seatbelts light went off, Abby stood up to get her briefcase from the overhead bin and, sitting back down, opened the case and found the papers for the closing. She carefully scanned the pages, making quick notes on her yellow pad of items that she wanted to further clarify for her client. Giving a final glance through the contract and her notes, she gave a sigh of deep contentment, again feeling the satisfaction of being back in her professional routine.

Abby replaced her briefcase in the overhead bin and settled herself back in her seat just as the pilot announced they were beginning their descent into Denver. Once again she watched out the window as the large city of Denver sprawled beneath her window, homes and buildings covering the ground below. She felt a surge of excitement build within her at returning home for the weekend. It would be wonderful to see her mother again, though she wished her father was not out of town. And she was really looking forward to spending time with Scott. They certainly needed this weekend together. Suddenly, Blake's face surfaced unbidden in her thoughts, and her lips tingled with the memory of his kiss and the feelings it had stirred within her. She shook her head impatiently as if to clear the confusion and image from her mind. It was good she was coming home, if only for the weekend, so she could put things back into perspective again.

After landing, Abby picked up her rental car and started the drive to her office. As the traffic thickened and slowed, she found her hands tensing on the wheel and forced herself to relax. Driving in St. George had certainly been easier; she had forgotten the crush of traffic that clogged the freeways. When she finally arrived at her office building, she parked her car, picked up her briefcase, and walked to her office, calling out greetings to co-workers on the way. In her office, she put the briefcase on the desk and looked around. It seemed as if she had been away much longer than she had. A brief knock sounded on the open office door; she smiled and gestured her boss into the office.

"Glad you're back, Abby," Ben Forrester announced as he walked into her office. He was a large man, well over six feet tall, and heavily built. His manner and voice were jovial and friendly, but Abby knew that behind that laid-back facade lay a shrewd business mind; he did not tolerate carelessness in his employees. He respected honesty and integrity and rewarded it generously. She enjoyed working for him and knew that he drew the best from her.

"I'm glad to be back, Ben, even though it's just for a few days," she said, reaching out to shake his outstretched hand. "Hopefully, I'll be back permanently in a few weeks."

"Good, we've missed you. Everything ready for the Towers' closing? It's a big contract, and I know you've put a lot of hard work into it."

"Everything should be fine. The closing is scheduled for an hour from now, and I don't foresee any problems. I've talked to Mr. Arbogast several times this past week, and any concerns have been ironed out."

"That's fine, then." Smiling, Ben looked her over. "It looks as if you've been soaking up some of that desert sun, Abby. You look happy and healthy."

Abby laughed. "Believe me, I've worked harder physically these last few weeks than I remember doing for a long time. But I'm happy I've had the chance to do this. I really appreciate you understanding and letting me have the time off."

"You earned the time, Abby; you're a hard worker. Just keep me posted on when you'll be back for good."

As expected, the closing went off without a hitch, and Abby spent the next couple of hours reviewing the paperwork on properties that were still active, making several follow-up calls. Finally she cleared her desk, sat back in her chair, and looked around. It was good to be involved again, and she felt the usual keen sense of satisfaction that her job gave her. She glanced at the clock on her desk as the phone rang.

"Abby, I'm so glad you're back in town," Scott said enthusiastically. "I can't wait to see you. Are we still on for seven tonight?"

"I'm excited to see you too, Scott," Abby responded with a smile in her voice. "Yes, pick me up at seven. I'm just leaving my office now."

"I'm about to leave as well. I made reservations at the restaurant for eight, so that will give us plenty of time. See you shortly."

Fighting the rush-hour traffic, Abby was glad she lived close to her work. She parked the rental car in the garage and unlocked the door to her condominium. Inside, the air was stuffy; after raising the blinds, she opened the windows to let some fresh air blow through the condo. She walked quickly to her bedroom and through to the adjoining bathroom. Giving a sigh of appreciation, she started the water flowing into the large spa tub then opened the closet to choose something to wear for her date with Scott. Laying out a black dress on the bed, she picked up the phone on the nightstand and entered her parents' phone number. The phone rang several times before the answering machine came on, and she left a message.

"Mom, it's me. Just wanted to let you know that I arrived okay, and I'm looking forward to seeing you tomorrow. Scott's picking me up at seven, so I'll talk to you in the morning."

It does feel good to be back, she thought as she lowered herself into the warm water and turned the jets on. She allowed herself to relax for a while before turning the jets off and getting out of the tub. She dressed carefully, wanting to look her best, aware that she was both nervous and excited to see Scott again. A lot had happened since they had last been together, and she hoped that the weekend would clarify the confusion she felt when she was around Blake.

The doorbell rang just as Abby was putting on her pearl earrings. Quickly, she gave a last glance at herself in the mirror and then rushed to the door and opened it. Scott gathered her into his arms as soon as she had closed the door.

"Oh, Abby," he whispered, holding her close to him. "I've missed you so much."

She laughed breathlessly, glad to see him as well. "I've missed you, too." She returned his kiss and then stepped back to look at him. He was an attractive man and was meticulously dressed in a charcoal gray suit and crisp burgundy-and-white-striped dress shirt. She smiled at him, noticing that he was looking her over as well.

"You look wonderful, Abby—all tanned and glowing," he said, giving her another kiss. Releasing her, he looked at his watch and reached for the jacket she was holding. "I guess we'd better go so we make our reservations."

Inside the restaurant they were seated at a table by the window, and Abby gazed out at the city, the windows on the tall buildings reflecting faint hints of gold as the last rays of the setting sun reflected on the glass. Scott watched her then reached out to lay his hand on top of hers. "It seems like forever since we were here the night before you left, doesn't it?"

She turned her head back toward him and sighed. "So much has happened—it really does seem like a long time. I'm so glad to have this weekend home so we can spend some time together. I've missed you, Scott." She squeezed his hand and smiled over at him. "How's the trial going? You and Dad are a lethal team, so I'm sure it must be going well, even with him out of town."

Scott laughed at her comment. "I like to think we are. It's going well and should have a final verdict the first of next week. It will be good to focus on the next case. So, what do you want to eat tonight?" he asked, opening his menu.

After the waiter had taken their order, Scott leaned toward Abby. "Tell me, how are you really getting along? It sounds as if it's been a lot of hard work."

"It has, Scott, but I'm so thankful I've been able to find the time to do this. In many ways, I've really enjoyed being in St. George, and I'd forgotten how much I loved the town and people. As I was driving to the office from the airport this morning, believe me, I realized I haven't missed the rush-hour traffic."

He laughed. "Yes, I'm sure that's a plus."

As they ate their dinner, Scott updated Abby on news relating to friends and events that she had missed, and she found herself comparing her two worlds. She was enjoying the atmosphere of the five-star restaurant and had relished dressing for the occasion. She had missed feeling and being part of the pulse of this vibrant, bustling city and the feeling of achievement she experienced with her work. On the other hand, she found her mind reflecting on the quiet and peace of her days in St. George, where she'd had the time to step back and really feel life instead of the constant rush to keep up with the hectic schedule that was demanded of her here. Suddenly she became aware that Scott had stopped talking and was looking at her.

"What are you thinking about?" he asked quietly.

"I'm sorry, Scott. I guess I'm just tired. It's been a long day," she answered, giving him a reflective smile.

"Do you want any dessert, or shall we just go?"

She folded her napkin and placed it beside her dinner plate. "I'm so full I couldn't eat another bite, but it was a wonderful dinner."

He put his arm around her as they walked back to the car then helped her inside. She leaned back in the soft leather seat and fastened her seat belt. After starting the car, Scott turned to her. "Do you want to go any place else, or shall I take you home?"

"Do you mind if we just go home? I'm really tired. We'll see each other tomorrow, and I promise to be more lively then."

"All right, Abby, but get some good sleep tonight. I don't want you to use the excuse of being tired when I beat you at our golf game tomorrow," he joked.

When they arrived back at her condo, Scott helped her from the car and walked her to the door. After unlocking the door, he drew her into his arms and kissed her. Raising his head, he looked into her eyes and drew her close again. "I don't know if I'll be able to let you go back," he said huskily, lowering his mouth to hers and kissing her deeply. He embraced her one more time before walking to his car. "Sleep well tonight, Abby. I'll see you tomorrow."

Closing and locking her door, Abby breathed deeply several times before she headed upstairs to bed. It was wonderful to be back home with Scott.

Abby woke early the next morning, unable to sleep any longer. Getting out of bed, she knelt by the bedside for her morning prayer. As she arose, a sense of gladness filled her spirit for this new habit and the peace it gave her. She pulled on sweats and running shoes, ran a brush through her hair, then quickly brushed her teeth. Locking her front door, she looked up at the sky, grateful that it was clear with just a few thin clouds. After a few warm-up stretches, she started off. The streets were fairly empty this early on a Saturday; only an occasional car passed by. She entered the park near her condo and joined other early-morning runners.

Taking deep breaths as she ran, Abby felt herself relaxing. Yes, it was good to be back, if only for the weekend. She was looking forward to a morning shopping trip with her mother. Mid-afternoon she was going to meet Scott and play a round of golf, and that evening they would attend the black-tie dinner at the home of George Ross. Abby was glad she had made it back for the affair, as this was an important evening for Scott.

Finally she turned her steps toward home. Inside, she headed directly to the bathroom for a shower. She stood under the spray of water for a few minutes then washed her hair. After pulling on dress slacks and a soft cashmere sweater, she walked to her small kitchen, opened a can of juice, and poured it into a glass. She took a slice of bread from the loaf in the freezer and made a piece of toast. As she was rinsing her dishes, the phone rang. She was glad to hear her mother's voice on the other end of the line.

"Mom, I'm anxious to see you! What time shall I pick you up?"

Mary laughed. "I can't wait to see you as well. I'm just finishing up here at home, so about an hour would be good. Anything special we're shopping for?"

"I want to get something glamorous to wear for the dinner tonight. It's a black-tie affair, and I want to buy something special. I'm also celebrating the closing of the Towers' deal, so lunch is on me."

"Sounds good to me. I'll see you soon."

After hanging up, Abby retrieved her grandmother's scriptures from her suitcase. She settled herself on the sofa and opened the Book of Mormon to the place where she was reading. This morning she read the book of Fourth Nephi. *What would it be like,* she mused as she closed the book, *to live in a world without war, selfishness, and fear? The power of Christ's appearance to the people in America had been so compelling that over two hundred years passed away before corruption and evil was able to take hold in men's hearts again.* As Abby reflected, she knew that she was also undergoing a "change of heart," that blessings had come into her life since she went to St. George—the testimony she was gaining being the biggest blessing of all.

Abby put the scriptures on the end table; sadness filled her heart for the years that had passed without her having the gospel in her life and the richness it could have added. She couldn't help wondering what her life would be like now if she had stayed active in the Church and made it a prime focus. She was grateful that she had not made serious life-altering mistakes during those years that would have added more remorse to the sorrow she already felt as she walked through the steps of repentance. She had drunk an occasional glass of wine at social functions and once in a while a cup of coffee with friends; fortunately, these had not been daily habits. But even these sins caused her to regret their presence in her life. Abby was also painfully aware that there could have been years of opportunities to grow and serve in the Church that were now lost forever.

***

Her mother answered the door before Abby had a chance to ring the bell. After giving her daughter a firm hug, Mary held her away and looked her over closely, finally giving a relieved smile.

"You look wonderful, Abby, and I'm glad. I've worried about you. I know how close you were to your grandmother and know it must be an emotional roller coaster ride for you to pack up her things."

Abby grinned at her mother. "You're right, and you know from my calls home how hard it's been for me. But, Mom, it's also been very rewarding. My life is slowly changing for the better, and I'm finding peace with her death." She helped her mother on with her jacket, and they walked back to Abby's car. "I'm looking forward to shopping for my dinner dress where there are lots of choices. Not that St. George doesn't have its shops, but there definitely are not as many as there are here, and you know how I love to shop, even though I'm always so rushed when I go."

Mary laughed, too. "Remember, I grew up in that town. All right, let's go."

Abby became frustrated as they went from store to store. Most of the formal dresses she saw were made with plunging necklines and backs, and she became aware of another way that she had changed. She wanted a dress that was modest and conformed to Church standards.

Just before lunchtime, they entered a small boutique, and Abby walked to where she could see several formal dresses hanging. She looked each one over carefully and then let out a deep breath of excitement. "Look, Mom," she said, holding out a dress for her mother to see. It was a gown in a deep emerald green, so dark it was almost black. The dress was plain by modern standards with its rounded neckline and short sleeves, the skirt dropping from the bust in a straight line. The elegance of the dress was in the cut of the soft crepe fabric and its matching short beaded jacket.

"Oh, Abby, I think it's just right. Is it your size?"

"I think so. I'm going to try it on and then decide." As she slipped the dress over her head, the soft material draped itself lovingly to her figure: a perfect fit. She walked out of the dressing room to the large mirrors; her mother stood and walked to where she moved slowly in a circle.

"It's beautiful on you!" Mary said appreciatively.

Abby studied her reflection in the mirrors; the elegant cut of the gown and matching jacket flattered her trim frame, and the color of her eyes deepened with the dark green in the dress. "It's been worth the chase!" she said happily.

As she paid for the dress, Abby reflected that it was a good thing she had the commission coming from the sale because the gown cost more than she had planned on spending. Once she found a pair of shoes to match at another store, the hungry but contented women decided to break for lunch.

"Now remember, Mom, it's my treat today," Abby reminded her mother as they were seated in the restaurant and had opened their menus.

"How was your evening with Scott last night?" asked Mary after they finished their meal. "Did he bring up marriage again?"

Abby put down her fork and looked across at her. "Thankfully, he didn't. In fact, it was a really nice evening, and Scott went out of his way to make it so. I hadn't realized how much I'd missed him until I saw him again. I was glad, though, that he didn't mention the ring. I just don't want to think about marriage until I'm home again for good. I know that I need to resolve some issues within myself before making any kind of commitment."

Mary was silent as she studied Abby's face. "From what you've said to me earlier, it sounds as if part of the problem is Blake. Is that the dilemma?"

Abby pondered the question for a few seconds before answering. "I don't honestly know. They are both good men, and I don't know how I can have serious feelings for two men at the same time. I wish Scott was interested in the Church, but we have so many other things in common, and I enjoy being with him. And I think if we married, he would at least support me in my desire to be active. And I hope he would join the Church sometime in his life. As far as Blake is concerned, I'll admit he has many qualities that I admire, his spirituality and gentleness being a couple of them, but at this point, I'm just not sure how deeply I really feel about him either. He has certainly been a lot of help to me, though, and I feel a real friendship with him."

"I'm glad that if you marry Scott he would encourage you to stay active," Mary said quietly, her thoughtful gaze resting on her daughter. "Going back to church now, I'm much more aware of what's been missing these past years from my life with your father, and I'm glad to have it as part of our lives again. I don't want you to have to wait for that. I want you to have it in your home always, but you need to make that decision for yourself. I know that Scott is a good man and would make a good husband." She folded her napkin. "Well, I'm certainly full. Are you ready to go?"

Abby stood up. "Yes, I guess I'd better get back. Scott is picking me up around two-thirty; we're going to get in a game of golf this afternoon."

"This was a wonderful morning, Abby," said Mary as they pulled into her driveway. "Are you sure you can't come in for a few minutes?"

"I'd better not, Mom. I'm sorry I'm running short on time this trip. I'll just walk you to the door, and then I think I'd better get back. I need to change my clothes before Scott picks me up." As she felt her mother's arms go around her, Abby wondered if daughters ever outgrew their need to feel the emotional security their mothers' arms afforded.

"I'm so glad you and Dad are coming next weekend for Easter, Mom! I've missed seeing Dad this weekend. Next week is going to be so busy with more packing and then preparing that presentation on the St. George temple for the Relief Society activity. I'll be glad for your help when you come."

Mary chuckled. "We can't wait to get there. In fact, your father is taking a couple of extra days off so we can stay longer. Now that the trial is almost over, he's anxious to get away." She released her daughter and turned to open the door to the house then faced Abby again. "I wish I didn't have that big charity luncheon on Wednesday, or I'd come early and go to the activity with you. But you'll do fine Wednesday night; you just take good care of yourself until we get there."

Abby laughed. "You know I will. I'll see you next weekend. Give Dad a hug for me, and good luck with your charity luncheon." She gave her mother another quick hug and then walked back to her car. As she was getting in the car, her mother called to her. "Just a minute, Abby. I almost forgot that I put together some family stories on the St. George Temple for you. I'll just run and get them and you can take them back with you instead of my emailing them."

Mary emerged from the house again, carrying a large brown envelope. "I've put them in here for you," she said, handing the envelope to Abby through the open window.

"Thanks, Mom," Abby said as she placed it on the seat. "I'll call you Sunday when I get home."

Returning to the condo, Abby sorted through her closet for something to wear, aware that she could be home for good in a few weeks. She found herself thinking about Blake and the evening they had spent together after Megan's fall. She sighed as she thought of the differences between him and Scott. They were both professional men, well-respected in their chosen occupations. Scott was every bit the product of his privileged upbringing. He loved the good life and all that it entailed. He loved the arts, good food and wine, and his close personal friends were those that belonged to the same life of privilege that he enjoyed. Though particular about his leisure activities, Scott was not snobbish, but generous with his good opinion and his resources. Abby knew he had a good heart. His environment and home life was similar to hers in many ways, and she felt comfortable with their circle of friends and activities and the life he could offer her.

Blake, on the other hand, was a man who was as happy eating at the local café as he would have been having dinner at a gourmet restaurant. He loved a large variety of music, but she secretly thought he preferred the old ballads and folk songs. Megan had mentioned he played the guitar and had sung with a group before his mission. She knew he loved the outdoors and horseback riding. Blake was also a deeply spiritual man, governing his life by what he knew was right. She recognized that he, too, was very generous with his resources, both time and money. Again she thought, *They are both good men.*

As she was bringing out her golf clubs from the entry closet, the doorbell rang. Quickly she opened it to admit Scott.

"Hi, Abby. Ready to go?" he asked. He reached for her clubs.

"You bet! I'm looking forward to it," she replied, picking up her jacket.

Scott put the clubs in the trunk then helped Abby into the car. "I've made a reservation for three o'clock at the club, so we'll have to hurry to make it."

As he drove, Scott glanced over at her. Satisfaction and relief washed over him at having Abby back with him, if only for a short time. He wanted to question her about the doctor who had been spending so much time with her in St. George, but he reminded himself to just enjoy the time they had together. He wanted Abby to have only positive feelings about this weekend.

At the clubhouse they rented a cart and loaded their bags. The weather was perfect as they wound their way to the course.

When they reached the fairway, Scott gestured to Abby to go first. "Do I need to give you a handicap?" he laughingly suggested, aware they were both competitive players. "I bet I've played more times than you this past month."

"You just stand out of my way, mister, and I'll show you who needs the handicap," Abby retorted, and stepping forward she raised her driver and swung. They both watched as the ball sailed in a straight line toward the flag.

He gave a soft whistle as he stepped up to tee off. "Are you sure that you haven't spent your time playing golf instead of packing?" Scott followed through with his drive, his ball landing a few yards in front of Abby's.

As they continued playing through the various holes, laughing and egging each other on, Abby was reminded of all the common interests she shared with Scott; so why was she hesitating to marry him?

Standing on the green at the eighteenth hole, she watched as Scott studied the distance and angle for his shot. So far they were tied, so this hole would determine who won the game. She held her breath as Scott stepped up to the ball and positioned his putter for the shot. Instead of going into the hole, the ball stopped at the rim. She laughed gleefully as he tapped the ball into the hole.

"I guess I'm not as out of practice as I thought," she said. "I think you owe me one hot fudge sundae."

Scott, picking his ball up out of the hole, laughed as well. "I'm sorry, Abby, but you were just too big of a distraction for me today. I had a hard time concentrating on my game with you so near me. And," he continued, "it's written in the official golf rules that the winner has to give the loser a kiss."

She laughed again. "I haven't seen that version of the rules yet, but I guess in the name of good sportsmanship . . . " She reached up and gave him a quick kiss.

"Hey, that's not a real kiss," he replied, reaching for her again.

"Sorry," she replied, "but I now remember reading that rule, and it says that one quick kiss is all that's required."

He laughed and glanced at his watch. "Well, I'll collect my due later this evening. I guess we'd better go if we're going to have time to get ready for tonight."

Back at the condo, Abby put her things away and walked to the bathroom to start the water running in the tub. Scenting the water generously with her favorite lily of the valley fragrance, she allowed herself time for a good soak. The warm water felt wonderful. Abby sighed contentedly. Her time home had been well-used thus far. Abby mulled over the events of the day and her mother's counsel. Eventually her thoughts turned to the lovely gown she had picked out with her mother that morning. Abby savored the warm, aromatic water for a few more moments then reluctantly pulled the plug on the drain. She was just giving herself a final check in the mirror when Scott arrived to pick her up. When she opened the door, his eyes swept over her, admiration showing in his look.

"Wow," he exclaimed, "you look absolutely stunning tonight, Abby. What a dress!"

"Thanks, Scott." How handsome he looked in his tux! The dark black of the suit brought out his blond good looks. "You're pretty stunning yourself."

"I'm going to be the envy of every man there tonight," he said, smiling as he helped her on with her coat.

Mr. and Mrs. George Ross lived in a large estate set on five acres of land located in Boulder, Colorado. After introducing her to their hosts, Scott led Abby into the formal living room. The floor-to-ceiling windows of the room looked out on the awe-inspiring Rocky Mountains, the peaks of the majestic mountains still covered with snow. Abby caught her breath at the beauty of the scene in front of her.

"It's such a beautiful setting for a house, isn't it, Scott," she said.

"Someday—I promise, Abby—I'll build you a home that will equal this one," he said, squeezing her hand.

"I don't need a big house like this one, but I love a stunning view," Abby answered. "The mountains are so beautiful."

Abby glanced around and was pleased to see several people that she knew, and she and Scott were soon absorbed into a group of friends.

Pre-dinner drinks were being handed around, and as the tray was passed, Scott handed her a glass of white wine. Abby shook her head. "May I have a glass of ginger ale or juice, please?" she asked. Scott took a glass of wine for himself and handed Abby a glass of orange juice, his eyebrows raised at her choice.

She enjoyed the dinner and the evening, but as the conversation flowed around her, Abby felt anew the changes that she was making in her life. The wealth and comfort this evening offered were no longer major goals for her; she now found happiness in many simpler experiences. She found herself thinking of her time in St. George and of the friendships she had renewed. Yes, her life had definitely changed.

She was silent on the drive back to her condo. Scott glanced over at her. "Abby, you haven't said a word since we left the Rosses'. What are you thinking about?"

She turned and smiled at him. "I'm fine, Scott. I'm just thinking about what a nice evening this has been. I'm so glad I was here to go with you. I really have missed my life here, and I enjoyed today so much."

Scott turned the car into Abby's driveway and shut off the motor. "Can I come in for a few minutes?" he asked.

"Of course," she answered. He walked her to the door and waited while she let them both into the condo. Closing the door after him, she slipped off her coat and hung it in the front closet. He settled himself on the sofa and patted the seat beside him. "Come and sit down, Abby, and let's talk."

She let him take her hand and draw her down beside him. "It's been a good weekend, Scott, and I know we really needed this time together."

He drew her head to his shoulder and put his arm around her. "I hate the thought of you going back. When are you going to be home for good?"

"It's only going to be another few weeks. You know Mom and Dad are coming next weekend for Easter, so that will help a lot. It won't be long now."

"You keep talking about the changes you are making in your life, Abby, and it scares me a lot. Am I going to be one of your changes? Are your feelings for me altering?"

Abby raised her head from his shoulder and turned to face him. "Scott, I've told you the ways I'm changing several times. I've found my testimony in my church again, and I love being part of it. The changes

I'm making in my life are good ones, and I will be a better person for them—a better wife and mother."

"You haven't answered my question, Abby," Scott told her, his face deepening with worry. "Are your feelings toward me changing? I still love you as much as ever and want to marry you."

Abby's eyes dropped as she pondered what to say. "If I'm honest with you, Scott, there are times I feel uncertain about what our life together would be like. I care so much for you, and we've had a lot of fun together this weekend. You're very good to me."

"Then what's the problem? Since we're talking through things, I'll admit I'm increasingly nervous about Blake Matthews being around you so much. Is he the reason for your concerns about me? Are you falling for him?" He looked at her intently.

Abby stood up and walked around the room then sat down again next to him. "I like Blake, and he's been very good to help me, but part of the problem is that I just don't know whether I want to marry outside of my faith," she said quietly. "Megan and Ryan have been a good example for me of what it means for a husband and wife to both have the same spiritual goals."

Scott leaned over and took both her hands in his. "Abby, I've told you before that I haven't felt the need for any church in my life, but you know I believe in God. I'll not interfere in your desire to attend church. I'll even go occasionally with you when I can. I can't see how this should be a problem for us. We can work anything out together. If it takes making changes in my life to keep you, I'm willing to consider it rather than lose you."

She laid her head on his shoulder. "I'm sorry, Scott. I just wish life weren't so complicated."

"You're the one making it complicated, Abby." Scott's gentle touch offset the slight frustration in his voice. "If we love each other enough, everything else can be worked out later."

She sighed deeply and stood up. "I know what you're saying, Scott, but I find myself wondering if we need to give ourselves a little more time to be sure we both want the same things out of our marriage." Abby looked down at her watch. "It's late, and I still have a few things left to do tonight." Scott stood as well and drew her into his arms. "I just know I love you very much and miss you every second you're not with me. I don't feel I need more time, Abby. I'm sure now that we could be very happy."

She tightened her arms around him and felt his lips touch hers, first softly and then more earnestly. Finally, she raised her head and looked at him. "Oh, Scott, what am I going to do? I'm glad we've had this weekend, and I've enjoyed being home."

"That's because you've been where you should be," he said. "As far as what you should do, just come back to me as quickly as you can, and we'll address those issues you're concerned about."

Abby paused, considering his words. *Maybe he's right, that I'm overanalyzing everything, that things will be different when I'm back.* She raised her head and smiled at him. "You're right, Scott. I'll be back soon, and then we'll have the time to really talk things through."

She gave him a final hug then walked him to the door and watched as he got in his car and drove away.

***

1 June 1845

Today was my wedding day. How different it was from what I had planned my entire life, and how I wished that we could have married before leaving home! As we stood in front of Captain Sanders to repeat our vows, I thought how I had visualized standing in front of my father, his voice somber as he performed the ceremony. I thought I would have been married in a beautiful new dress, which Mother would have made for me, and we would have shared hours of companionship as we prepared the food and the house for the wedding. Instead, I was married in my brown merino traveling dress, a little wrinkled after the long hours of travel it had endured. For a festive touch, Abigail sewed green ribbons on my old bonnet, and Mrs. Fisher gave me a fresh linen handkerchief to hold. I thought also of how the old church at home would have been filled with family and friends, all wishing us well. There would have been bouquets of wildflowers gathered from the fields spread around the church, their fragrance spicy and sweet and filling the chapel with beauty. The organ would have swelled with music, adding the richness of song to the occasion. But instead I was married with the backdrop of the blue Irish Sea, the waves rocking the ship gently and the only sound that of the gulls' constant harsh cries as they flew overhead. I felt such an ache in my heart without Mother and Father, but as Tom took my hand, overwhelming joy flooded my soul from knowing that I was now truly his and that we are one. I felt, also, the blessing of his family at our sides. I now belong to a family with brothers and sisters; his dear mother and father will now be mine.

Before we left Liverpool, Tom and I had our photograph taken, and it is another keepsake that I have placed in my little oak box of memories.

It felt so peaceful tonight to say my prayers with Tom at my side. For the first time since leaving home, I am beginning to look ahead with excitement to my new life.

Chapter 15

The flight back to St. George late Sunday morning was uneventful. Abby had spent a restless night after Scott left pondering their last conversation, and she had finally resolved not to spend as much time with Blake. She dozed most of the way and was glad when they touched down at the airport. When she unlocked the door and stepped inside, the house seemed to welcome her back. She carried her suitcase and briefcase up to her bedroom then returned to the kitchen. After calls to her Mother and Scott, she spent the rest of the evening reviewing some of the things she had learned about the St. George temple.

Monday evening after dinner, Abby gathered together her materials for the Relief Society activity and began laying out what she wanted to say. She was amazed at the amount of information she had collected and spent the next couple of hours trying to decide what to use. She opened the envelope her Mother had given her on Saturday and scanned through these as well. At eleven o'clock she gathered up her papers, placed them in a folder, and went upstairs to bed.

* * *

Abby wasn't able to return to her notes until Tuesday evening. As she reviewed them, she felt a desire to go to the visitors' center at the temple and was preparing to leave when her phone rang.

"Abby, it's Blake. Just wanted to make sure you'd returned safely. Were you able to complete your business obligations?"

Abby smiled, glad to hear Blake's voice on the other end of the line. "Everything went fine with the closing, and it was so good to be home again, if only for the weekend. What about you, did you have a good weekend?" she asked.

"I kept pretty busy but missed seeing you on Sunday. Abby, one of the reasons I called was to see if I could come by and see you tonight. Or we could go for another short ride."

"I'm sorry, Blake, I'm not going to be here," Abby said. "I'm just getting ready to go to the visitors' center at the temple. Tomorrow night I'm giving a presentation for a Relief Society activity on the building of the St. George temple. I've wanted to see the center, and I guess now would be as good a time as any to go."

"Would you like company, or is this something you would rather do on your own?" Blake asked.

She paused a few seconds, considering. "Actually, if you have the time, I think I would enjoy having someone with me. Can you meet me there in thirty minutes, or is that rushing you?"

Blake sounded enthusiastic as he replied, "I can meet you there, or I would be glad to pick you up."

"I have to make a quick stop on the way, so let's meet at the center. Shall we say seven, in the lobby?"

"Seven's fine. I'll enjoy going. I think it's been about a year since I was there as well. See you shortly."

After hanging up, Abby sat for a few minutes, her heart beating with anticipation at seeing Blake again. So much for her resolve. Last weekend she had enjoyed her time with Scott and thought she could hold firm with her resolve regarding Blake. But all it took was hearing his voice, and she found herself eager to see him again. Finally, with a shrug of her shoulders, she gathered up her purse and left the house.

After a quick stop at the cleaner's, she drove toward the temple. Abby found a parking place in front of the visitors' center and walked inside, feeling a little nervous. The first person she saw was Blake. He was standing in the reception area waiting for her, and her heart skipped a beat when he smiled at her and came forward. "Shall we take the tour from the missionaries first? Then we can view the films we want to see," he said.

"That sounds fine with me." She looked about her with interest, already feeling the sweet spirit that filled the building.

Sister Espinoza, a young missionary from Brazil, came forward to greet them. Abby and Blake seated themselves where she indicated and, in faltering English, she introduced herself and told where she was from. Though the missionary's language was limited, Abby had no difficulty understanding the Spirit that testified of her words as she guided them through the center. Abby was impressed with the presentations on the family and thought of Scott. She knew now she wanted more in her life, a richer base, and if she married him she could only hope that he would be willing to make changes in his life as well.

When they reached the area where the Christus was situated, Sister Espinoza left them to sit and ponder for a few minutes while soft music played. The Christus was beautiful. It stood about fifteen feet high on a pedestal and was sculpted from white marble. Christ stood with His hands outstretched toward them, the prints of the nails visible in His palms, compassion and love showing in His face. Tears filled Abby's eyes as she gazed toward the statue, and Blake reached over and took her hand. A feeling of peace and love entered her heart along with a determination to continue on the spiritual path she had started down. She glanced over at Blake to find him watching her, tenderness in his eyes. When the music was finished and the first part of the tour was completed, Sister Espinoza shared her testimony. As Abby listened, a warm feeling enveloped her as the Spirit confirmed the truth of what she had heard and seen.

They finished their tour by viewing a film called *The Testaments*. Once again, Abby found her eyes flooded with tears as the message of the film resonated with her heart and soul. She watched the Savior's appearance to the people in the Americas after His resurrection and found her body consumed with love for this beloved older Brother who had sacrificed Himself for her. She fumbled through her purse for a dry tissue to wipe her streaming eyes. Blake put his arm lightly around her and handed her his handkerchief. She gave him a tearful smile in return. As the lights came on in the theater at the end of the film, another sister missionary bore her testimony. Then they stood to leave, Abby still wiping her eyes. She winced at the thought of what a mess her face must look, her eyes and nose red from crying. They thanked their guide for the tour and walked outside.

Abby looked at the wet handkerchief she held and then at Blake. "I must look dreadful. I've cried all my makeup off, and I'm sure my eyes are red, but I'm glad you came with me tonight, Blake. I enjoyed the tour so much."

He smiled at her tenderly. "I'm glad I came too. And, Abby, you always look beautiful to me. Didn't you notice me wiping my eyes during the movie? That particular film is overpowering. It would take a hard spirit to sit through it and not be touched by its message."

"Thanks, Blake. You make me feel better, but I wish I could have seen you with tears in your eyes. You always seem so strong to me."

"Believe me, Abby, during difficult times in my life, I've shed my bucket of tears." He knew now that if he were not able to keep her here with him, he would again fill that bucket several times.

She flashed him a grateful smile then looked at her watch and thrust the handkerchief in her purse. "I'll wash this and get it back to you. I guess I'd better start for home. I need to go over my presentation again now that I've been to the center." She reached her hand out for his, and Blake held it gently as he walked her to her car.

After helping her inside, he leaned on the doorframe before closing the door. "Thanks again, Abby. Good luck tomorrow night."

When Abby arrived home, she pulled out the folder on her presentation, tried to concentrate, and realized she was too emotionally spent to do any work on it that night. She left her papers on the table, turned her laptop off, and went upstairs to prepare for bed. Later, kneeling by the side of her bed for her evening prayer, Abby was overwhelmed with the love she had felt for her Savior. She stayed on her knees, trying to find the words that would express her thankful heart.

***

Wednesday morning, Abby put the final touches on her talk, including the stories of her ancestors building the temple, their sacrifices, and the hardships they had endured. She connected it to the temple that now stood as a beautiful beacon to welcome those worthy to enter its doors. She added the final note, realizing that it applied especially to her, that if those who were worthy to attend did not do so faithfully, then the sacrifices that had been made by so many would be wasted in their behalf.

Later that evening as Abby prepared for the activity, she felt butterflies in her stomach and tried to calm them. She told herself that she was used to being in front of people and giving presentations. The truth was, she had never attended an evening Relief Society meeting and wasn't sure just what to expect. She knelt to ask for Heavenly Father's help to strengthen her weakness and afterward felt a little calmer. As she was preparing to leave, a knock came at her door, and she found Agnes standing on the porch.

"Would you mind, dear, if I rode with you tonight for the activity? My car seems to be acting up again."

Abby smiled. She was sure Agnes had sensed her need to have someone with her. Taking Agnes's arm, she walked with her to the car. "Believe me, I'm glad for the support tonight. I don't know why I'm so nervous; I'm just grateful you're with me."

"You'll do fine, dear," Agnes said, patting her hand.

When Abby entered the Relief Society room, she was glad to have Agnes at her side. Sister Richardson greeted them at the door. "I'm so glad to see you, Sister Peters and Sister Givens. We'll start with a prayer and a short lesson then we'll turn the time over to you."

Once again, Abby felt Agnes lead her to the front row and, sighing, thought she should be used to it by now. Oh well, maybe tonight was a good time to sit at the front. The room slowly filled, and many of the ladies made a point of coming by to greet her. Gradually, she found herself relaxing and feeling the warmth of fellowship in the room.

When it came time for her turn, she gathered up her talk, along with a few special pictures she had found on the building of the temple, and walked to the front of the class, placing her papers on the small pulpit in front of her. Abby placed the early pictures of the temple during construction on one side of the board then hung a beautiful picture of the temple as it now stood on the other side. Taking a deep breath, she began her talk.

As she spoke she felt the words and impressions she should share flood her mind. She told how the foundation of the temple was finally built then went on to talk about Tom and Dorothy Fisher. She relayed how hard life had been here in the desert and the great sacrifices that had been made in building the temple. This was the first temple to be constructed in Utah, and after it was dedicated on April 6, 1877, the temple work for all the Saints in the entire church was done here in St. George until the Logan temple was dedicated seven years later. Abby's voice carried emotions of love and appreciation for the sacrifices that she had learned about as she had prepared and studied. Finally, glancing at the clock on the side wall, she noticed her time was up and completed with her statement of how she had now set a goal to be able to enter the temple and receive the covenants and blessings that would enrich her life. She sat down, her hands trembling.

Agnes reached over and took hold of her hands, tears in her eyes. "That was beautiful, dear. You are so much like your grandmother; she would have been so proud of you tonight." Abby flashed her a grateful smile as her heart started to calm down.

After the closing prayer and a blessing on the refreshments, Abby found herself surrounded by sisters thanking her for sharing the stories of her ancestors with them.

That night as Abby said her prayers, she gave heartfelt thanks for the opportunity she had been given. She knew that tonight had been another turning point in her life, a life in which she wanted the temple to play an important part. As she lay in bed and thought over the evening, she acknowledged that already her heart and life were full of new treasures that would bless her life as long as she continued her spiritual journey.

***

5 June 1845

Four days ago I left England and everything that I love there to travel across the seas to Zion. I stood at the ship's rail and watched as the soft and gentle green hills receded from my vision. With each beat, my heart seemed to whisper "home" to me, and my eyes filled with the tears I had not permitted myself to shed since leaving my home and beloved parents.

Now on this fourth day at sea, my world has shrunk to the size of the ship, surrounded by endless water. Our accommodations are very small, but the Saints on board are joyous to be on their way. I have found that I am a good sailor, being unaffected by the rocking and heaving of the ship. However, many are sick, among them Susan and Father Fisher. Mother Fisher has been busy trying to administer to the needs of those who are ill, and her soothing hands and herbs have comforted many. Tom is also a good sailor, and we have tried to help those who are suffering as well.

England and home now seem a dream to me, and yet I find myself at different hours of the day picturing what Father and Mother must be doing, and the ache of my parting from them once again floods my spirit with anguish. Our journey across the ocean should take us approximately six weeks before we land in New Orleans, Louisiana, and then we will travel by steamship to Nauvoo.

Chapter 16

Friday evening, Abby arrived early at the same small airport in St. George that she had flown out of last weekend. The airport was located on a bluff on the west side of town, and the views from the windows of the building were fantastic. It was a little after eight-thirty in the evening, and the sun was just setting. As she stood at the window, watching for her parents' plane, she could see the city of St. George set out below her, like a jewel in the desert. The setting sun cast its brilliant evening rays against the surrounding bluffs, highlighting them into a golden-orange blaze of fire.

She tapped her toe restlessly as she waited, anxious to see her parents again, especially her father since she had missed seeing him last weekend in Denver. Her mother had called yesterday morning to say that her father was definitely taking Monday off as well, and Abby was glad to have the extra time with them. She was excited to show them what she had accomplished and also wanted to talk to them about keeping the house. Impatiently, she glanced at her watch, and finally the announcement came over the intercom that her parents' plane was landing. She watched as the plane came into view and then as the passengers began departing onto the tarmac. Finally she saw them coming down the steps of the plane. Her father was a tall and distinguished-looking man, his head of thick brown hair mixed with strands of gray. He was holding her mother's hand as they walked across the tarmac. Abby moved to a place where they could see her as they entered the building, and a few minutes later found herself enfolded in their arms.

"How was the flight?" Abby asked. "These small planes can feel the turbulence if there are strong winds. Oh, Mom and Dad, I'm so glad you've come and that we can spend Easter together."

"The flight was fine—quiet most of the way," her father replied then stood back to study his daughter. "You look wonderful. I take it the new suntan isn't the result of hours on the golf course," he joked.

"She does look nice, though, doesn't she," Mary confirmed.

"Thanks, you two," Abby rejoined. "Are there any more bags, or is this all?" she asked, pointing to their two small suitcases.

"This is it," her father replied and reached down to pick up his and Mary's bags.

Abby led the way out of the airport and to her car. As they began the descent down the road from the airport, her mother looked out the window and drew a deep breath. "David, look at the clearness of the air and how beautiful the town is."

"It is something," he said. "And look at the new construction. This place is really growing."

"You bet it is," Abby responded, turning the car onto Bluff Street. "It's exciting to see all that's happening. The real estate market is still pretty strong. Every once in a while I find myself wanting to be part of this new growth."

Her father, sitting in the front seat beside her, turned and studied her face. "So, are you having second thoughts about coming back to Denver?"

She thought for a few seconds before answering lightly. "No, I don't think so at this point, but let's leave that subject for later. Right now I just want to enjoy seeing you again."

A few minutes later they turned into the driveway of the old home. Abby unlocked the front door and turned on the outside and entry lights then returned to help carry in the luggage. "I've made up the bed in Grandmother's room for you, so I hope that's all right," she said as she followed her parents into the house.

Abby noticed her mother glancing at the neat row of boxes in the living room and then saw her shoulders straighten with determination as she continued down the hall to the bedroom. As Abby placed her mother's small case on the bed, she looked over at her mother, who was still standing in the doorway. Abby felt her heart constrict as she saw the silent tears falling from her mother's eyes as she looked around the room. David and Abby both put an arm around Mary and guided her to the bed, where they helped her sit down.

"I'm sorry," Mary said, "I didn't think it would affect me so much. But it's like having to face her death all over again." David put his arm around his wife and handed her his handkerchief.

"I know, Mom," Abby said quietly. "I have had the same feelings. I don't know how I could have stood it without Blake's and Agnes Givens's help. It's been so difficult going through her personal belongings and packing them away. It makes everything seem so final." Abby paused to reflect before continuing. "But you know, there is a real feeling of Grandmother and Grandfather in this house, a feeling of peace and love."

Mary looked at her daughter through her tears. "I know, dear, I feel it too." She blew her nose and gave her eyes a final wipe with the handkerchief. "Well," she said shakily, "let me put a few things away, and then your father and I will meet you in the kitchen. Is there any chance of having something to eat? We really didn't have much of a dinner tonight."

Abby stood up. "Actually, I have some plates of fresh fruit, veggies, and cheese and crackers ready for you. I knew you would probably be hungry. I'll just set them out, so take all the time you need."

After Abby left the room, David stood up and pulled Mary to her feet, still holding her hands. "I'm glad we're going to have a few days here, Mary. You need time to savor the memories and have a chance to help, too. It's a way of adding closure, a chance to do some final things for your mother."

At his statement, new tears threatened once more, but Mary threw back her shoulders. "You're right; David, I'm so glad you were able to come with me. Our going back to church has given me some strength and comfort, and," she waved her hand around the empty bedroom, "without it, this would have been so much harder for me."

They quickly unpacked their small suitcases then made their way to the kitchen, where Abby had just finished setting out a plate of cheese and crackers. While they ate, Abby updated her parents on the strides she had made in the cleaning and packing process.

"I can't wait for you to see the backyard. Blake," at his name, she found herself smiling, "has helped me a lot, and it looks so nice." Her father noticed Abby's smile as she pronounced Blake's name and looked over at Mary with raised brows. "I haven't done anything with Grandmother's clothing and jewelry, Mom, because I thought you should be the one to decide what to do with them." Looking around the kitchen, she went on. "I haven't done any real packing in here, since I'm still using it every day. Plus, I don't know what you want to do with everything. It seems like a waste of time to pack things and take them back to Denver if you don't want them. We could just take them to the Deseret Industries here in town."

Her father gave her a big smile. "Good thinking, Abby. I'm proud of you and thankful for all you've done. It will save us a lot of time."

Mary smothered a yawn. A glance at the clock told her that it was already after ten. She picked up her plate and walked to the sink. "I'll help clean up, and then let's all go to bed."

"Good idea," David seconded, picking up the glasses and placing them on the countertop. Abby wrapped the fruit and vegetables, placed them in the refrigerator, then wiped down the table and counters.

"You go ahead. I'll just put these in the dishwasher, and then I'm off to bed as well." Abby gave her parents a final hug and watched as they left the room, thankful to have them with her. There was so much to show them and tell them about in the next few days. Plus, she was hoping to convince them not to sell the home. She gave one last swipe with the dishcloth before rinsing it and hanging it up to dry. Giving a final glance around the room, she turned out the lights and went up to her room.

***

Saturday morning after breakfast, they took a tour of the home so Abby could show her parents what she had done in the last few weeks and what still needed attention. In the study, she pointed out the boxes that David needed to sort through and the boxes of family history her grandmother had worked on for many years. These boxes she had left unsealed so her mother could go through them while she was here if she wanted to. As they went from room to room, she pointed out the beautiful aspects of the old house with the idea still firmly in her mind of trying to persuade her parents to keep the house. Abby reminded them of how beautiful the wood floors and the staircase were that Tom Fisher had built and laid. As she talked, Abby noticed her mother lovingly running her hands over the staircase railing and her father's appraising look as he contemplated the old lighting fixtures and the claw-footed tub in the bathroom.

"I don't know, Mary, but I think we should reconsider selling," David said. "There's not another home like this in the world. Your family has lived here for generations, and it seems a shame for us to end that legacy."

They were standing in the dining room, and Mary was fingering the china that still lined the old hutch and sideboard. "I remember we always used this for special dinners. My mother and grandmother told me stories of this china, how Tom and Dorothy Fisher gave it to their daughter, MaryAnne, on her wedding day to Daniel Sayer. It's remarkable that only one cup has been broken in all that time." Turning to face her husband, she asked wistfully, "Do you really think we should keep the house, David? We could use it for holidays and vacations. Someday you will be retiring, and we can spend more time here, and," she laughed, "just think, St. George is full of golf courses."

Noticing the look on his wife's face, David grinned back. "I think a very positive case can be made for keeping it. We'll think about it this weekend and make a decision before we leave for home."

Abby breathed a sigh of relief. This was going to be easier than she'd hoped. "Okay, we've seen the inside. Now let me show you what Blake and I have accomplished in the backyard." They walked through the kitchen to the back door and stepped out onto the patio.

It was a beautiful spring day, the cloudless sky a deep, intense blue. A slight breeze lazily blew, its soft sigh echoing through the trees and bushes and releasing the intoxicating fragrance of the last of the spring hyacinths and lilacs. The flower gardens were full of color: the bright red of trumpeter tulips; the yellow of daffodils; and the pink, lavender, and white of spring-colored tulips, their buds just starting to open. Smaller bushes of desert lilac added a dash of bright color with their deep purple blossoms. Abby had fertilized the lawns, and their deep green coats witnessed with pride of the care they'd received. Blake had managed to get the waterfall running, and the musical sounds of the water as it cascaded and splashed merrily into the small pond gave the yard a feeling of peace and serenity.

Mary gave a sigh of pure bliss. David, looking around, was clearly impressed. "You *have* been busy. When we were here for the funeral, I remember thinking of all the work that would need to be done. It's beautiful, Abby. You've done a terrific job."

"Oh, Abby," Mary exclaimed. "Mother would be so proud of you. Her flower gardens were always her pride and joy, and she loved spending hours out here. I swear she used to talk to them, calling them her 'little beauties.' I think you must have inherited her green thumb."

"It has been a lot of work," Abby admitted, "but I've loved working outside. It's been emotionally healing, working in the soil and the sunshine."

"You say Blake Matthews helped you with the heavy work?" David asked.

"He's been so good to help; he's spent long hours pruning and trimming and then hauling away all the junk. And Dad, he did offer to help while you're here, if we need him. Frankly, I don't know what I would have done without him."

David glanced over at his wife thoughtfully. "Does this mean he is becoming more than a friend?" he questioned, looking at Abby closely.

Abby sat down on a lawn chair, thinking how best to answer. "Truthfully, Dad, I don't know. Blake is a very good man, and he has made me question some of the things I thought were important. He's strong in his faith, and it spills over in the way he treats others. He's also very considerate and kind, and I'm sure this is why Grandmother adored him."

Her father dragged a chair next to her and sat down as well. "Does Scott know about Blake? I've felt some worry in his voice when he talks about you, but he hasn't said anything to me about what's going on. I attributed a lot of his nervousness to the trial. You know, Abby, he did show me the engagement ring he had bought to give you, and I've wondered since then if there's a problem because, obviously, you're not wearing it."

"I still have deep feelings for Scott, but I've also told him I'm changing in many ways, such as going back to church and reading my scriptures. And I've told him I'm starting to have doubts about whether I want to marry someone outside of the temple." She hesitated for a minute before going on. "It's been frustrating that Scott doesn't seem to understand," she motioned at the yard, "just all I've had to do and how emotionally difficult it has been for me to pack up this house of memories. And yes, he's questioned me quite a lot about Blake. But on the other hand, I really enjoyed spending time with him last weekend; I've missed him a lot. We have so many things in common, and we have such a good time when we're together. We did talk some about my activity in the church, but I need to ask myself about what I want spiritually in my marriage partner before committing myself to anyone."

"Don't worry, David," Mary said, sitting down as well. "Abby's a very responsible young woman, and marriage is a big step. I'm sure she'll consider her situation well before making any decisions." She gave the yard one final look. "Let's go back inside and decide where to start and how much we want to do if we're not going to sell."

They trooped back inside to the living room. Abby stopped long enough in the kitchen to pick up the list of jobs she had made. "Grandmother's clothing and jewelry, the kitchen, and the storage room still need to be packed," she said, scanning her list. "By the way, we are celebrating Easter Sunday tomorrow by going to church and having an Easter dinner, aren't we?"

"You bet." David looked fondly at his wife and daughter. "I can't wait to take my two favorite women to church with me. Besides, it will give me a chance to check out this Blake Matthews and see him as someone other than just Elizabeth's doctor," he said, looking at Abby with a twinkle in his eye. "In fact, Mary, I think we should invite him to Easter dinner tomorrow. I'm sure if he has no family here that holidays are probably lonely for him."

"I think that's a very good idea," Mary said. "Abby, why don't you call and invite him to come for dinner, let's say around four in the afternoon."

Abby looked at her parents, speechless. There they sat with innocent smiles on their faces. But she thought they had a point. Blake would probably be alone for Easter, and it would be a good chance for her parents to be around him for a few hours. "Okay, I'll call and invite him. But I'm also going to invite Agnes Givens from next door. She has been so good to me, and I bet she'll be alone as well."

"Fine," Mary said. "Why don't you go and call them so we'll know how many are coming, and your father and I will go through the house again and decide what we want to accomplish today."

Abby, giving a last look at her parents, sighed, and went up to her room for her purse. She found the card Blake had given her and pulled out her phone. She looked at the card for a few seconds before taking a deep breath and punching in his number. She almost hoped he wouldn't be home and she could just leave a message. But after the second ring, she heard his voice.

"This is Abby, Blake." Taking a deep breath, she continued. "My parents arrived last night and are so grateful for all your hard work. They would like a chance to thank you in person, so we'd like to invite you for Easter dinner tomorrow, say at four?"

Once again she held her breath, waiting for his answer. "I'd enjoy that, Abby," Blake said cheerfully. "That's kind of your parents to think of me, and I'd enjoy seeing them again. I'll admit holidays are usually pretty lonely, so it will be nice to have special people to spend it with. And," he laughed, "it gives me a chance to spend more time with you."

She let out her breath, aware she was very glad he was coming. "Well, we'll see you tomorrow at four then, and I guess we'll see you at church as well."

"See you tomorrow, Abby," he concluded happily before hanging up.

Agnes was also delighted to be asked to dinner and offered to bring her homemade rolls. Abby was glad she had thought to invite her, and there was a lighter spring to her step as she headed back downstairs.

She heard her parents in the kitchen making sandwiches for lunch. They were laughing and talking together, and as she watched from beyond the door, David pulled Mary into his arms for a light kiss, and laughing, she pulled away. "Abby should be down any minute, David," she said.

"I can't help it," he replied. "The last two months I've been rediscovering just how much I love you, and I know a lot of it has to do with our commitment to put our lives back together spiritually. I see you now, Mary, as my eternal sweetheart, as I did years ago. I think I had forgotten that we were celestial soul mates. It's been good to put our lives back in the proper perspective again." Mary gave him a light kiss before turning around to finish the sandwiches.

Abby felt a lump form in her throat as she watched her parents and backed farther out into the hall. She wanted to give them a few minutes before entering the room. How happy and unified they seemed! This was the kind of marriage she wanted, and, she thought, another reason to be spiritually in tune with her marriage partner.

"I've talked to them both, and they each accepted, so we'd better plan on feeding five," she said, entering the room casually. "I bought a ham yesterday and thought we could make salad and deviled eggs to go with it. I'm not going to worry about calories tomorrow. Agnes said she would bring her homemade rolls. So, Mom, what do you think we should make for dessert?"

Mary thought for a few minutes. "Let's have strawberry shortcake. The strawberries are nice right now, and it won't be any work. We can just buy an angel food cake for the base."

"Sounds good to me," Abby said. "Did you two decide where we are going to start this afternoon?"

"I think I'd like to sort Mother's clothing and jewelry, and, Abby, I want you to help me. I'm sure there are pieces you would enjoy having as keepsakes, as well as some of her other things. We'll let your dad get started on the papers in the office."

They ate lunch on the patio and, after cleaning up, parted for their separate jobs. Mary and Abby started with the closet, pulling out the clothing and piling it on the bed. They laughed together at the styles of the older dresses stored at the back of the closet before packing them in a box. "Mom, I wonder if the community theater here in town would want to go through these and see if there is anything they could use for costumes," Abby said thoughtfully.

"That's a good idea, Abby. Let's pack them in a box and then call them. If they don't want the clothing, we'll take the box to the Deseret Industries."

Two hours later, they had exhausted the closet, and clothes and shoes were stacked neatly in boxes. Mary decided to keep a few of her mother's jackets, and Abby had selected a favorite robe she remembered her grandmother wearing, feeling that when she put it on it would be like having her grandmother's arms around her.

"Oh my," Mary said as she opened the jewelry armoire and looked at the array and amount of jewelry displayed in the drawers and sides of the chest. "This is going to take a while to sort. I didn't remember Mother having this much jewelry."

As she and Abby looked through the drawers and the organized rows of rings, earrings, brooches, and necklaces, they were impressed. Mary picked up an old gold chain with a locket and opened it. Inside was a picture of a young man with a moustache and a smiling young woman, her hair piled high on her head. She held it out to show Abby. "I remember Mother showing me this locket when I was a little girl and telling me that Dad gave it to her on their first anniversary. This is definitely something I will keep and treasure, and someday I'll pass this down to you."

Abby was busy looking through her grandmother's rings. Her grandmother had had beautiful hands and loved rings, so the drawer was full of them, with a variety of stones and settings, many of them very old. Among the pearl, amber, turquoise, and diamond rings, she found a simple gold band. The gold was tarnished, and the ring looked very old. Abby picked up the ring and handed it to her mother.

"Mom, was this Grandmother's wedding ring? I don't remember ever seeing her wear it."

Mary took the ring, turning it over in her hand. "No, I don't remember this ring at all. It does look old. I know it's not her wedding ring." She held it up to the light to look at the inside of the ring. "Look, Abby, there's an inscription." She studied it carefully. "I can just make out the letters *C-A-T*." She studied the inscription a few more minutes then shook her head. "I can't make out anymore letters. But I think Mother used to keep a magnifying glass in her nightstand for reading in bed." While she was speaking, she was busy looking through the small table. "Yes, here it is. Now let's see if we can make out more of the letters. Yes, it is definitely *C-A-T*, and the next letters are *H-E-R-I-N-E*. It says 'To Catherine.'" She handed the glass and the ring to Abby.

Abby took them and looked through the glass to study the inscription. A small shiver of excited anticipation ran through her body. "Mom, do you mind if I keep this ring? When I was going through the stack of old pictures, I found one with just the name of Catherine on it, and for some reason, I felt drawn to the girl in the photograph and wished I knew who she was. She looked a lot like Grandmother. This ring must have belonged to her." She gave a self-conscious laugh. "Sounds pretty silly, right?"

"No, dear, you keep it. I'd also like to see the picture sometime. It's strange that I don't remember my mother or grandmother ever talking about a Catherine being part of our family."

Abby smiled her thanks and placed the ring aside.

They spent another happy hour going through the jewelry, recognizing many of the pieces. Abby selected two additional rings, several pairs of earrings, and a necklace and bracelet to keep. She knew that wearing them would bring back happy memories of her grandmother.

They were only halfway through when David entered the room, running his hands through his hair. "You did a good job, Abby, sorting through the papers. I think I'll just take a few things home with me when I leave that I can peruse at leisure." Looking at the amount of jewelry laying around, he groaned. "Good heavens, aren't you two through? I'm hungry, and I think we should go out to dinner. I'd like to see a little of the town before we decide what we are going to do. Can this mess just be put back and finished later?"

Abby and her mother looked at each other and burst out laughing. "Isn't it just like a man to want his dinner on time," Mary said. "Okay, we'll put these back and clean up. How soon do you want to go?"

"How about in half an hour. That should give us a chance to wash up and change."

Once again they laughed but hurriedly put the jewelry away and rushed to their rooms to change for dinner. Locking the front door, Abby held out the car keys for her father. "Do you want to drive, Dad?"

He shook his head. "You drive, Abby. You know your way around. After dinner I'm going to want you to show me the town. Your mother and I have not explored St. George for quite a few years, and if we're thinking of keeping the house, we need to see just what this city offers."

Abby got in the driver's seat then turned to her parents. "So, what do you want for dinner? We have some good restaurants—what are you hungry for?"

"I don't know about you two," David responded, "but I want a good steak. I worked up a real appetite this afternoon."

Abby laughed and started the car. "So, Mom, you okay with going to the Outback? They have good steaks."

"Anything is fine with me," Mary replied. "I'll admit I'm hungry too."

After dinner, Abby drove her parents through many of the areas surrounding St. George, pointing out the new stores and houses that stretched from one bluff to the next.

"It doesn't have the shopping and restaurants that Denver offers, but it's definitely growing," David said, eyeing a large new hotel that was under construction.

"This is not the only part that's growing," Abby said. "If we get a chance, I'll have to take you for a drive to Hurricane. It's located a few miles north of here, and you should see the big homes and golf courses that are going in. That's also where Megan and Ryan live, and the Hurricane valley is really beautiful."

***

29 June 1845

It has been several weeks since I have had time to write in my journal. The weather has become calm and peaceful. Many that were sick are now able to come up on deck and enjoy the fresh air. At night after dinner, the Saints gather on deck and the sounds of the fiddle and harmonicas rend the night air. The music uplifts my spirit. It is humbling to me to walk around the deck with Tom and view the magnificence of the sky and the creations of my Father in Heaven. At night the stars are so bright and appear so close that it seems I only need to reach up and pluck one from the sky. I seem such a small part of His creations, but I know He loves me and is aware of my needs.

Two weeks ago a terrible storm battered our ship, and we feared we would all be drowned at sea. The mountainous waves flooded the decks, and the ship began to lean dangerously to the side. The winds were fierce, howling their fury, whipping all around us. The captain ordered us to stay below the upper decks for our safety and told the Saints to prepare for the worst. Fathers and mothers gathered their little children to them, and we huddled together in thick darkness, fearful and silent. As the ship continued its violent heaving I thought surely we would all be drowned in the depths of the sea. Suddenly, the deep silence was broken by one of the missionary elders returning home from England. In a strong, firm voice he commanded the storm and winds to cease and blessed the ship to stabilize and steady so we could continue our journey. As he finished his prayer, the turbulent heaving and tossing of the ship ceased, and the waters became steady and calm. Tears of gratitude stung my eyes as once again I realized I had witnessed the miracle of God's love for His children and the power of the priesthood.

The captain came below and said surely it was a miracle that the storm had dissipated and the sea calmed. Humbly we knelt on the wet floors and with grateful tears gave our thanks to Heavenly Father, who would see us to our new home safely.

Chapter 17

Abby awakened early Easter Sunday morning. As she lay in bed, she looked around her room with gratitude. She had not realized how much she had missed both her parents, and it felt good to know that in a few hours they were all going to church together. It had been a long time since they had done so. She smiled to herself, thinking of their meeting Blake. He was certainly different from Scott, but he was impressive in his own way. Getting out of bed, she knelt down. Her prayers had now become a habit, and she exulted in the peace it gave her day. After her prayer, she climbed back in bed and pulled her grandmother's scriptures toward her. This, too, had become a habit, and she eagerly turned to her place in the Book of Mormon and read for the next hour. Finally, glancing at the clock, she hastily climbed out of bed. She would need to hurry to be ready in time. After taking a quick shower, she did her hair and makeup and then pulled on the floral skirt and sweater.

Entering the kitchen, Abby found her parents already sitting at the table with toast, cereal, and juice in front of them. Sitting down, she saw they were gazing at the bay window view of majestic Pine Valley Mountain with a few clouds flitting across its face.

"How beautiful it is," Mary said with a sigh. "So many memories keep surfacing. When we came for the funeral there were so many people around, so much pressure not to let myself think of the past so I could cope with everything that had to be done. But now my mind feels crowded with memories everywhere I look. I was so blessed to have such good parents." Brushing a few tears from her eyes, she arose and carried her bowl and glass to the sink, where she rinsed them and placed them in the dishwasher. "Are we going to pick up Agnes this morning?" she asked Abby.

"When I talked to her yesterday, she said she had her car back and didn't need a ride. Between you and me, Mom, I think her car has been fine since that first week. She just wanted to make sure I kept going. She is such a sweet lady." Abby grinned at her mother. "And last week she insisted we sit right next to Blake! Believe me, she loves involving herself with people."

Mary chuckled. "Well, it will be good to see her again and thank her for the love and support she has given you. I'm glad she's coming to dinner today. Come on, David, we need to leave in a few minutes."

David stood up and took his dishes to the sink. "I'm ready. I just need to put on my tie and suit coat. I'll get our scriptures." At the look on Abby's face, he looked sternly back at her. "And you, young lady, go get yours." Abby laughed as she ran upstairs to brush her teeth and put on lip gloss. Grabbing her scriptures and purse, she walked downstairs to where her mother and father were waiting for her. Seeing them there, Abby felt a lump come to her throat.

Abby was proud to introduce her parents to Bishop Lindsay, who was standing at the door, and then led them down to the front of the chapel, where Agnes Givens was sitting by herself. "Sorry," she whispered to her parents, "but I can't leave her here alone, and this is where she always sits." Her parents slid into the row after Abby, and Agnes leaned across Abby to shake Mary's and David's hands, a delighted smile on her face. "How good it is to see you again! I appreciate the invitation to dinner today. Holidays are always a little lonely with no family around. It's been such a delight for me, having Abby close by."

David took both her hands in his. "You've become part of our family, taking such good care of our daughter. We're glad you're coming for Easter dinner."

Abby, glancing around the chapel, noticed Blake come in and take a seat on the side. He spotted her and gave her a smile and a quick wink before turning to shake the hand of the man sitting next to him. She settled back in her seat and listened to the organ prelude music, aware of her parents sitting next to her. Her thoughts turned to the Atonement. Her heart filled with emotion as she thought how fitting it was that on this Easter morning, the celebration of the Atonement and Resurrection of the Savior, she now understood first-hand what the chance to repent and come back to Heavenly Father and Jesus Christ truly meant. He had prepared the way so she could be here with her beloved parents, who had also availed themselves of Christ's sacrifice. As the meeting commenced, Abby rejoiced in the hymns and sang the words about the empty tomb with grateful heart. As she partook of the sacrament, the words of the sacrament prayers held new meaning. She bowed her head and humbly covenanted to do all she could to make up for her years of inactivity. Raising her head, she looked over at her mother and noticed that she, too, had tears in her eyes and was holding David's hand. For just a second, Abby felt the whisper of a sigh, as if her grandparents, too, were aware of their beloved family attending church together on this beautiful Easter morning.

Many people stopped to greet Mary and David as they left the chapel. And when they finally entered the Relief Society room for Sunday School, Abby noticed that the only seats left were on the front row next to Blake. Self-consciously, she ushered her parents to the front and sat down. Blake gave her a smile then reached across with an outstretched hand to her parents as Abby introduced them. Mary took Blake's proffered hand and gave him a smile. David reached for Blake's hand as well, looking him over the entire time. "We're grateful for all the help you've been. Abby would have been lost without you."

"Somehow she'd have managed, but thanks. And thanks for inviting me to dinner today."

Abby introduced her parents to the class, and after the opening prayer, Blake rose to give the lesson. David sat back and watched him closely. From the way Abby acted whenever his name was mentioned, he thought they might be more involved than what Abby recognized, and he was determined to find out all he could about this young man before he left town. In spite of himself, he was impressed. Blake's sincerity and love of his subject showed in the way that he presented the lesson. After Sunday School, David made a point of shaking Blake's hand and telling him what a fine lesson he had given, and they left for priesthood meeting together.

Before Relief Society started, Sister Richardson rushed over to be introduced to Mary. After shaking her hand, she said, "I wish you could have been here for our activity Wednesday evening. Abby gave such a fine presentation on the St. George temple. She made us all feel what it must have been like to have lived here at that time, and I know we all left with a greater appreciation for the sacrifices and dedication of those pioneers who labored so diligently to fulfill the assignment that the Lord had given them."

"I wish I could have been here, as well," Mary returned with a smile, "but knowing Abby, I'm not surprised. She always puts her heart and soul into everything she does."

After returning home from church, Abby debated what clothing to change into and finally settled on dress slacks and a light blue sweater. Running downstairs, she found she was humming, and with a smile on her lips, she hurried to the kitchen.

Mary had changed her clothes as well and was studying the array of cookbooks in the pantry. "My goodness, I had forgotten there were so many." Pulling one from the shelf, she handed it to her daughter. "Look, Abby, this is an old pioneer cookbook. My, there must be some real treasures here."

"I know, Mom. I looked through many of them when I had to take a dessert to Megan's. Do we need to make Dad a snack to tide him over until dinner?" she asked.

Mary shook her head. "I made him a sandwich along with some of the fruit left over from last night, and he has settled himself on the patio to read." Reaching for an apron, she tied it around her waist and then handed one to Abby. "Shall we just make two salads? I think with the ham, deviled eggs, and the rolls Agnes is bringing, that should be ample."

"I agree. I thought maybe we could make a pasta salad and a fresh fruit salad and then do a plate of veggies."

Mary gave a laugh. "As usual, you have everything organized. So let's start the eggs boiling for the deviled eggs, and if we each do a salad, we'll have this finished in no time."

They chatted happily together as they chopped, mixed, and tossed, and in just a short time they had everything chilling in the refrigerator. Looking at the clock, Abby took the ham from the fridge and put it in a roasting pan and into the oven. The ham was pre-cooked and only needed to be warmed. Mary and Abby quickly straightened the kitchen, started the dishwasher, and, taking off their aprons, went outside to enjoy the warmth of the afternoon.

Abby and her mother wandered around the flowerbeds, discussing and looking at the new plants starting to push through the soil, as well as looking at the early flowers that bloomed in profusion. Abby pointed to the roses. "These should have been trimmed a little earlier in the year, and I almost cried when Blake cut them back, but they look so healthy now. Look, Mom, new leaf buds are starting to form." Looking at the bushes, she added wistfully, "I wish I were going to be here to see them all in bloom. Remember how proud Grandmother always was of her roses?"

"It wasn't just your grandmother who loved the roses. That bush," Mary said pointing to one growing at the side of the house, "has managed to survive for a very long time. Your third great-grandmother, MaryAnne Sayer, planted this from a start she received from a pioneer neighbor. Each generation has added to this rose garden. And, Abby, do you remember how wonderful they smell? The old fashioned roses have such a wonderful heady fragrance. So many of the new hybrid varieties just don't have much scent."

They continued strolling through the lush yard. Mary stopped in front of the large cottonwood tree and asked, "Do you remember, Abby, the tire swing that hung on a limb in this tree? Your grandfather hung it when I was a little girl, and it stayed there until you had grown too old to be interested in it. There are so many memories in the yard, as well." She gave herself a mental shake. "Well, it's getting late. We had better decide where we should eat. Dining room or patio, what do you think?"

Abby looked around. "Do you think it's too hot to eat outside on the patio? Shall we set the dining room table with the old china and have our feast inside?"

Mary thought for a minute, considering. "I say let's eat inside on the china. It hasn't been used for a long time, and this weekend has certainly been a journey of family memories. Shall we set the table?"

"I think I'll cut a bouquet of flowers for a centerpiece, if you don't mind, and then I'll be right there."

"Good idea, Abby," Mary said. "I'll start setting the table. Those plates will need wiping off, I'm sure." She turned to go back inside, stopping to give David a hug on the way. Abby retrieved the clippers from the garage and wandered around the flowerbeds for a few minutes, deciding what to pick. She then started clipping a bouquet of tulips, daffodils, desert lilac, and hyacinths.

David laid his book down and watched his daughter as she bent over the flowers, deciding the best ones to pick, and he smiled to himself. She had been such a blessing in their lives. He remembered the early years of despair when he and Mary thought they never would have a child of their own. When Abby was born, she added a sunlight and joy to their family that had been missing. He hadn't recognized how much he'd missed her until he had seen her waiting for them at the airport. He sensed her confusion over Scott. Scott was a fine attorney and would be able to provide Abby with a very financially secure future; plus, if Abby married him they would live close by. On the other hand, much as he hated to admit it, he had been impressed with Blake, even the little he had seen of him. And if Abby married him, she would have the priesthood in her home. As her father, David wanted her to have that from the beginning of her marriage. Not that Abby had said she was considering a serious relationship with him. But you would have to be blind not to see the look in each of their eyes when they saw each other. He was glad Blake was coming for dinner today, as it would give him a chance to observe him more. But Scott was also a fine man in many ways, and maybe he would be interested in taking the missionary lessons.

By now, Abby was coming toward him, her arms full of flowers, and David caught his breath. She was so beautiful, and he was so proud of her. All he really wanted was for her to be happy, to have a wonderful life.

Abby gave her father a kiss on the top of the head as she passed him and hurried into the house. Her mother was busy wiping the plates of china, humming as she did so.

"What do you think, Mom, do these look all right?"

Mary turned, smiling at Abby and the mass of flowers in her arms. "It looks as if you have enough for several centerpieces. I think Mother used to keep her vases on the top shelf in the pantry."

Abby used the step stool in the pantry to look at the vases on the shelf, finally selecting one that would be perfect with the arrangement she had in mind. She washed the vase then used the clippers to cut and arrange her bouquet. When she was finished she stepped back to look at it, made a few changes, then carried the flowers to the dining room, where she placed the vase on the center of the old oak table. The table looked beautiful with the flowers and old china. The silver was a little tarnished but still gleaming.

As Abby entered the kitchen, her nose caught the smell of the ham, and she looked around her. *I needed the alone time of the past few weeks, but family really makes a house a home*, she thought. Looking at the kitchen clock, she saw it was just a few minutes before four and ran upstairs to run a quick brush through her hair and freshen her lip gloss. As she stepped back from the mirror, the doorbell rang, and she hurried downstairs.

Her father had answered the door and was ushering Agnes into the house. She was holding a tray of hot rolls in her hands, and the aroma of warm bread drifted through the air.

David leaned over to take the tray from her hands. "Boy, am I glad you came. I haven't had homemade rolls for a long time. These smell so good." He leaned down and inhaled the aroma again.

Agnes laughed. "It just seemed good to make them. I always loved to bake. Now there's no one to eat it if I make it, so I don't bake much anymore."

The doorbell rang again, and Abby opened the door to let Blake in. He, too, sniffed the air appreciatively. "This must be the right house by the good smells coming out of it." He had brought a box of candy for her and a bouquet of roses for her mother.

She took the box and smiled up at him. "I'm glad that any food we eat on Easter has no calories, because if it did, we would be eating enough today to count for the next month!"

He laughed and followed her to the kitchen. After greeting her parents and Agnes, he asked what he could do. Mary was busy removing food from the refrigerator and thrust a bowl of salad in his hands. "Could you carry this into the dining room, Blake, and set it on the table? I think we're almost ready to eat." She looked at the roasting pan holding the ham. "David, would you please cut this ham and take it in to the dining room?"

Abby gave Blake another smile as he passed her on his way to the dining room. "This is where everyone has to help," she said, picking up the other bowl of salad and following him to the dining room. As she was starting back to the kitchen, her cell phone rang. She stopped and pulled it from her pocket to answer it.

Blake heard her say, "Hello, Scott," and his heart turned over. He watched her face as she answered and then walked back to the kitchen to see if there was anything else he could carry in.

"I couldn't let the day go by without calling you," Scott said, a smile in his voice. "How are you doing? I bet you're glad to have your parents there for this holiday."

"I'm fine, Scott," Abby told him. "It's really nice to have Mom and Dad here, and we're getting a lot done. But we're just sitting down to eat, so I don't have much time to talk. What are you doing today?" She heard her mother's laugh as her parents, along with Agnes and Blake, came back into the dining room.

"I'm just on my way to meet some friends for a game of golf. For once, the weather is warm." Abby heard the hesitation in Scott's voice as he casually asked, "I hear a lot of voices in the background. Who is there besides your parents?"

Abby glanced around before answering, "We invited Agnes Givens from next door and Blake—"

"Was it really necessary to invite Blake Matthews to a family dinner?" Scott broke in, frustration showing in his voice.

Abby, aware that everyone was seated at the table and waiting for her, interrupted him. "Scott, we're just sitting down to eat, so this is not a good time for me to talk. I'll call you later. Have a good game of golf." Without waiting for his reply, Abby terminated the call, positive she'd left Scott fuming on the other end of the line.

Soon they were seated around the table and, after a blessing on the food, proceeded to enjoy the feast before them. As they were finishing their dessert, David looked across at Blake. He had noticed the way Blake had helped to bring the food in and the courtesy he had shown in seating Agnes and Abby before sitting down himself. David pushed back his chair, folded his napkin, and placed it on the table. "Would you ladies excuse Blake and me from the cleanup? I want to get his opinion on how many trips we need to take to put all those packed boxes in storage."

Abby looked over at Blake. She knew what her father had in mind. She had not been able to fool her dad about her feelings toward Blake. She watched as Blake stood as well, thanked her mother for the delicious dinner, then followed her father from the room.

Mary smiled reassuringly at Abby as she stood and started to stack the dishes.

"Let me help too," Agnes said, picking up plates and carrying them to the kitchen.

Abby picked up a bowl of salad and started for the kitchen. She stopped at the living room door to see Blake and her father standing over the packed boxes. She jumped when she felt her mother's hand on her arm. "It's all right, Abby, it's just that your father is very protective of you. Let's leave them to it."

Following her mother, Abby retorted, "I just hope he won't ask Blake what his intentions are. I don't know how he feels about me, and I don't know what I would answer if Blake were to express it to me. I still care for Scott and haven't decided just what I want to do yet."

Inside the living room, Blake was saying, "I told Abby I could help tomorrow afternoon, so I would be happy to bring my truck, and we could get these boxes to storage."

"I'd appreciate that," David said, looking around the room. "If we could get some of these out of the house, it would help." He looked Blake in the eye and continued. "Mary and I are debating whether we want to sell this house. Right now I think we are leaning closer to keeping it, but we'll have to see. But in any case, if we do keep the house, we'll need to do some painting and fixing up, so everything still needs to be cleaned out. Are you sure you can break away from work tomorrow?"

Blake returned David's look. "I do have a very busy practice, but I usually take Monday afternoons off. When my father died, I took over his practice as well as mine, and for the next few years I wasn't able to take much time off. Now there are two additional doctors in the clinic. This has taken a lot of pressure off me and allowed me to free up my schedule somewhat, so I'll be happy to help tomorrow."

David weighed Blake's answer in his mind. Obviously, this young man was a very good doctor and a good son. Abby had told him that his mother had developed some pretty significant health problems after the death of her husband, and Blake had been patient and helpful with her until she, too, had passed away.

David, in lawyerlike fashion, managed to find out over the next hour what hobbies Blake enjoyed, what he did with his free time, where he'd served his mission, and finally his future goals. As they headed back to find the women, Blake smiled. He knew he had just been given a good cross-examination by a very experienced attorney and just hoped he had passed the test.

Abby, along with her mother and Agnes, was sitting on the patio, enjoying the lovely evening. The men pulled up chairs, and soon they were talking about their memories here in this house. Mary shared with them her stories of growing up here, and Abby loved listening to her mother's experiences. She felt closer to her grandparents now more than ever. She was starting to see them as people who had been young, romantic, and had done both fun and foolish things, just like her.

When the evening light faded, Agnes stood up. "I think I'd better go home. I go to bed fairly early now, but I had a wonderful day. You were so kind to invite me to share your Easter with you. I want you to know that when I say my prayers, I ask Heavenly Father to impress you with the desire not to sell this old home. It needs to be lived in by the people who have loved it for generations."

Blake stood as well. "I think I'd better be going now, too. I have early appointments tomorrow, but I'll be here at two in the afternoon." After shaking both Mary's and David's hands, he added, "I also had a wonderful day. You've made me feel very welcome." He turned to Abby and took her hands in his. "Thanks, Abby. I've had a good time; and thanks again for letting me share your parents today."

Abby walked to the side gate with Agnes and Blake and opened it for them. She watched as Blake bent his head to hear what Agnes was saying to him, her arm through his. She thought of the courtesy Blake always seemed to show those around him, and her heart again lifted as she observed him.

Abby told her parents she needed to call Scott back and went upstairs to bed early. After getting ready for bed, she lifted her phone from the nightstand and held it for several minutes before punching in his number. Her fingers paused on the connect key. She was sure there was going to be another argument and knew that it was her fault. She should not have cut Scott off without giving him a chance to say good-bye. However, the phone rang four times before his voice mail came on and, relieved, she left a message.

***

The next day Abby and her parents worked through the morning, sorting the last of the things in the office and her grandmother's bedroom. They also packed up the china, silver, and other valuables in the dining room. When they entered the kitchen, Mary looked around the room and shook her head. This room had so much that needed to be packed, and if they decided to keep the house, it would then need to be unpacked.

"I don't think I want to do anything in here until we decide for sure what we're going to do. If we decide to sell, we'll come for a weekend and finish," she said wearily.

"Good idea," David agreed. "Let's have lunch. It's almost time for Blake to come."

Blake arrived promptly at two, and they spent the rest of the afternoon packing the truck with boxes, unloading them at the storage unit, then returning to the house to repeat the process. By six o'clock, all the boxes to be stored were out of the house. Tired and hungry, the Peters family and Blake wandered through the rooms for a final analysis.

David put his arm around Blake's shoulders. "I don't know how we would have managed without you and your truck this afternoon. I'm buying dinner out tonight. We're all too tired to fix anything here, so come and share one last meal with us."

Blake looked at Abby, wondering if he should accept. This was her last evening with her parents, and he didn't want to intrude. But she nodded at him encouragingly, so with a lift in his heart he said, "Thank you; I'd like that."

After arranging to meet Blake at the restaurant, Abby and her parents took quick showers and changed into clean clothes. This time, Abby gave her father the car keys and got in the backseat so Mary could sit by her husband. They found Blake waiting in the lobby for them. It was a cheerful meal, and Abby found herself looking around at the three other people seated at the table. She was dreading placing her parents on a plane for Denver tomorrow, and she knew the house would seem more lonely and empty than ever. Abby looked over at Blake, who was laughing at something her father said, and her heart turned over. What she was going to do about him, she had no idea. Scott had not called back, so she was sure he was still angry with her, but she knew she still had deep feelings for him as well.

Arriving back at the house, her father headed for the study, where he could watch the news on the small TV. Abby and her mother seated themselves in the living room. "Oh Mom," Abby said, laying her head on her mother's shoulder for a minute. "I'm so glad you were able to come. I think this has been the best Easter weekend of my life. It was wonderful to go to church yesterday as a family and know that we are all on the same path."

"It was wonderful, Abby," her mother replied, putting her arms around her. "You are such a dear daughter, and you add so much to our lives." Looking around the room, empty now of boxes, she continued. "You've made taking care of this house so much easier for me with all the work you've been willing to do." Mary took Abby's hands in hers. "Abby, do you want to talk about things? After meeting Blake and spending some time with him, I can see why you care for him and why you feel attracted to him. He's a wonderful man, both in body and spirit."

Abby nodded her head. "I just feel conflicted so much of the time. I thought I wanted to marry Scott, and I still do in many ways. I care for him a lot, and he and I share so many common interests. But Blake has dimensions that Scott lacks, and the sad thing is that

Scott doesn't seem to feel a need for them in his life. And I don't really know just how Blake feels about me." At her mother's look, she smiled. "Oh, I know he cares for me, but he hasn't said anything, and I don't know what I would answer if he did. There are still so many issues I'm struggling with, and I haven't written Scott out of the picture yet either. I have a few friends that married outside their faith, and they have happy marriages."

Mary gave her daughter's hands a quick squeeze. "It will be all right, Abby. With your life on track, you are entitled to receive personal revelation, and the answers will come. Your Heavenly Father loves you very much and will help you make the right decision."

The next morning, Abby drove her parents to the airport. As she hugged her father good-bye, he whispered in her ear, "I do approve of Blake, more than I thought I would."

She hugged him again then watched them board the plane.

Returning home was as hard as she had thought it would be, and the house seemed so lonely and quiet now. She spent the day cleaning cabinets and washing the walls in the kitchen. By evening the hard work had lightened her mood, and she was tired.

She was sitting in bed reading when her cell phone rang, and she leaned over and picked it up off the nightstand.

"Abby, it's Scott."

"I really did try to call you back Sunday night, Scott," Abby said. "I felt so sorry for cutting you off like that."

"I know. I overreacted, too. But I get frustrated thinking that he's there and I'm here. I just wanted to remind you again of how much I miss you. And I'm trying to find a weekend I can come and help you finish. I think a lot of our problem is that we have spent too much time apart from each other."

"I know, Scott. If you're coming, it will have to be soon. I'm almost finished here."

"Good. I'll let you know when I'll be there."

After Abby finished the call she held the cell phone for a few more minutes before placing it on the nightstand and turning out the light. She listened in the dark to the music of the night, the crickets chirping, and the soft breeze blowing the curtains at her open window.

Through the window she could see a few stars winking down at her, and, feeling comforted, she slept.

***

10 July 1845

The captain says that we are about two weeks away from land, and it feels good to be near the end of this sea journey. Life aboard ship has been hard, and there has been much sickness. The Fisher family and Tom and I have been blessed to have withstood the hardships so far without succumbing to the devastating sickness that seems to be all around us. Mother Fisher is tired from her constant care of the sick and does not have much chance to rest as she makes her daily rounds to those who are ill.

Today has been a heartbreaking day. Sister Jones gave birth last week to a baby boy, but within a day of giving birth she came down with milk fever and has not been able to feed her little one. In addition, he is so sickly. Mother Fisher did all that she could, but the little baby died early this morning. Sister Jones is so ill, and her mind cannot comprehend that her baby has died, and she pleads for us to bring him to her. It is heart-wrenching to hear her cries and see her outstretched arms reaching for her child.

I helped bathe the tiny body, my tears dropping on his perfect little face, his eyes closed as if he were sweetly sleeping. After wrapping him in his baby quilt, I held him close for a few minutes. There have been several deaths at sea, but this time as the little body was lowered into the water, I thought my heart would break.

Chapter 18

Abby was awakened early Wednesday morning by a telephone call from Ryan. "Megan went into labor last night about ten, and at 4:36 this morning, Katie Megan Fellows made her entry into our family." His voice was filled with pride and love.

Abby gave an excited laugh. "Oh, Ryan, I'm so glad! And what a beautiful name! Is everything all right? Is the baby okay? And Megan, how is she?" Questions tumbled out of Abby's mouth.

"Everything went fine. The pediatrician doesn't see any problems with the baby at this point. She weighs just five pounds ten ounces, so she's small, but considering she's early, that's understandable. As for Megan, she's tired but thrilled with her new daughter."

"I can't wait to see her," Abby said with enthusiasm. "How long will they keep Megan and the baby in the hospital?"

"If everything continues to be all right, they will let her go home tomorrow afternoon. Come and see her tomorrow evening. She's so excited to show you the baby." Ryan sounded tired but happy, and Abby knew he probably had other calls to make.

"Tell her I'll be there, and give her my love. I'm so thrilled for you both! And, Ryan, thanks for calling me."

"You bet! See you tomorrow."

After hanging up, Abby leaned back on her pillows, a happy smile on her face. She was so glad both Megan and the baby were doing well. She had been blessed to carry the baby almost three additional weeks after the fall—long enough that everything was fine. The Lord had truly confirmed the blessing Ryan and Blake had given her.

Finally, glancing over at the clock, Abby threw the covers back and got out of bed. She could not believe how the weeks had flown by! All that was left now was the storage room, and she would be going home for good. At the thought, an ache came into her heart. How was it, she thought, that she could be excited at the thought of going back to Denver and simultaneously feel such a loss at the thought of not being here? She acknowledged quietly that some of those feelings had to do with Blake. And she would not be the same person when she returned home as when she had left. She had rediscovered her spiritual legacy and would do all she could to keep her testimony shining bright.

Abby took a quick shower and then headed to the kitchen. She was glad her parents had decided not to sell the house, partly because she would not have to pack the kitchen goods. Her mother had decided if they would be using the house eventually, she would go through that room herself at a later time. Abby carried her bowl of cereal and fruit out to the patio and then went back for her grandmother's scriptures. She returned to the patio, scriptures in hand, and turned to Moroni as she sat down. Abby had been diligent in her reading and was close to finishing the Book of Mormon. As she read the last chapter of Moroni, her eyes paused over the promise that was given, that if she would ask of God with a sincere heart and real intent, He would reveal the truth of the book to her by the power of the Holy Ghost. She savored the words, pondering them in her heart. She truly wanted to put this promise to the test.

She carried the book inside the house and mounted the stairs to her room. Kneeling by the side of the bed, Abby closed her eyes and waited a few minutes before beginning her prayer.

"Dear Heavenly Father, my heart is so full of gratitude and thankfulness for the blessings that have come into my life these past few months. Even though my heart has been heavy with sorrow over the loss of my grandmother, I have felt Thy comforting Spirit as I have begun this journey of spiritual rebirth. It has helped to heal my grief. I'm grateful for the opportunity to repent and feel the blessing of the Atonement in my life as I strive to move forward, willing to serve Thee and live Thy commandments. I love the Book of Mormon and have found peace and comfort in its pages. I'm thankful for the Prophet Joseph Smith and his willingness to sacrifice all in order to translate this sacred text, finally sealing his testimony with his blood. Now, at the completion of my reading this book, I kneel before Thee in humility, seeking a confirmation of the promise given in Moroni. I have read with real intent to know the truthfulness of its words and promises. I pray that I may receive that answer, that my spirit will feel the confirmation and burning of testimony."

Abby ended her prayer reverently and stayed on her knees, waiting for an answer, and slowly a feeling of peace and love flooded her body. Tears fell as she personally felt the confirmation of truth and knowledge that her Father in Heaven and her Savior loved her deeply. Tears continued to flow as she basked in the glow that enveloped her being until she again began a prayer of thanks for the answer she had been given.

Rising from her knees, Abby clasped the book close to her heart. It had become a treasure of great worth to her. She placed the book reverently by the side of her bed. Abby grabbed a tissue from the bathroom and wiped her eyes as she went back downstairs. She had a difficult time forcing herself to do the routine chores of cleaning the kitchen and watering the plants. With this new confirmation of a testimony burning within her and the love she had felt as she ended her prayer, Abby knew that she could not ever again take her membership in the Church lightly. She also recognized that she was ready to serve and move spiritually forward in her life.

Abby finished with the smaller chores and turned her attention to the task of the day. She picked up the packing tape and extra boxes needed for the storage room and went back upstairs to tackle this last big project. She had not entered this room since peering inside it the day she arrived. As she opened the door fully and stepped inside, she noticed the thick dust that lay on everything. Clearly no one had entered or cleaned this room for many years. The room, silent and lonely, seemed full of the memories of those who had lived in the old home. She looked around at the stacks of boxes, trunks, and old furniture, trying to decide where to start. Finally, drawing a breath of resolution, she dusted the top of an old table sitting in the center of the room. Picking up the nearest box, she placed it on the table, opened it, and began the process of going through what was there.

The hours went by swiftly as she sorted through several boxes of old fashion magazines and laughed softly at the styles of long-ago years. Another box yielded her grandmother's fabrics. Abby remembered wistfully the doll's quilt made from scraps from this box. When she was ten years old, her grandmother had patiently taught her how to cut out the squares, sew them together, and then quilt the small blanket.

Abby's work in the storage room was only interrupted by a brief break for lunch as she worked methodically through stacks of old boxes. By evening, Abby had only managed to go through part of the room and was tired and dusty. When she finally quit for the day, she looked around once more at the day's accomplishments then turned off the hanging overhead light and closed the door.

***

The next morning after breakfast, Abby called both her mother and Scott to let them know that she was nearing the end of her tasks and would be home soon. Abby could hear the relief in Scott's voice as she relayed this message to him. She worked diligently in the storage room until early afternoon then, after another quick lunch, showered and changed her clothes. By this time it was already after three; Abby wanted to pick out a gift for Megan's new baby and decided to give Megan a quick call to make sure she was feeling well enough for a short visit later that evening.

Megan was resting when Abby called, but Ryan assured her that Megan was excited to see her and show her the new baby.

Grabbing purse and car keys, Abby drove to the mall, anxious to find something for the baby. She was amazed at the variety of newborn merchandise as she wandered from the baby department in one store to another. She finally settled on a soft green dress with lace inserts and matching sweater and booties. As she was leaving, she passed a table of baby blankets and couldn't resist buying a delicate cream shawl. Finally, armed with her purchases, she left the mall. On the way home, she stopped at a florist and bought a huge spray of spring wildflowers for Megan.

Seven o'clock found her standing on the Fellows's front porch, purchases and flowers filling her arms. Ryan answered the door and smiled to see her hidden behind the flowers. "Looks as if you've been shopping," he said with a twinkle as he took the flowers from her. "Come in; Megan's waiting in the family room."

Abby followed him into the family room.

"Honey, Abby's here." Ryan grinned and held out the flowers for Megan's inspection. "And she's come bearing gifts."

Megan was seated in a rocking chair, gently holding a small bundle. She looked up as Abby entered the room and gave her a luminous smile. "Oh, Abby, I'm so glad you came. I've been dying to show her to you!" She held out the baby.

Abby laughed. "Let me put these down so I can take a really good look at her." She put the presents on the table next to Megan's chair then bent over the baby. She was so tiny and fragile-looking. Abby didn't think she had ever seen a baby this young or little. Katie Megan Fellows's little head was covered with fine red hair, and Abby was glad she had settled on something green. "She's beautiful! Her name fits her."

"Doesn't it, though? Do you think she is going to be cursed with freckles all her life like me?" Megan asked with a laugh. "I spend hours just looking at her and can't believe how perfect her little body is. And Ryan's just as bad. He's already giving her father-daughter chats!" She laughed again.

As Abby sat down on the sofa next to Megan's rocking chair, the doorbell rang, and Ryan left the room to answer it. He returned a moment later with Blake. When Blake saw Abby he gave her a smile then turned toward Megan and the baby. "Just thought I'd better stop by and see this new addition to the Fellows family," he said. He bent over Megan's side so he could see the baby. "I knew it," he exclaimed. "This one is going to be a beauty, just like her mother."

Megan blushed and laughed, holding out the baby to him. "Here, take a good look and then pass her to Abby. She hasn't had time to hold her yet."

Blake took the little bundle and held her in his arms with the air of experience. He walked over and sat down by Abby on the couch, holding the baby so they both could see her. "She's perfect. I'm so glad for you both." He smiled down at the baby, unwrapping the blanket for Abby so she could see the little feet and hands.

Blake held the baby with a tenderness and confidence that impressed Abby. With a quick breath, she fingered Katie's tiny feet and fingers. Blake gently wrapped the blanket again around the baby and held her out for Abby.

"Oh, Blake, she is so tiny and perfect," Abby said and reached out to take the baby into her arms. She drew the infant close to her, breathing in the fresh baby smell and feeling a deep desire to protect and care for a baby of her own. *This little one must still feel so near to the world of our Heavenly Father; she brings part of heaven with her,* she thought.

Blake looked at Abby and the baby in her arms and was flooded with love. He knew he wanted to see her holding their child in her arms. Abby looked at him over the head of the baby and smiled, and it was all he could do not to take her in his arms and declare his love.

"Here, Ryan, you'd better hand Katie back to her mother before I run away with her," Abby laughed. Ryan quickly held out his arms, and she placed the baby in them.

She stayed another few minutes then stood up. "I'm not going to stay long. I'm sure you're tired, Megan, but she is beautiful, and I'm so glad she's here and everything went well."

Blake got up from the couch. "I have to leave, too. There are patients I need to check on at the hospital before I go home. I'm glad that she's here. She was really worth the wait."

Abby gave Megan a hug and then walked with Blake and Ryan to the door. Giving Ryan a hug as well, she stood back as Blake said good-bye. Blake walked with her to her car and opened the door for her. But instead of closing it, he stayed where he was.

"How much longer are you going to be here, Abby?" he asked, an ache in his heart at the thought that she would be leaving soon. He knew he needed to let her know how he felt about her before he lost his chance.

"I think I'm going to be able to finish in a few days. I'm down to the last room, and I've made a good start there." Abby looked up at him, saddened at the thought of not seeing him again. "Blake, I don't know how I'm ever going to thank you for all your help; I couldn't have finished without you. I appreciate it so much."

"If you really want to thank me, then there is something I would like." Abby held her breath at his words. "I'd like to take you to dinner this Friday."

Abby let out her breath. In her heart she was afraid to go, afraid of her feelings for this man, but the pull of wanting to be with him was hard to resist. She looked into his eyes. "I'd like that, too, Blake." She tried to put a lighter tone in her voice and smiled. "That's the least I can do for all your help."

He relaxed; he had been so afraid she would refuse. "I'll pick you up at seven Friday night."

***

22 July 1845

Today, after seven long weeks at sea, we landed in New Orleans, Louisiana. Tom and I stood on deck and watched our new country draw close to us, so grateful to come to this land that is choice above all others, a land that has been blessed and prepared for the restoration of the gospel. When I placed my feet on the firm land, I found they were unsteady; I had become so used to balancing myself to the rocking and heaving of the ship. The earth smelled sweet and, as my steps became more sure, it was good to be on land again.

This morning before leaving ship, we as Saints gathered together for a final prayer and testimony meeting. Our hearts were filled with thanks for our safe arrival in America. We have truly bonded as a group of people with love toward one another.

New Orleans is very different from my little village of Fornham St Mary. It is a large, bustling city filled with many people. Their colorful accents sound so strange and are different from any I have ever heard. The city is both beautiful and frightening. The sidewalks and window boxes are filled with bright flowers of all colors; however, the city is full of the noise of hundreds of people, the hammering of workers erecting new buildings, and the rumble of horses and carriages in the streets. Tomorrow we will board the steamship that will take us up the large Mississippi River to Nauvoo.

Chapter 19

Abby knew she was tempting fate by accepting the dinner date with Blake, but she wanted to see him one final time. She told herself that this was one way of facing her attraction to him. She would go to dinner, tell him good-bye and thanks for his help, and that would be it. Even so, when it came time for her to dress for the evening, Abby wanted to look her best. She spent several minutes trying to decide what to wear, finally settling on the deep violet dress she had bought on her shopping trip with Megan. She spent extra time on her hair and makeup then stepped back from the mirror to view the results. The luxurious deep violet of the dress brought out the highlights in her hair. The green eyes reflecting back at her shone with excitement and just a hint of nervousness. She sprayed a quick spurt of scent then picked up her purse from the bed, gave one final glance in the mirror, and started downstairs just as the doorbell rang.

At the sound, her nervousness increased. She opened the door and invited Blake in. He, too, had dressed for the evening. The crease in his gray slacks was razor-sharp, and his deep red pullover sweater contrasted nicely with a navy blue blazer. Abby gave a smile as she noticed the polished boots on his feet. Blake gave a soft whistle of approval as he looked at her. "You look beautiful, Abby."

She felt her heart flip-flop within her and tried to respond lightly. "You look really nice too. Shall we go?"

They walked to the car, and Blake opened the passenger door for her. "I thought tonight we would go to the Lodge in Springdale for dinner. It should be a nice ride."

"It sounds wonderful," she said, trying to calm her beating heart.

Abby enjoyed the drive and slowly found herself relaxing. The hours of light were becoming longer, and even though it was after seven in the evening, the sun was still bright and just beginning to touch the edge of the horizon. The few clouds in the sky were becoming tinged with purple, pink, and gold as the sun's rays reflected behind them. Soon they passed the subdivision where Megan and Ryan lived. "I'm glad everything turned out so well for them," she said, pointing to their home high on the hillside. "The baby is so cute, and I'm glad they were able to bring her home."

"I know," Blake answered. "You'd think they were the only two people to ever have a baby, they are so happy. But that's the way it should be."

Abby could understand their joy. As she'd held the baby, she was surprised at the maternal instincts she'd felt and the desire to hold one of her own. She glanced at Blake, remembering how comfortable and natural he had been holding the baby in his arms. Of course, she told herself, he was a doctor, but she knew he loved children. She could easily picture him as a father and knew that he would be a good one.

They arrived at the restaurant and soon were seated at a table near the window. Once again, Abby exulted in the beauty of the area, made even more beautiful by the setting sun. The waiter handed them menus, and Abby directed her attention to the entrées offered. She considered the options and finally settled on fresh trout. After giving the waiter their orders, she sat back and looked across at Blake to find him watching her.

"So you think in a few more days you'll have finished what you need to do? Have your folks decided whether they are going to sell or not?" he questioned.

She shrugged. "I'm almost through now—a few more boxes in the storage room is all I have left. I can't believe how much work it's been." She paused, looking at him. "It's going to be difficult to leave in many ways."

The waiter arrived with their salads, and after he left, she went on. "Mom and Dad have decided for sure not to sell, and I'm so glad. I've just hated the thought of selling the old home. When they were here at Easter, they could see the advantages of keeping the place as a holiday home. So," she paused, pushing the last of her salad around on the plate. "So, I guess I'll still come back occasionally."

She glanced up. His eyes were studying her face. "Are you sorry to be going back, Abby?" Blake probed. "Or are you anxious to get back to your life in Denver?"

She laid her fork down, pondering her reply to his question. "I'm not sure how to answer that, Blake. I feel torn in two. I've really enjoyed being here and will miss so much of what I have grown to love. But, on the other hand, I have a job and family there waiting for me; my life is in Denver."

The waiter brought their main dishes, and they moved on to lighter subjects. After sharing a piece of raspberry cheesecake for dessert, Blake paid the bill, and they left. Instead of going to the car, he took her arm and led her to the path that ran along one side of the lodge. It wound its way to the river, where the trail paralleled the river's path. Occasionally, they passed a bench. "I hope you don't mind a little walk before we head back," Blake said as he reached for her hand, holding it firmly in his.

Abby wondered why it was she felt so secure with Blake and why it seemed so natural to be walking with him, her hand in his. "I'm grateful for the walk. I'm so full from dinner, which, by the way, was very good."

They walked a few minutes longer in silence; then Blake led Abby to a secluded bench, and they sat down. The full moon was just beginning to rise in the evening sky, its golden beauty bathing the world around them in soft light, the faint breeze scented with pine. Abby took a deep breath, trying to remember her resolve to just enjoy the moment and not become involved. She glanced at Blake, and her breath caught in her throat. He was looking at her with such tenderness that she found herself turning toward him. He took both her hands in his and gently caressed them.

"Abby, I know you are still involved with Scott, but I need to tell you how I feel. Several years ago I was engaged to be married and was devastated when my fiancée gave back my ring. I thought I would never find anyone else I loved as much as Emily. Without realizing it, I've kept my heart pretty protected these last few years. But Abby, your smile and sweetness has filled my heart and brought me joy." He took a deep breath and drew her toward him. "I'm in love with you in every possible way, and you add a completeness and richness to my life I never dreamed was possible. I want to marry you, raise a family with you, and grow old with you. When I think of eternity, even that doesn't seem a long enough time to be with you. You are everything and more I want in my soul mate, and I can't imagine life without you by my side."

Listening to his words, Abby felt herself move closer to Blake. As he gathered her close to him in his arms, her heart started to pound, and her resolve to distance herself from him melted away. She eagerly turned her face up to meet his and waited breathlessly as his mouth descended on hers. Time lost itself as she gave herself up to the rapture of his embrace and welcomed the feeling of his strong arms around her. When he took his lips from hers, he tenderly rubbed the corners of her mouth with his finger and looked deeply into her eyes, seeking an answer to his unasked questions. She felt herself trembling at his touch and raised her eyes to meet his. Once again he gathered her close to him and kissed her. This time she put her arms around his neck, feeling his thick hair with her fingers. Abby could feel his heart beating rapidly and knew hers was racing as well. When the kiss ended, she gave a soft sigh and let her head fall on his shoulder.

"Blake, I care for you too! I think about you constantly and can't wait to see you. You bring out feelings in me that I haven't felt before, and I feel a unity of spirit when I'm with you." As she spoke, her words touched his heart with happiness, and he reached toward her once again, but she sadly shook her head. "But, Blake, I've felt so much turmoil inside myself as I've thought about what I should do. I thought I loved Scott, and I still do care for him in so many ways. We have so many things in common. And if I marry you, I don't know if I can meet all your needs. I'm becoming 'spiritually reborn' and have experienced 'a mighty change of heart,' as Alma said, but I haven't been really active for many years. Plus, I love living in a big city. I love the hustle, the challenges it offers, the good theaters and restaurants. I know your life is here, and I don't know if I can adjust to living in a small town year-round." By this time, tears had gathered in her eyes and threatened to overflow as she looked at him and noticed the unhappiness reflected in his eyes. "Please, Blake, give me time to think and pray over this." She smiled tremulously through her tears. "Yes, I'm going to do some serious fasting and praying over this. My heart and testimony are entrenched in the gospel now, and I have faith that Heavenly Father will answer my prayers. I finally have learned just how much He loves me. Would you mind giving me a little time before I give you an answer?"

Blake's look softened as he gazed into her eyes. "I can live with that answer because I know Heavenly Father loves us both. I'll give you your time, but I want you to remember just how much I love you and want to marry you. I want to devote my life to making you happy."

Once again he drew her to him, loving the feeling of holding her close. In his heart he felt everything would be all right but knew he would worry until she agreed to marry him. He could not imagine going on with his life without her. "Don't make me wait too long," he sighed as he lifted her face to his for a final kiss before pulling her to her feet for the walk back to the car and the drive home.

Chapter 20

They kept their talk light on the way back to St. George. Even with all that had happened, Abby found herself laughing at the stories Blake told her of his childhood. As he turned the car into her driveway, she became aware of another car parked there and caught her breath as she saw Scott sitting on the front porch, a large bouquet of yellow roses laid across his knees.

Blake said under his breath, "I take it that's Scott. Are you going to be all right, Abby?"

Abby felt her body tighten with tension as Blake stopped the car and helped her out. Scott stood up and placed the roses on the chair. He slowly walked toward them, his eyes never leaving Blake's face.

"I didn't know you were coming today, Scott," Abby said, trying to calm her voice.

"Obviously not," he answered, his eyes narrowing. "I take it this is Dr. Matthews."

"Yes, Scott, this is Blake Matthews, and Blake, this is Scott Shafer." Blake offered his hand to Scott, and after a few seconds Scott took it, his eyes still sizing up the other man.

"I'd better go, Abby, it's getting late," Blake said, a knot forming in his chest. He hated leaving her there to face Scott alone; but staying would only make matters worse.

"Thanks for the farewell dinner, Blake, I really enjoyed it," Abby said, giving Scott a pleading look, her eyes begging him not to cause a scene.

Scott looked away as Abby kissed Blake's cheek. Blake smiled reassuringly at her before getting in his car and driving away.

"Why didn't you let me know you were coming?" Abby asked as she unlocked the door and stepped inside. Scott followed her into the house, picking up the flowers off the chair.

"I wanted to surprise you, so I came without calling." He handed her the bouquet of roses. "I thought you'd be glad to see me, and I could help you this weekend to finish up here."

Abby buried her head in the flowers, inhaling deeply as she tried to relax. "The flowers are beautiful, Scott. You remembered that yellow roses are my favorite."

"Where have you been tonight, Abby? And why did you go with Blake Matthews?" Scott demanded, his irritation surfacing once again. "It seems I've been right in my suspicions that *Dr. Matthews*," he said the name with sarcasm, "has ulterior motives concerning you."

Abby blushed as she remembered Blake's proposal and kisses. "I'm sorry, Scott, but Blake has been so much help to me that when he asked for a farewell dinner before I left, I decided to go," she replied hesitantly. "And Blake's been nothing but kindness and help to me since I came. He's become a good friend."

"Friend!" Scott shouted accusingly at her. "I saw the way he looked at you. He's in love with you, Abby. Did you neglect to tell him that we're talking about getting married?"

Abby walked into the living room and sat down on the sofa, laying the flowers on the table in front of her before firmly replying, "Please sit down, Scott. You don't need to stand and shout at me."

Scott looked at her face then sat down in a chair opposite her, his voice filled with emotion. "I'm sorry, Abby, I don't mean to shout. I just don't understand what's going on here. Couldn't you have just thanked him for his help with a card or a small gift without going out to dinner with him? You've been gone from Denver for quite a while now, and I've certainly felt no need to be looking around for someone else to date."

Abby felt weariness wash over her. The night had held too much emotion, and she was tired. "I don't know the best way to answer you, Scott, but I guess honesty is the right solution. I can't deny any longer to myself or to you that I do have some pretty serious feelings for Blake, but I certainly didn't purposely set out with those intentions.

He has been willing to give of his time to help me get this place in order—I needed someone, Scott. I couldn't do some of the work by myself."

Scott felt the anger building inside him again. "So I was right, Abby. He's forced himself into your life, and now you feel a debt toward him."

"Blake knew from the beginning that I had a serious relationship with someone from home, and he's never tried to force anything on me," she said patiently. "And no, my feelings toward him aren't because he's been there for me when I needed him. He's helped because he saw I needed it." She looked at Scott and went on. "When we were together that weekend in Denver we talked about how I felt toward my involvement in my church, and you said you felt no need for it now in your life but that you'd go with me."

"That's right, I will." Scott nodded.

"But Blake is fully committed to the Church *now*, and there are many goals and values we share because of that love for the gospel," she said gently.

Scott leaned toward her. "I'll admit that I didn't think you were going to get so absorbed in it, but if it's that important to you, then I'll take the missionary discussions. Maybe I'll even join your church."

Abby smiled sadly at him and shook her head. "It doesn't work that way, Scott. I don't want you to join or participate to please me. You have to want it for yourself, to feel the need for it in your life. I know from experience that unless it's something you really desire and value, it can easily slip away and become lost. Real commitment involves something more than just going to church once a week. Our love for the Savior and desire to live the way He wants us to has to come first in our lives; it has to be the focus in all our decisions."

Scott looked intently at her. "I'm trying to understand, Abby, and I do respect your beliefs. I'm willing to compromise on this religion issue, but you also need to remember how many other things we have in common right now. We both love living in Denver, near our families and friends. You love your career and are good at it. You have talents and ambitions that need a larger area to flourish."

Abby smiled at him. "You're right; there are many things we have in common, and I still have deep feelings for you, too. But another decision I've made since being here is that I want to start a family after I'm married. When Megan had her baby and I held her, I realized I don't want to wait several years before starting a family." At his look of astonishment, she continued. "I know what you're going to say. If I want a baby, then I can have a baby. But I don't want it to be my decision, my baby. I want it to be a shared decision, out of mutual love and joy for a family, something we both want."

"I want a family too, Abby," Scott ran his fingers through his hair. "And we can negotiate the timetable for a baby. The important thing to remember is that we both love each other. With that love, we'll learn how to compromise, and I'm sure with all my heart we'll be happy. You and I know several married couples with different faiths, and they have very successful marriages. We both know that marriage requires sacrifices in order for it to work. We're realistic adults and can face together the issues that come up."

"I know, Scott. That's why I'm so confused. There are so many things I appreciate and admire about you. I love your sense of humor and," she indicated the roses lying on the coffee table, "the romantic things you do for me. I've appreciated your support in my desire to build my career, and we have such a good time together. In addition, I still feel a bond of closeness with you that I'm not sure I want to give up."

Scott felt his mood lighten; he hadn't lost her completely yet. "Abby, I'll always try to show you how much I love you."

The tiredness was beginning to take its toll on Abby, and fatigue showed in her voice. "I know, Scott. But right now I just haven't decided what I'm going to do or where I'm going to live. There is so much I love in Denver, and part of that is my job. Plus, my family is there, and so are you." She felt her eyes beginning to fill with tears. "Please, Scott, try to understand what I'm going to ask. I really appreciate your gesture in coming here, but I want you to go home tomorrow morning. Right now I'm filled with so much turmoil that I need time alone to think things through and decide just what the right decision is for me to make."

He looked over at her, frustration showing on his face. "I don't understand, Abby, why I should leave. If I go, then Blake will still be here to push his case. Besides, you've had the past two months to be alone."

Abby shook her head. "No, I told Blake I needed time as well, so I won't be seeing him again until I know what to do."

She stood up. Scott, after a careful look at her face, rose to his feet as well. He put his arms around her and drew her close into his arms. "Okay, Abby, you win. I'll go back, but just remember we do love each other. If you had kept that in mind when you came here, you would not have allowed yourself to develop feelings for Blake. Being away from home has brought this confusion to you, and when you come back, everything will be fine." Resentment surfaced briefly in Scott's voice then faded as he added gently, "Just remember, we can work anything out together."

Abby nodded at him, her eyes pricking with tears. Scott held her away from him, looking into her eyes, then gave a disappointed sigh and leaned forward to kiss her. She put her arms around him and kissed him back, confusion still raging inside of her. Scott drew his arms away from her and walked quickly to the door without a backward glance. She could tell by the way he got in the car and slammed the door that she had hurt him, and tears flooded her eyes as she watched him drive away.

After Scott left, Abby dissolved into tears. Too much had happened in one night. How was it possible to love two such different men? She felt in her heart she loved Blake but doubted her ability to adjust to all the changes in her life that marrying him would require. But she also felt she loved Scott; he was a very good man in so many ways. Maybe if he took the discussions and went with her to church he would feel the same commitment that she did. Later, lying in bed, she cried softly for a long time until finally falling asleep.

Chapter 21

Abby woke early the next morning, eyes aching from her restless night. She slid out of bed and knelt in prayer. Again she poured out her heart to the Lord, seeking help and guidance as she fasted today about what she should do.

After showering and dressing, she called her mother. When her mother answered, tears flooded Abby's eyes as she related everything that had happened.

"I worried when your father told me that Scott was going to surprise you with a visit," Mary said. "I'm glad you're fasting today over your decision. They are both fine men. But, Abby, a lifetime and beyond is a long time to live with a decision like this one, so be sure to make it for the right reasons."

"I know, Mom, but if I do decide to marry Blake, can I really make him happy? Will I be able to adjust to life here?"

"Only you can determine that, dear," her mother said patiently. "But real love does require compromise and sacrifice. While you fast today, you need to visualize what your life would be without Blake in it. On the other hand, your marriage may work with Scott, but you also need to remember that there are no guarantees that Scott will ever love the church and the gospel as you do. Can you accept your life without that?"

"I know I need to consider that. Thanks, Mom, for being there for me. Here I am at twenty-six still needing advice and help from you. I'll give you a call when I've reached a decision. And Mom, please pray for me."

Abby felt better after talking with her mother and spent a few minutes outside watering the flowerpots on the patio and front porch. Already the day promised extra warmth. Entering the house again, she went from room to room, feeling the emptiness of the home now that everything was boxed and out of the house. She smiled to herself as she thought of her parents having to go back through things now that they were going to keep the house.

Blake called as she was preparing to go upstairs and finish the sorting in the storage room. "I won't keep you long," he said. "I just needed to be sure you were all right after I left last night."

"I'm fine, Blake," Abby responded, "Scott's gone back to Denver this morning, and I'm fasting today; I need to feel the confirmation of the Spirit as I make my decision."

Blake felt relief at her statement that Scott was not there. "Abby, I want you to know I'm fasting today as well. Hopefully we'll both come up with the same answer."

"Thanks, Blake. I'm sorry to make you wait, but I appreciate your patience with me."

"You're welcome." She could hear a smile in his voice. "Abby, I love you."

Her eyes filled with tears. *This is silly*, she thought. *I never used to cry, and now I cry at everything.* She thanked him again and promised to call later.

Eventually she entered the storage room and, going down on her knees, dragged a large box toward her and opened it. She smiled with delight as she carefully lifted out old books of children's classics. She had always loved to read these as a child, and she pulled many worn friends out of the box; she spent several hours reading parts of her favorite books. These were wonderful. A few first editions were in the box, and these she handled carefully. Packing the books in a new box, she sealed the lid with tape and carefully labeled it. Someday she would open this box and read these stories to her own children. Again, she felt the importance of making the right decision.

Abby sorted through several more boxes, finding more treasures from the past, wishing she knew the stories behind the elaborate old dresses and dance cards she found. Finally she had exhausted the boxes that needed to be sorted and, with a feeling of satisfaction at finishing, stood up and dusted her hands on her jeans. She needed to clear the dust from the room, and then she'd be through. On her way downstairs to collect cleaning supplies, she glanced at her watch. It was just after two in the afternoon. As she passed the kitchen her stomach growled, reminding her of her fast. Once again, she took a minute to pray and ask for help.

As she was collecting cleaning supplies, her cell phone rang again. This time it was Scott, letting her know that he was back in Denver.

"Scott, I'm so sorry for the way things are. I'm going to fast and pray for an answer today."

"I'm sorry too, Abby. It really wasn't fair for me to just show up at your grandmother's house without letting you know I was coming. I just want to remind you again that I'm willing to make some compromises. I love you and will be looking forward to your coming home."

Tears filled Abby's eyes again. "Thanks, Scott, for trying to understand. I never meant to hurt you, and I'll talk to you soon."

Once again Abby gathered up the cleaning supplies and headed back to the storage room. She was amazed at the amount of dust that had accumulated over the years and opened the window before starting to sweep. She swept the room several times before it was clean and then walked to the closet to give it a final sweeping and dusting. She was running the feather duster over the high top shelf of the closet, trying to remove the dust, when she felt the duster hit something at the back of the shelf in the far corner. Standing on tiptoe, Abby tried to see what was there but couldn't see that far back. Pushing again with the duster, she tried to move the object forward, but to no avail. *Oh well,* she told herself, *I'll have to use a ladder.* She ran down the stairs and out to the garage. Carrying the ladder and being careful not to trip, she carried it upstairs to the storage room closet.

After setting it in position, she climbed up the steps until she could see the back of the closet shelf. In the far corner was an object covered in a thick layer of dust. It looked as if it had not been disturbed for many, many years. Abby moved up the next step on the ladder so she could reach the box. She sneezed several times from the dust but managed to lift the box carefully from the shelf and start down the ladder with it.

Abby set the box on the table in the center of the room, retrieved her dusting cloth, and started wiping it clean. As she worked, she could see the box was made of wood, and hearts and leaves had been engraved on the top and sides of the box. When it was clean, she carried the box to the old couch and sat down with it in her hands.

Heart beating rapidly, Abby held her breath as she opened the box. Several items were inside, a small book lying on top. She carefully wiped the light dust from the book's cover then opened it. The book seemed to be an old journal. Laying it back in the box, Abby dragged the old table near the couch and placed the box on it. The fading light in the room was too dim to see clearly, so she turned on the hanging overhead light. Once she had settled herself back on the couch, she opened the box again, took out the book, and opened it. The name *Catherine Anne Moore* was written in black ink on the first page. Abby felt chills run over her body. Catherine was the name on the picture and the ring she had found. Surely this must be the same woman! Now she had a last name as well. Eager to know what Catherine's connection was to her family, Abby ran to the study to retrieve her grandmother's genealogy book and carried it quickly back to the storage room and sat down. She scanned the pedigree charts at the first of the book quickly but found no such name. Sighing with frustration, Abby laid it aside.

She opened the old journal again, turned to the next page, and with beating heart began reading.

25 December 1844

My name is Catherine Anne Moore . . .

***

31 July 1845

This morning we arrived in Nauvoo. After so many months of travel and afflictions, I cannot believe we are finally here, united with the Saints in this beautiful city. The journey here has been long, and it seems a lifetime ago since the day I left my parents and the gentle, green hills of my village in England. I thought the journey by ship to America was difficult, but these last miles from New Orleans to Nauvoo by steamship were the hardest of all.

To save money, many of us purchased tickets to sleep on the decks, and the conditions have been almost unbearable. The traffic up and down the Mississippi River is very busy, and the air is filled constantly with the noise of passing ships and their continuously clanging bells. The humid, wet heat has been suffocating, and the mosquitoes drift in thick clouds among us, biting our necks and faces. It seems all we can do to tolerate these new afflictions. It has been impossible to sleep at night with the noise, heat, and the constant biting and buzzing of bugs. In addition, we are limited to only washing our faces and hands. I long so much for a full bath! I have felt so nauseated and tired these past few weeks that it has been a struggle to keep my spirits up. At first I only suspected that I might be pregnant, but Mother Fisher confirmed my feelings. Tom is overjoyed with the news, as am I. A baby, to me, is a confirmation of the love Tom and I have for each other.

It has taken one week to reach our destination. As we drew close to the city of Nauvoo, which is situated at a bend of the Mississippi River, the Saints gathered on deck to watch as the city drew near. It had been raining most of the day, but as I stood watching with tears of gratitude in my eyes, the sun emerged from the clouds and illuminated the temple on the hill, the white of its walls shining forth with purity and hope. The city appeared so large and is scattered on the banks of the river. On board, we started singing hymns of praise to our God in gratitude for surviving the journey here. As the steamship drew close to the shore, we could see hundreds of people gathered on the banks where we would arrive. As we left the steamship, many embraced and welcomed us here. One of the missionaries on board pointed out a man standing at the front of the crowd on shore as Brigham Young, President of the Twelve Apostles. As I left the ship, he shook my hand and welcomed me to Nauvoo, and I felt tears gather in my eyes as the Spirit confirmed that I was in the presence of a special servant of God. My spirits rose, and my soul felt at peace. We have finally arrived home!

Tom and I will be staying with George and Margaret Snaith until we can build our own house. Brother Snaith is about sixty years of age and is a carpenter by trade. He has been working at the temple to help with its completion, and he and Sister Snaith have been with the Saints since Kirtland. Sister Snaith is about fifty-five years of age and is a small, thin, bustling type of woman. She reminds me of my mother, and I already feel a special bond to her. They live in a brick, two-story home in the main part of the city. The Snaiths have two children, but they are both married. Their daughter and her husband also joined the Church and live close by.

Tom and I were given a small bedroom, and I was overcome with emotion to see the cleanliness of the home; Sister Snaith had even placed a bowl of wildflowers in our room. It seems years since I have lived in a house, and we can finally unpack some of our belongings. Another blessing for me was to take a real bath and feel clean again. Tom and I have not had our own private space for a long time. Tomorrow we will explore Nauvoo. Because of his experience working as a carpenter, Tom has been assigned to work with Brother Snaith on the temple. The Fisher family will be staying with another family nearby. Tonight my heart is overflowing with thanksgiving to finally be here in the city of the Saints.

***

1 August 1845

Our first day in Nauvoo. What a joy to wake this morning in a bed and see sunshine streaming through the open window. Sister Snaith, knowing how tired we must be, let us sleep as long as we wanted. She made a wonderful breakfast. Tom and I enjoyed it but ate quickly so we could explore the town.

The city is spread from the hills to the river, and the noise of hammers and saws fills the air. The streets of the city were still muddy after yesterday's rain, and the mud clung to our shoes like glue. The houses in the main part of the city are beautiful, many being made of brick. Gardens and fences surround the homes, and several have orchards. As new Saints arrive, many have built simpler homes of logs and other humble materials. With so many Saints pouring into the city, every available bit of land is used to grow food. Vacant lots and open land areas are planted with grain and vegetables. After walking around the city, Tom and I climbed to the temple site and were amazed at the glorious view. We could see into Iowa and for many miles up and down the winding Mississippi River.

Although the community seems to be well-organized and growing daily, there still seems to be some unrest in the air. One of the men working in a wagon shop told us there has been so much mob violence that Brigham Young is preparing the people to leave Nauvoo sometime soon. He further said that since January of this year, the Nauvoo charter has been revoked by the Illinois legislature, leaving the citizens of Nauvoo without any city government, militia, or any real legal protection from the armed mobs that are constantly attacking the city. We felt sorrowful that our arrival should be overshadowed by further unease.

After helping Sister Snaith with dinner and the clearing up, I spent the evening finishing a letter to Father and Mother. At dinner Brother Snaith mentioned there are missionaries leaving in the morning for England and that they would be glad to take letters back with them. I have been writing on this letter since boarding the ship at Liverpool, so it is quite long. I want my beloved parents to know how happy I am with Tom and that I have arrived in America safely. I also wrote and told them of the new baby. Just the thought of having the baby without Mother close by makes my heart ache with sadness.

***

18 September 1845

We have been in Nauvoo now for several weeks, and life has settled into a routine. Each morning Tom leaves early to work on the temple, and I help Sister Snaith with what needs to be done at home. There is always so much to do. We are busy now drying the last of the summer harvest for the winter. We have also been gathering the flax from the fields and preparing it for spinning and weaving, and my hands are cut and chapped from working with it. I also help take care of the animals, the family washing, and the making of soap and candles. I often think of my lazy days in England and how much more I could have helped Mother.

The women have been organized into an organization called the Female Relief Society of Nauvoo, and I love the fellowship I feel with the other women. It has become one way of meeting other sisters and becoming friends with them. Many evenings we meet and sew shirts for the men working on the temple.

One of my special friends has become Sister Snaith's daughter, Dorothy Stokes. She is very pretty and has black hair and blue eyes. She is like her mother in that she is full of laughter and compassion. She is married to Charles Stokes, a somewhat frail man, who, before joining the Church, was a music teacher at a private school. He has a good singing voice and gives music lessons here in Nauvoo. Another thing Dorothy and I have in common is that we are both expecting our first babies within a week of each other. Tom and Charles have become good friends as well. Nauvoo has a concert hall for musical evenings, and the four of us often go together to listen to the lovely music. Both Charles and Tom's sister, Emily, perform frequently at the hall. We also have a Nauvoo Quadrille band that has played for many special events. Sister Snaith said the Prophet Joseph Smith encouraged the Saints to use their talents, and there is evidence of that all around us in theater entertainment and the music of wonderful musicians. President Young continued the practice after the death of the Prophet. How blessed we are to have so much to enjoy in this beautiful city!

Tom loves working on the temple. He says it is a purifying and humbling experience to be part of the force laboring on such a sacred building. They are working hard to complete the temple as soon as possible. There is so much unrest and mob activity surrounding us that President Young wants to have the temple completed so that endowments can be performed as soon as possible.

***

25 September 1845

The days now seem to fly by so fast! Everywhere around us we see evidence pointing to an exodus from Nauvoo. I remember on the ship traveling to America visualizing in my mind that Nauvoo would be the end of our long journey, and Tom and I would live here with our family for the rest of our lives. But I could never have imagined the unrest and violence that surrounds us here. It seems every day there is some new manifestation of the world's hatred directed toward us, and I know in my heart we will be leaving here soon, wanderers again. I think often of how so many of

God's children from times past have had to leave homes and travel to new lands. As they have hearkened to the prophets and obeyed, they have been blessed, and this comforts me. However, my heart is heavy at the thought of leaving this beautiful city and the temple in our midst. I pray I will be equal to the challenges that lie ahead.

***

6 October 1845

Today was a wonderful day. A special conference was held in the temple, even though it is not fully completed. President Young encouraged the Saints to prepare to leave Nauvoo, directing that we should be sure our debts are paid and start setting aside goods for the journey so that every family who wants to can go. He promised if we do all that we can, the Lord will pour out His blessings upon us.

Sister Lucy Mack Smith, the mother of the Prophet Joseph Smith, also spoke to us. She could not hold back tears as she told of her eleven children. Of her seven boys, all but one are now dead. She told of the love she has for them and now how her heart sorrows for the loss of her family. She expressed the hope that those of her family who remain would go with the Saints, and if they did, she would go too. While she talked I thought of the new life growing within me, and my heart ached as I thought of how I would feel if this baby were taken from me.

I also felt anew the absence of my father and mother and the anguish I feel at knowing they are lost to me in this life. In my prayers every night, I pray the way will be provided that I can be sealed to them and we can be united as a family in eternity.

***

20 October 1845

How can mankind be so cruel and unfeeling toward one another? Tonight the smell and feel of smoke is so thick in the air that it burns my eyes. We had just finished dinner this evening when Tom looked out the window and saw flames pouring from Brother Snaith's barn. I ran to get help while the others tried their best to put out the fire, but all to no avail. We were fortunate to be able to free the horses and cows from the barn before they burned as well. When I was running for help, I noticed several other fires burning in Nauvoo. Sister Snaith said the Saints have been persecuted and threatened from the early days of the Church. With tears in her eyes and voice she told of the dreadful day that the Prophet Joseph Smith was taken away and then murdered at Carthage jail along with his brother Hyrum.

I realize now even more why President Young is preparing us to leave this beautiful city. We will never find the peace to live our lives quietly here in Nauvoo. Even with all the efforts of President Young and the Apostles to help us endure the mob violence and hatred, there is constant unrest. Many evenings Tom's younger brothers, Carl and Jonathan, join together with a group of boys and young men, equipping themselves with Bowie and jackknives and sticks. They then watch for any suspicious person who walks through Nauvoo, surround him, and, whistling and whittling, follow him closer and closer until the stranger leaves.

As Tom and I kneel to say our prayers, we pray for strength to endure and do all that we can to be faithful to our Heavenly Father. I know Mother and Father would be worried for us if they were aware of the turmoil that surrounds us here.

***

·*2 November 1845*

I have been asked to teach some of the children in school, and I am glad to do this. As I look into their sweet faces and quick smiles, I find myself thinking of the new life inside me, and I already feel such love for this baby. The days are passing quickly now, and we are so busy that the days never seem to hold enough hours to accomplish all that needs to be done. Tom and the other brethren are working long hours on the temple, trying to complete it before the Saints are forced to leave Nauvoo. He comes home so tired at night that often he falls asleep eating his supper. Before he goes to bed, I try to knead the knots from his shoulder and neck muscles so he may rest more easily through the night. Many nights he goes back to the temple with some of the men to guard it through the night from any who may wish to cause harm and damage. He seems tired all the time but filled with joy as the work on the temple nears completion.

Tonight Emily has announced her engagement to William Walters, whom she met on the ship here from England. Her quiet manner cannot hide the new sparkle in her eyes and voice as she talks about her William. He is a kind young man with a quick sense of humor, and he will be good for Emily. Of course, Abigail is hoping that Emily will have a big wedding with a white silk gown and lots of flowers, but with all that is happening right now in Nauvoo, I don't think this will happen. Mother and Father Fisher are pleased with the engagement. Even though there is much tribulation surrounding us here, there is much to celebrate.

***

27 November 1845

We had a holiday today to celebrate the harvest, and Tom and I left early this morning to spend the day with family and friends. A month ago, Mother and Father Fisher moved into a tent home made of canvas, but they are glad to have a place of their own. The day has been so beautiful, with the sun shining and the autumn air cool and crisp. As Tom and I walked to his parents' home in the early morning light, I could barely see the river for the clouds of mist that hung over it. The mornings are very cool now, and the promise of winter snows and storms are coming. What a joyous day of celebration it has been to give thanks for so many blessings!

Even with the holiday, the city is filled with the noise of hammers and saws as the Saints prepare for departure from Nauvoo. Every available house, store, or space has been devoted to the building of the hundreds of wagons that will be needed for the exodus. President Young has said we must be ready to go when the order is given. Between the work on the wagons and the work on the temple, Nauvoo is a very busy and noisy city. Tom and I, along with all the Saints, have been preparing to leave soon.

***

25 December 1845

Christmas Day! How different my life is from a year ago. I have thought constantly today of England, and I have felt a full measure of homesickness for what I left behind. For months I have pondered in my mind on what Mother and Father are doing and how their health is. Even though my letter was carried to England more than two months ago, I have not heard from them. I wonder if they have forgiven me for leaving. This morning as I pinned my hair brooch to my dress, tears came to my eyes as I remembered the love that had been given with this birthday gift. I thought of the old church at Fornham and Father, in his gentle voice, telling again the story of the birth of the Christ child. He has such a love for Jesus; why wouldn't he listen to the gospel message that would have added more light and peace in his life? I continue to feel in my heart that someday, somewhere, they will listen and accept.

I am sure another reason this has been an emotional day for me has been the gratitude I feel for the life I am carrying. As I feel the baby move, I am filled with overwhelming love for this child and feel the heartbreak my mother must be feeling without me being there, a part of her life. I have also thought much today of Mary and the birth of the baby Jesus, the love and tears she shed for her baby as she raised Him, watched others reject and scorn Him, and witnessed His final gift of sacrificing His life for us. How could she bear the pain of watching Him suffer?

Next year at this time Tom and I will have our child with us to celebrate Christmas. What dimensions of love this baby will add to our lives!

***

5 January 1846

Tom and I, along with so many of the Saints, are gathering together the things we will need for the journey west. We have been given a list of goods that we must take with us, and we have been fervently striving to accumulate them. The mob violence and beatings increase daily. The temple is now completed to the point that the first endowments were performed in December. The number of families wanting the sealing blessings of the temple is tremendous, and the building is filled every day with waiting couples. Tom and I, along with the Fisher family, are praying we will have these blessings given to us before leaving Nauvoo.

Tom and I have been deeply worried for Dorothy's husband, Charles. He has been sick with cold and fever for the last several days but is so concerned with completing the temple and the preparations for his small family's departure from Nauvoo that he is not taking the time to rest and get well.

***

5 February 1846

Today has been the most beautiful and important day in my life. I received the ordinances and blessings of the temple this morning, and then Tom and I were sealed for time and all eternity. I wish I had the power of words so I could express the joy and peace that entered my heart as Tom and I knelt across the altar of the temple from each other and, by the power of the priesthood of God, were sealed as husband and wife for all eternity. Death has no power to separate us; we will be together forever. My spirit was flooded with the feelings of love that my Heavenly Father and Savior have for me and all His children, and in my mind, I envisioned the gates of heaven opening before me. What in this world can surpass this great gift of eternal families? No earthly possessions or achievements can ever equal the blessings I have received. I know I can never repay my Heavenly Father for all I have been given, and my sacrifices in leaving my family in England are small compared with the great richness and peace I have received in this new life.

Mother and Father Fisher and their family were sealed after Tom and me, and for one grief-stricken moment, I was overwhelmed with heartache and sorrow and wished that Mother, Father, and I, too, were kneeling around the altar to be sealed together. But even as I wished it, the Spirit whispered peace to me, that Heavenly Father knew the desires of my heart and that it would happen someday.

Emily and William Walters were also married today and sealed together. Poor Abigail, her dreams of a big wedding party did not happen again.

The mob violence has increased to such a point that the first wagons have already left Nauvoo. We will be leaving in a couple of days, and with the blessings of the temple in my life, I am now ready to go.

***

11 February 1846

Tonight I write this journal entry by firelight in a camp across the river from our beautiful city of Nauvoo. Last night we loaded the last of our

*personal belongings in the wagon, and this morning at daybreak crossed
the frozen Mississippi River. As we waited in the bitter cold morning for
our turn to cross, I clung to Tom's hand and prayed I would be equal to
the journey ahead. I am in the last stages of my pregnancy; it is awkward
for me to move now, and I tire so quickly. Dorothy and Charles were
just ahead of us. Charles's cough has become steadily worse, and today
he shivered constantly with chills and fever. Dorothy has had to shoulder
much of the burden with her husband ill. I know she must be feeling the
same anxiety as I, as she is expecting her baby a week before I am, but her
attitude is one of cheerfulness and energy.*

*Tom's family was behind us with their wagons, lending us comfort
and support. His younger brothers are excited about crossing the plains,
but I fear that the journey will be long and taxing before it is completed.
The frozen river was like a miracle to us, much as the parting of the Red
Sea was for Moses and the children of Israel. It has provided a road across
the waters to Iowa and safety. Even so, my heart ached for those who are
older and feel the cold so desperately.*

***

15 March 1846

*This evening we arrived at Sugar Creek, Iowa. As we approached the
camp, we could see the tent city that has been created among the trees. The
evening air, heavy with the thick smoke of fires burning and the smell of
food cooking, enhanced the feelings of hunger and weariness I am feeling.
Even though it should be spring, the weather continues to be so cold and
harsh that tonight as I listen to the wind's fury beating against our wagon
bed, I long for comfort and shelter from the storms that beat against my
body and spirit. I know I have been given many blessings, but tonight
I feel lost in a world of ice and snow and fierce winds. Today is also my
nineteenth birthday, and it seems so long ago since last year's celebration.
I long to feel my mother's arms wrapped around me in comfort, her
soothing words and touch healing my spirit. I have taken my hair brooch
from my small chest of memories and held it close to my heart, and it
has brought me a measure of comfort and peace. As always, Tom and his
family are by my side with their love and care.*

The conditions in the camp are grim. Many have come on this journey without adequate food and shelter, but there is much sharing and giving. There is also much sickness here. Abigail has come down with chills and fever along with so many of the Saints. Charles continues to worsen, and I fear for Dorothy. Her time to deliver her baby is near now.

***

25 March 1846

Music is truly a gift from God. Tonight we have had a musical celebration that has lifted our spirits and given us strength to endure. Brother Pitts and his brass band have arrived, and this evening the sound of music filled the night air with dancing and laughter. Abigail was well enough to dance, even though she is still frail, and I am glad she is recovering quickly.

I sat by the edge of the fire with Tom's hand in mine, the dancers twirling by, and felt again refreshed and renewed. As I watched, I reflected on the events in my life that have brought me to this point. I am not the same woman that left the green hills of my homeland less than a year ago. My life there now seems a story that happened a long time ago to someone else. I have learned what it means to walk by faith, knowing not what challenges each day will offer, but trusting in the Lord with all my heart. I have found great joy in the simple gifts in my life and know that each day must be celebrated and appreciated. I have learned that with the Lord's help, I can endure beyond what I would have thought possible. I know that God loves me. Tonight, as I gazed into the heavens, the star-studded sky seemed to wink at me as if to assure me that truly all is well.

***

28 March 1846

Today has been a day of double tragedy and heartache. Charles passed away in his sleep last night; when Dorothy awoke this morning, he was already gone. Within a few hours, she started labor, and at four this afternoon her tiny baby girl was born without life in her little body. During the birth process, the baby became caught in the umbilical cord and died. Brother and Sister Snaith are heartbroken, but I am grateful they are here to help and comfort Dorothy. My heart is full of so much pain and grief for Dorothy. I have truly come to love her as a sister, and I cannot imagine the magnitude of the loss she must be feeling. Her body and spirit seem paralyzed with grief, and I know not how to comfort her. I cannot think of any words to offer that will give her peace. When I left her tonight lying in her wagon bed, tears silently flowed from her eyes, a look of utter desolation on her face. My heart breaks for her. Mother Fisher has given her something to help her sleep, but she seems past the point of utter exhaustion. How would I bear my life at this point without Tom beside me? I cannot even begin to imagine it.

Tonight, Tom, along with his brothers, dug the grave, the earth still hard and frozen. A small service will be held in the morning before the bodies are buried, the tiny baby being laid in her father's arms for the burial.

***

1 April 1846

I am taking time to write early this morning because I have just started labor and want to put my words to paper so our baby will know how excited I am to welcome it to our family. Tom is beside himself with worry and excitement, and Mother Fisher finally sent him outside to do his chores. What thoughts fly through my head! Surely a baby must be the closest thing to heaven we can hold in our arms, a chance to hold a little part of eternity next to our hearts.

My thoughts also turn to England and home. If Tom and I had never heard the gospel message, we would be having this baby there, and Mother would be by my side, encouraging and helping me. Father would be planning the christening date, his heart full of the pride and joy that a grandchild would bring into their lives. Instead I am here in a tent, far from home, and missing my parents grievously. Even with their absence in my life, I am not sorry this is the path I have chosen, for I have been truly blessed beyond all reasoning. My afflictions have only brought me closer to my Heavenly Father and Savior as I have leaned on Them for needed strength and then felt Their love for me. The greatest blessing I have been given is that Tom and I have been sealed together for eternity. This new baby will be a bond and a link to us, a part of us forever. My heart is at peace, for the Spirit continues to assure me that someday Mother and Father, too, will accept the gospel, and we will be united as a family.

***

12 April 1846

We are preparing to leave Sugar Creek to continue our journey to the West. As I was going through Catherine's things, I found her journal in the small box I made for her more than a year ago. I have spent the last few hours reading her words and living our journey over. Catherine died in childbirth. Shortly after our little daughter was born, Catherine started to bleed, and despite all that Mother could do, she passed away, taking part of my heart with her forever. Our baby looks like Catherine, her small head covered with dark curly hair, and so I have named her MaryAnne Catherine, after her mother and grandmother. I know this is what she would have wanted me to do. Dorothy was helpful to me in the following days and took the baby to nurse. She told me that caring for MaryAnne filled her own empty arms and that she would continue to help with the baby on the long trip west. Both Dorothy and I are trying to cope as best we can with the tremendous losses we have suffered.

As I read Catherine's journal, I have felt more at peace. I have blamed myself in the depths of my grief for taking her away from England and her home, but her journal has let me know this is the path she wanted to take with all her heart, and I know that someday we will be together again. I leave this final entry in her journal as a written testimony of my love for her and our daughter, our love of the gospel, and the knowledge that the Lord is just and merciful.

Tom Fisher

Chapter 22

Abby lowered the journal to her lap, tears running down her face. Catherine Anne Moore Fisher was her great-great-great-great-grandmother. Heavenly Father, through Catherine's journal, had answered her fervent prayer for help. As Abby read of Catherine's struggles in leaving home, family, and country only to endure want, cold, and death, she thought of the divine nature of Catherine's spirit and courage shining through the journal pages. Catherine had sacrificed much but had found great peace and joy in her short life. Her testimony and love for the gospel strengthened with each trial. How could Abby not follow her example? It was not the soft and smooth road that brought eternal joy and happiness but the road that twisted and turned and climbed ever upward, offering at every bend challenges and trials that humbled the spirit and brought the traveler to the feet of the Savior. Abby's answer was in the journal pages, the choice that would allow her to grow spiritually and enjoy the blessings of the gospel every day in her life and in the lives of her family. On her earthly spiritual journey back to her Father in Heaven, if she married Blake, they would walk the road together, spiritually matching their steps as they worked toward the same goals and dreams. However, if she married Scott, she would find herself alone on that path, constantly listening for his footsteps behind her and pausing occasionally to watch for him. Her heart would ache at the sorrow of going down that spiritual road without him, forever hoping and praying that he would catch up and they could finish the journey together.

Suddenly, Abby felt shame wash over her. She thought of herself as a modern woman, yet she herself had been clinging to the known and secure path, afraid to fly on new wings. Home was where her heart was, and it was here in St. George, with Blake. As she made her decision, peace filled her heart, and the Spirit bore witness that this was the right choice for her, the one that would allow her to live her life with the beauty of the gospel wrapped around her like a warm cloak of protection and security.

Abby sat quietly for a few minutes before opening her grandmother's genealogy book, anxious now to check again for Catherine's name. Looking over the pedigree chart, she gasped in surprise. Catherine's name was not listed on the sheet as MaryAnne's mother. Tom Fisher had married Dorothy Stokes, and future posterity must have assumed that MaryAnne Fisher was their baby. Catherine had been missing for a long, long while and become forgotten over time. Her name had been lost for generations, her legacy unknown.

Abby reached into the box and drew out the hair brooch, holding it closely to study. She could see the colors of the entwined hair and remembered from the journal that the black and gray hair was Catherine's mother, the light brown her father's, and the dark black hair Catherine's. It also reminded Abby of Catherine's desire to be sealed to her parents, to have their lives joined together for eternity.

The final object in the box was a photograph of a young couple posing for a final picture before leaving England. The man had his arm protectively around the woman in the picture, but it was the woman's face that drew Abby's eyes. This was the same young woman she had seen in the other photograph. In this picture, however, Catherine was looking into the camera with a shy sweet smile. Her hair was pulled back into a low knot, but a few curly strands had escaped their pins and softened the outline of her face. Her eyes reflected tiredness but also mirrored the strength of her spirit and determination, further enforced by the forward thrust of her chin. This was a picture of Catherine as a woman, full of spirit and courage to meet the challenges ahead.

Abby carefully laid the journal and photograph in the box, then set the brooch on top, and, with a heart full of compassion and love for Catherine, closed the lid. Several minutes went by as she reflected on the story in the journal. Finally, she knelt down on her knees, eyes again brimming with tears, and offered up a heart full of gratitude to her Heavenly Father for the answers she had received to her prayers and the life now open to her. She also expressed love for Catherine and the life of courage and testimony that she had lived. After her prayer, Abby stayed on her knees for several more minutes, overcome with appreciation and gratitude.

Finally, she stood and dusted herself off. *Blake,* she thought excitedly. *I need to tell him what's happened.* She glanced at her watch. The hours had truly flown by! It was now after nine in the evening, and Abby saw it was already dark. So lost had she been in the journal pages that time had slipped by without her noticing.

Tucking the box tenderly under her arm, she hurried to her room and rummaged through her purse for the card Blake had given her with his address and phone number. When she found it, she pulled her phone from her pocket and began punching in the numbers. Her finger paused on the connect key. What she had to say, she needed to tell him personally, not through a phone call. Abby terminated the call and pushed the phone back in her pocket. Running down the stairs, she fished out both the house and car keys from her purse. She locked the front door and hurried to her car, carrying the small wooden box. She found the address quickly, grateful it was only a few blocks away. Abby turned the motor off and sat for a few minutes, trying to calm her beating heart. Then, getting out of the car, she walked to the front porch and rang the doorbell.

The porch light came on, and Blake opened the door. Abby noticed the weariness and worry etched in his face. He stared at her for a few seconds, as if unable to believe she was really there, his eyes never leaving hers. Abby's face broke into a smile of pure joy, and Blake breathed a sigh of relief and opened his arms. She rushed into them eagerly and nestled closely, overwhelmed with her love for this man. Her heart, soul, and body had found its home.

"You're the answer to my prayers," she whispered as she lifted her face for his kiss.

Epilogue

Eighteen Months Later

Abby awoke early, excitement and anticipation making it impossible for her to sleep any longer. The first streaks of golden light coming in through the open windows announced that it would be a beautiful morning, and she lay quietly thinking of the day ahead. Blake was still asleep beside her, his breathing soft and even, and she looked over at him with tenderness. What joy and happiness she had experienced in this new life with him! A few days ago they had celebrated their first wedding anniversary, and it was hard for her now to even think of life without him. She placed her hands gently on her stomach, feeling the soft mound. In four months they would welcome a new baby to their family, a daughter. They were going to call her Catherine. The name would honor a woman long past who had affected their future.

Yesterday her parents had arrived to participate in the important event that would happen later that morning. They had also brought news that had eased some of the sadness she still felt when she thought of Scott and how hard it had been to tell him of her decision to marry Blake. Her dad reported that Scott was planning on being married in a few months, and Abby was pleased that he had moved forward and found someone else.

"Are you ready for today?" Blake asked, and she saw that he was now awake. Abby leaned over and kissed him.

"I'm so ready and excited I can't stay in bed any longer," she announced as she swung the covers back and climbed out of bed. "Hurry up! We need to be there at nine this morning, and we still have to get ready and then pick up Mom and Dad."

Later, Blake and Abby, hand in hand, entered the St. George temple along with her parents. Finally the day had arrived to fulfill Catherine's fervent wish. Abby took the place of Catherine and her parents acted as proxy for Catherine's parents. As they knelt around the altar in the sealing room of the temple, the dreams and hopes of a young English woman were to become a reality. Finally the words were uttered that would seal Catherine to her parents. Abby felt Catherine's spirit, as well as the spirits of Catherine's parents, there in that holy place, and tears of joy ran freely down her face. Raising her head, she looked across the altar to the mirrors reflected on both sides of the room. It seemed almost as if she could see Catherine and Tom, along with their parents and the generations who loved them, gathered to witness this important event, and her heart was overcome with thankfulness for the privilege of performing this sealing. Finally, after more than one hundred fifty years of waiting, Catherine's voice and prayer across time had been answered. A family link had been welded together for all eternity. Her legacy of faith and courage would be known, and her name called blessed in the generations to come.

Author Bio

My husband and I had the opportunity to visit England and house-sit for our daughter's English husband's grandparents for two months at a time over a period of a few years, and we availed ourselves of the chance to visit the villages of our ancestors. The old church where my Todd family had worshipped for hundreds of years was no longer in use, and its flint walls stood amid a jungle of wildflowers and briers—the silence only broken by an occasional bird call or the buzzing of bees. It was not hard to imagine that time stood still, and I found myself visualizing what it would mean to leave all this to follow a new faith to a new land, leaving behind family, friends, and country. After spending many years writing software training manuals for my company, I have loved writing this book of romance, mystery, and faith.

In addition to traveling, I also enjoy reading, cooking, family history, and spending time with my family. We currently live in Hurricane, Utah.